Praise for
VIRGINIA EUWER WOLFF'S
The Mozart Season

◆"A luminously realized character, Allegra is gifted not only musically but in her sensitive, intelligent responses to events. Her season of discovery—of Mozart, her own roots, and the creative balance between life's traumas and trivia—marks a fine achievement."

–*Kirkus Reviews,* pointer review

"Wolff gives readers a delightful heroine, a fully realized setting, and a slowly building tension that reaches a stunning climax."

–*School Library Journal*

"A distinctive novel, with intriguing characters and a touch of romance…. Readers who are musically inclined and those who enjoy a story with strong and intriguing characters…will savor each word."

–*The Horn Book*

An ALA Best Book for Young Adults

An *SLJ* Best Book

An ALA *Booklist* Editors' Choice

A *Hungry Mind Review* Book of Distinction

Other Signature Titles

THE

Mozart
SEASON

VIRGINIA EUWER WOLFF

SCHOLASTIC
Signature

an imprint of
SCHOLASTIC INC.

New York Toronto London Auckland Sydney
Mexico City New Delhi Hong Kong

Acknowledgments

Thanks to Dorothy McCormick, Mildred Edmundson,
Roby Reid, Anthony Wolff, Juliet Wolff,
Carol Sindell, Sophia Tan, Michael Parker, Tom Bessler,
Vincent Heitkam, Nick Wheeler, the staff
of the Hood River County Library, and most
emphatically to Brenda Bowen.

∾

*This is a work of fiction. Apart from Ernest Bloch (1880–1959)
and other celebrated figures in the world of music, all characters
in this story are imaginary. As of this writing, there is
no Bloch Competition for Young Musicians of Oregon.*

ISBN 0-439-16309-9

12   7 8 9/9 0 1 2/0

Printed in the U.S.A.   40

Scholastic Trade paperback reissue, April 2000

In memory of my parents,
Florence Craven Euwer and Eugene Courtney Euwer,
who gave me music

I learn by going where I have to go.
                    —Theodore Roethke, "The Waking"

1

In Mr. Kaplan's studio is a needlepoint pillow, on a chair. On one side of it is a violin. The other side says, *A teacher is someone who makes you believe you can do it.* Somebody who took lessons from him a long time ago made it. When I was little, I couldn't read it clearly because needlepoint letters have odd shapes.

"Now that you're warmed up, let's revisit Mr. Mozart," said Mr. Kaplan.

It was a gorgeous June morning and in my mind I heard another voice: "Now that you're warmed up, let's demolish those Vikings." My softball coach and my violin teacher were overlapping each other.

With my softball coach, it was stairsteps and laps and stretches and endless batting practice. With Mr. Kaplan it was eight repetitions of very fast B-major scales and five minutes of octaves. Two weeks after being the shortstop on the team that had lost in the second round of the district play-offs, I was at my lesson, looking for the Mozart concerto. People say I have a quirky way of holding my violin and bow way out to the side in my left hand while I bend over and sort through music with my right hand, as if I'm signaling to somebody. Mr. Kaplan said we were going to "catch up with Mr. Mozart. Do the concerto start to finish, no stops, to see what's going on in the totality of the thing." He was sitting on the piano bench, waiting for me. The Fourth Concerto, in D. I hadn't paid very much attention to it since February, and now it was June.

In the summer I get to have morning lessons twice a week, and I love it. The sun comes in the windows of Mr. Kaplan's studio, which is at one end of his house, and it lights up the rug's big, colorful designs. Mrs. Kaplan leaves for work early, and there's always some great smell left over, French toast or omelets or something. I work best in the mornings. Things haven't had time to get so cluttered yet.

Mr. Kaplan was wearing his "Pergolesi—a man for the '90s" sweatshirt. It's a joke. Pergolesi lived in Italy in the 1700s and he wrote operas and he died of consumption when he was twenty-six, five days after he'd finished composing something. Mr. Kaplan is better in the mornings, too. He says the Symphony keeps him up past his bedtime. He plays in the first violins in it with my mother. So he's up past his bedtime most of the time during the season. It's the Oregon Symphony. They don't play regular concerts in the summer.

I put the music on the stand and got ready. With Mr. Kaplan you don't whine or mutter. It doesn't help. "We want right notes, not excuses" is what all music teachers say, I guess. He doesn't have to say it very many times; you learn it fast. Mr. Kaplan and I'd been together for seven years, and he was going to know the instant I got to the top of the second page that I hadn't been practicing the Mozart. At that spot there's a fast shift from first finger to fourth finger on the G string, and you have to get ready for it. You can't let a shift like that take you by surprise.

"Straight through. Right, Allegra? Including cadenzas." A cadenza is the part where the violin plays alone; it's harder than the rest of the piece, and it gets the audience all excited when you do it in a concert. There are three cadenzas in this concerto, one in each movement.

"Right." Poor man.

The introduction is forty-one measures long. This time, instead of playing just the last two measures of it on the piano, Mr. Kaplan played the whole thing. He wears half-glasses, and he has a balding head with some blondish-gray hair on the back, and a mostly gray short beard, and he's a little bit slumped over when he sits at the piano. His ears stick out in a funny way. I love the way he looks. The introduction to the first movement, the part the orchestra would play, is bouncy, and it mostly announces what the solo violin will play when it begins. That way you get to listen to it twice.

While he was doing it, I practiced the G-string shift without making any noise, sliding my hand up and down the fingerboard.

I love this concerto. Mozart only wrote five of them for the violin. The year before, Mr. Kaplan had let me choose which one to learn, the third one or this one, and I'd taken them both home and spun my bow the way you spin a tennis racquet. If it landed with the hair toward me, I'd learn the third, in G; and if it landed with the hair away from me, I'd learn this one. When Mr. Kaplan and my parents found out I'd treated my bow With Such Astonishing Disrespect, they got very alarmed about it.

I'd worked very hard on it for several months, and in February we'd made a tape of it to send to a contest. I'd worried and fretted and trembled, but we'd gotten the tape made. After that, I'd sort of neglected it. In softball season I'd practically stopped being a violinist.

Mr. Kaplan, who was having fun playing the introduction, got to the BUM-*pum-pa-pum* part that comes right before the violin begins. I was ready. It starts on a high D and goes on up from there.

I got through the first movement all right, and I made some genuine messes of the beautiful double-stops near the end of the second-movement cadenza. Double-stops are two notes at once, on separate strings. And I was sure the last-movement cadenza was making it Abundantly Clear to Mr. Kaplan that I hadn't even seen it for a long time. But the end was fine. The *Blip-te-de-bip-bip-bip* came out very, very soft and nice.

Mr. Kaplan leaned back, smiling and saying a kind of "ah." Then he turned sideways on the bench. "Isn't this a beautiful song, Allegra?"

"Yep." It is. Mr. Kaplan calls overtures and symphonies and concertos "songs" sometimes. I waited for him to say the rest.

He leaned forward and flipped the pages. "Hmmm. I'm concerned about the articulation in spots, and some of the dynamics aren't at all what they should be—and you *know* that, young lady—and . . . Hmmm." Then he turned sideways on the bench again, straddling it. "Are you willing to play this concerto a thousand times by September?"

I laughed. That would be more times than I'd brush my teeth by then. He watched me thinking. He started to smile, then he got up and walked across the studio, away from me. Then he turned around. "Your tape was accepted," he said. "For the Bloch Competition. The finals are on Labor Day."

I looked at him. And I saw myself four months before, worrying and worrying and worrying about whether or not the sixteenth-notes in the first movement were vigorous enough, how satiny smooth the *Andante cantabile* was. . . . I remembered being a mass of nervousness, actually frightened of a tape recorder.

"Had you really forgotten about it?" he said.

The picture in my memory faded and Mr. Kaplan's face came in, looking at me over the top of his half-glasses. He has terribly vivid blue eyes.

"You're serious, aren't you?" I said.

"Indeed. You are one of the finalists. We have almost three months, if you decide to play. You may decide not to, of course."

I laughed. I held my violin and my bow out at arms' length, so I was kind of a V shape. "Really," I said. "Thanks, guys," I said to them. I dropped my arms, letting violin and bow dangle so they hung just above the floor. I thought of my grandmother in New York, Bubbe Raisa, who'd bought me the first violin I ever had. It was a one-eighth size. I can still hear her voice in my head, like an old radio program you think you remember, all jolly-sounding, saying, "Just tuck it under your chin, just tuck it. . . ." The whole violin was only seventeen inches long.

Mr. Kaplan bent his head to the side, a little bit like a bird listening. "Mr. Kaplan, do you think . . ." I purposely let my voice fade.

He shook his head back and forth. "You make your own

decisions, always, Allegra." I laughed again, and so did he. Mine was kind of an accusing laugh; I was thinking of the thousands of hours of finger-sickening exercises he'd put me through in seven years. Those nasty exercises were his decisions, not mine. "In important things of this kind," he added.

Spend three months with Mozart. My whole summer vacation. Go through the nervousness all over again. The Ernest Bloch Competition for Young Musicians of Oregon. Last year it was for piano, the first Beethoven concerto, and the boy who plays piano with the Portland Youth Orchestra won it. He played the concerto with the Oregon Symphony at a Sunday concert; that was his prize. I'll never forget his eyes when he came out on the stage to begin playing at the concert. They looked wild, as if he didn't know what a piano was. Daddy and I were sitting down front, and we could see him very clearly. Mommy said he'd been awfully jumpy in rehearsal but always came through in the clinch. He was eighteen. He played the performance wonderfully.

"How old are the others?" I asked.

"Allegra, will that affect your relationship with the concerto?"

I looked down to both sides of me. My violin was centered exactly over one of the dark blue curly designs on the rug. I centered my bow over another one. The designs weren't exactly alike. I'd had the rug designs memorized for years. I looked back up at Mr. Kaplan. He was standing with his hands in his pockets. "I don't exactly know," I said.

He moved his feet slightly. "Let's say I'm quite sure you're the youngest. Let's say that." He kept looking at me over his glasses. I put both violin and bow in my right hand. "How tall are you?" he asked.

I told him. Five feet one and three-quarters.

"Indeed," he said. "And you've had the full-size instrument since? . . ."

"Uh . . . I was just starting sixth grade. One and a half years ago. One year and nine months." The agreement was that if I started to slack off on the practicing, Mommy and Daddy wouldn't "take the payments very seriously," as Daddy said. If I got unmotivated or lost interest, away would go the violin, and I could use a rental. Same with the bow.

"I'm wondering if we can expect some growth these days. It would make the reaches a bit easier for your hand, you know. Your brother David, he's rather taller than you, yes?"

"David's five eleven."

"Indeed. Well, we'll see what nature has in mind." He began pacing across the rug. Then he stopped. "What do you think, Allegra? Would you like to play the competition? You mustn't play it unless you're willing. Com*plete*ly willing."

I'd never done such a thing in my life. I'd played auditions. One for the All-State Prep Orchestra, but I was so young then, that one hardly counts. I almost didn't even know what I was there for. And for the Youth Orchestra, the one I play in now. That was scary, because I knew exactly what I was there for.

"I've never—Mr. Kaplan, I've never played a . . ."

"I know, Allegra." His voice was full of—I didn't know what to call it. It wasn't pity. I had to have my own list of new words by September for school, and whatever it was in his voice would be one of them. I'd find it. It was something like pity, but not the kind that makes you feel bad.

"Does my mother know about this? When did you find out? Find out I'd made the finals?"

"Yes, she does. We've talked about it. Not long ago."

"What does she think? Why didn't somebody tell me?"

He sort of laughed but not really. "She thinks it's your decision. Naturally. We wanted to wait till after school was out—and your softball—so you could more accurately gauge how you want to spend your summer."

"Does my dad know?"

"I'm sure he does." Daddy doesn't play in the Symphony; he plays in the opera orchestra. And he teaches at a university and plays in a quartet. He's a cellist.

"What does he think?"

"That, I don't know. I have a hunch he agrees with your mother."

I loosened my bow. "What's it like? You don't have to play in front of a lot of people, do you? I mean, not the whole orchestra?" I looked down at the rug design on my left, where the blue and red come together. "Do you get more than one try?"

"This is the way it goes, Allegra. There'll be three, maybe four judges. They're the jury. Every contestant will play the entire concerto. Once. Without accompaniment. The judges listen and decide. Somebody will win. And there'll be a second prize, an alternate. The others will get a whopper of an experience. Then it'll be over for all the competitors except one. That one will play the concerto in January. With the Symphony, at a Sunday concert. If the winner should get sick, the alternate winner will perform."

Suddenly the idea of winning was the worst thing I could imagine. I'd be out there exposed to everybody. I'd rather lose.

Or would I?

"How many people are gonna be in the competition?"

"I'm not exactly sure. Fewer than ten, I think. The finalists have come from a field of eighty-five."

Eighty-five. "Are they adults or something? In college, I mean."

"There is no minimum age, just as in the Youth Orchestra. The maximum age is twenty-one. I expect the mean age to be about seventeen."

"I was twelve in February."

"I know, Allegra. Do you want to think about it for a few days?"

"I don't know. Maybe I'd better think . . . I don't . . ."

"Well. Then we have unfinished business, you and I. Let's do the Vitali for fun now."

My music says Vitali was born in 1660 and never died. It says, "Tomaso Vitali, 1660– ." It just has that blank. He wrote a ciaccona in G minor that I love. That was what I'd been practicing. It has a lot of trickery of crossing strings in it, and you have to play faster than your mind can think when you play the trickery parts. Automatic pilot is one way to describe it. It's a kind of automated finger memory. You let your mind go away and not interfere with your fingers. It's kind of like the way you write your name or ride a bike. First you learn how, and then you just go ahead and do it without thinking about how you do it. I love the ciaccona he wrote.

But when we got to four measures after letter M, I botched some trickery notes. And I stopped. I don't usually do that; I usually go right on.

"This section is still your Waterloo, isn't it?" Mr. Kaplan said. Somebody lost a battle at Waterloo; I don't remember who.

"Yes. I don't know if I can play any competition, ever, Mr. Kaplan. I . . ."

"Oh, come now. Don't start that. It doesn't do any good." He looked at me. "Remember, this competition is in memory of Mr. Bloch."

"Yes." Ernest Bloch was a Swiss-Jewish composer who came to Oregon and lived at the beach. Last year the Youth Orchestra played a concerto grosso he wrote, and it was so beautiful it made some people in the orchestra cry.

"And we're going to remember, you and I, that Mr. Bloch had tenacity and fearlessness and a great, great soul."

I looked at him in a question mark.

"Tenacity. Holding on when it would be more comfortable to let go."

I nodded.

While I was putting my violin away, I saw on Mr. Kaplan's desk a photograph of a string quartet I hadn't seen before. It had the most gorgeous guy holding a violin, with messy curly hair and an incredibly handsome roundish face, sort of smiling.

"Who's this?" I asked.

"That's the Juilliard Quartet. You must hear them in person someday."

"I mean who's *this*?" I pointed to the gorgeous one.

"Oh. That's Joel Smirnoff. Their second violinist. Excellent musician."

Instant crush. Lightning love. Allegra and Joel. Joel and Allegra. Duets.

"You'll think about the competition, won't you, Allegra?" he said as I was going out the door.

"Of *course*. Thanks. For the lesson. And . . ."

"You're welcome. Always. And do the Kreutzer double-stops this week?"

The terrible, nasty, tormenting Kreutzer double-stops. Kreutzer lived in the same time as Beethoven. He wrote a whole book of violin exercises, called études, and his idea of double-stops was to get you going good and fast and then throw one at you that your fingers can't possibly reach and make you keep going. Good old number 34.

I was just crossing the Kaplans' lawn when a catastrophe struck me: if I didn't at least *try* to play the competition, I'd be just one more boring violin student and Joel Smirnoff would never even think of looking for me in Portland, Oregon. He wouldn't even ever find out I was alive.

I turned around and ran back and knocked on the studio door. Mr. Kaplan opened it, and I told him, "Yes. I want to play the competition."

He looked a bit surprised, but not totally. "Good girl, Allegra. It's a deal. *Kreut*zer." He almost growled the last word, and smiled. I said good-bye again and he put his hand up in his flat-handed wave.

I walked home. I had to talk to somebody. My brother David was in the dining room making a cartoon. He was sitting in the chair he sits in for dinner. He's sixteen, and he's basically called Bro David. He makes a lot of cartoons. Last year he sold one of them to the *New Yorker* magazine by lying about his age. It had tragic, starving Africans opening up big boxes and saying, "Yeccchhh—not *more* spinach and rutabagas from the children of America!" He got some money for it.

When Bro David was thirteen, Bubbe Raisa paid for him to go to New York and visit her, and they went to eleven museums. Ever since then, he's been sort of Mr. Superior.

I stood in the dining room looking at him. I had to talk to somebody. Daddy was at work at the university where he teaches, and Mommy was at an all-day committee meeting, trying to make a playing contract so the Symphony wouldn't go on strike. "David, I did something today," I said.

"Good, Legs." He went on drawing. Some people think "Legs" is a decent nickname for Allegra.

"I mean, I made a decision today."

"Good."

He's exasperating. "Listen to me, David. You have to listen."

"Okay, I'm listening. Talk." He looked bored.

I told him, "I'm gonna play a competition. Maybe I'm crazy."

He didn't pay attention; he thought I meant an audition.

"A competition, David. You're not listening. There'll be about ten people. Do you know I sent in a Mozart tape way last February? To a competition?" The whole thing began to look in on me. The competition wasn't a thing I was looking at, it was looking at me, as if it had lots of eyes.

"What do you mean?" David asked.

I told him. I stood there in the dining room, with my violin case on the floor and my arms hanging all floppy at my sides, and told him the whole thing. How I'd have to play the concerto perfectly and be suddenly brilliant. I'd be the youngest. The cadenzas are very hard. The idea sounded insane.

David didn't see the point. "I don't see the point," he said. "If you win, you just get up out of your chair and you walk up front, and you stand there and you play it. If you lose, you sit there in your place and play your part. Look: you've won one spelling championship thing and you've lost one. That didn't annihilate your whole head or anything; you didn't go around looking for razor blades. You're a lousy twelve years old. Winning won't make you queen of the world. And losing isn't gonna terminate you. It's a concerto; it's not the future of the universe."

Sometimes I can be very frustrated and very quiet at the same time. I sat down in the chair I sit in for dinner, across the table from him, and I folded my hands. "I didn't say the Youth Orchestra, I said the Symphony." I said it very slowly.

He looked at me. "You mean Mom's symphony. Is that what you mean?"

"Yes."

I tried to remember what Joel Smirnoff looked like, but I could only picture his mouth and his hair.

"That's different."

"Right."

He rolled his eyes around, thinking. "What's it gonna do to you? Is it gonna make you a crazoid?" David thinks the world is a big insane asylum anyway. We're all inmates, just in different wards.

"I don't know."

"Well, look at you right now."

"Maybe that's because I just this morning found out."

"You don't want to end up like that Deeder person."

"Who?"

"You know. Mom's friend, the one that sings."

"Which one?"

"She sings concerts, and she's strange."

I couldn't remember anybody like that. "I wonder if I'll get strange," I said.

"Do you want to change your mind? You know, not do it?"

I thought of the way Joel Smirnoff held his violin in the picture: high up, kind of like a flag. Sometimes I feel my violin is out to get me—an enemy or something—and sometimes it feels like my best and only friend.

"I don't think so," I said.

He rolled a ball of Elmer's glue around on the table. "Do you think you can win?"

I looked at a cartoon he was making. It had a chimpanzee playing a piano. It was upside down from where I was sitting. "I don't know. Maybe. Probably not. I don't know. Eighty-five people sent tapes."

He picked up the glue bottle and started squeezing it lightly—just to hear the tiny little *pffft* it makes. "Well, you ought to go ahead and do it. But remember what I said. It's just a concerto."

Easy for him to say.

"I think I'm going to," I said. I had to hear myself say it out loud again.

He looked at me and *pffft*-ed the glue bottle four times. Then he put it down and said, "Look, Legs, I have to go to work in a little while. Nobody's home for dinner tonight. Dad has that park concert; Mom's gonna go hear him after her meeting."

"David, I'm afraid."

"Try not to think about it." He started cleaning up the paper and pens and glue mess.

"Yep. Try not to think about elephants." Somebody said

that when Bro David was in a little kids' art class at the art museum a long time ago, and he said it all the time for a while. I looked at my violin case on the floor, and at my briefcase with the Mozart and Vitali and Prokofiev and Kreutzer and all the other music inside it. "What does that word mean, the one with 'nigh' in it?" I asked him.

"I don't know. What word?"

"You said it. You said when I lost the spelling thing it didn't nigh-something my whole head."

He was sweeping scraps off the table with the edge of a magazine. "I don't know. Nigh-something. I don't remember."

"You *said* it."

"I don't know. I've got to go to work. Will you make me a salami sandwich?"

I went to the kitchen and made sandwiches for both of us. A breeze was coming up, blowing the hummingbird feeder around outside the kitchen window. David picked up his sandwich and put it in a bag and left for Safeway. I sat and ate mine. Mozart was nineteen when he wrote that concerto, plus the four other ones in the same year. I wonder if he thought they were the future of the universe. I wonder if he thought they'd make any difference to anybody. I wish somebody had saved his brain.

I was just taking out the Mozart, to look at the third-movement cadenza, when the phone rang. It was David. "It's 'annihilate.' Comes from Latin, *nihil*, n-i-h-i-l, means 'nothing.' It means 'destroy.' Bye."

It was time to start my list of new words. Summer goes very fast and you can end up with no list at all in September if you're not careful. I've seen it happen. I went upstairs and wrote it down on the clipboard beside the bed. Bro David hadn't spelled it for me, so I did my best. A-n-i-h-i-l-a-t-e. I put "tenacity" from Mr. Kaplan before it.

A long time ago, I'd thought I didn't even like David. He got to go to special art classes at the art museum every Saturday, and his paintings and collages and clay sculptures were all over the house. We had them not only on the refrigerator, but stuck to walls and doors and sitting on tables and chairs. I complained that I didn't get to go to any special classes, and I said Mommy and Daddy probably loved David more than they loved me, and that was when they began to figure out that I might be wanting music lessons. And my grandmother Raisa bought me the violin. So it turns out that here I was with a Mozart concerto to spend my summer with, all because when I was a little kid I'd whined with envy.

Later, when Bro David's art got to be all cartoons, they still were all over the walls and refrigerator, but by then I wasn't whining anymore.

I cleaned up the sandwich mess and went to the music room and practiced. I worked on Kreutzer no. 34, which is a good way to insult yourself if you haven't worked on it lately. I played it for almost an hour. It can torture your fingers, and it's good for you.

It's also very useful in distracting you from your problems, because you can't even think about them while you're playing it. Kind of like skiing: you keep your mind totally on what you're doing and give your mental problems a rest. You keep your mind right where your body is. I don't understand it all totally, but that's what you do. You keep doing it till you get convinced.

And after the Kreutzer, I went straight to the first-to-fourth-finger shift in the first movement of the concerto. I did it over and over and over again. Just that one shift; I did it maybe fifty times, and then I played a couple of Dancla études, which are different from Kreutzer's, and sometimes more fun.

Daddy came in late in the afternoon and said it was going to be windy for the concert, and he wanted me to turn pages. They don't always use page turners; only when there's a chance of wind. It was his quartet, the Multnomah Quartet, that was playing. They're named after an Indian chief. The same one Multnomah Falls is named for. And they weren't playing in a park; they were playing in a place called Pioneer Square, which is in downtown Portland. So sometimes there are lots of cars going past while the concert is having a really soft part, pianissimo. People make jokes about it.

I'd never turned pages for anybody in public before. You have to clamp the pages down with clothespins, and then unclamp a page at exactly the right moment and turn it at exactly the right instant so the person can go on playing, and then you reclamp everything and keep watching the music so you know when the next turn is coming up. There's another way to do it, too: with a sheet of Plexiglas laid on top of the music to hold it down when the wind blows. It can be as complicated as the clothespins.

"Daddy, I have to tell you something," I said. He was putting his cello case on the floor against the dining-room wall.

"Right. You have to tell me if you'll turn pages."

"No, I have to tell you something important—"

"Listen, if you won't do it I'll have to get somebody else. The concert's at seven."

"*Dad*dy, this is im*por*tant!" I heard myself sounding like a little kid.

He walked straight to me, looking confused. He put both arms around me, tight, and I put my head on his T-shirt.

"My tape got in the Bloch finals."

His arms got kind of rigid, as if he were bracing himself for something.

"And I'm gonna do it," I said. Just like that.

He didn't say anything. He just held me, and he found my left hand and kissed every finger on it. It's a joke he used to do when I was little and couldn't stand how badly I played. He kissed each finger to make it all better. He's always had a mustache, and the mustache kisses are hairy.

"I'll turn your pages tonight," I said to his T-shirt.

He laughed. "Pages aren't important. You're important. You're really going to play that competition. Allegra Leah Shapiro." He kind of sighed and just held me. Then he backed away and said, "Mommy knows you're going to play, does she?"

"Nope. I just found out at my lesson. Then I decided. I told David."

"Good. We get to surprise her. I'll heat up the chicken; you find something to wear. Something dark, okay? We have to leave in an hour. I'll show you the worst page turn. You'll have to be really nimble with the clothespins."

I was up the stairs. I put on a navy blue skirt and a grayish sort of shirt with little skinny white stripes. I guessed I looked dark enough.

"Set the table, will you, Allegra? Please?" Daddy called from the kitchen.

I brushed my hair first. It's kind of long. And thick and really dark. I've got blue eyes and dark hair, which is kind of an odd combination. Maybe it's from being half Jewish and half not. My friend Jessica has straight black hair to her waist, and she has really dark eyes and her skin is a perfect gold; it's because her dad was black and her mother is Chinese. Her father is dead; he was a geologist when Mount St. Helens erupted and he died there. Imagine having your father die that way. Jessica is gorgeous, the most beautiful girl I know. She's going to be an architect. While I was brushing my hair, Jessica was in Hong Kong with her mother and her sisters and brothers. They go there every summer, and she has to practice drawing Chinese characters so she doesn't end up all American and no Chinese.

And my other best friend, Sarah, was at ballet camp in California. Until that morning, I'd been the one with the dull summer ahead. I looked in the mirror at the bruise on the left side of my neck from the chin rest on the violin. It's a sort of rubbed place on my skin. Almost all violinists have them, just below the jawbone. That's how you can pick out a violinist in a crowd. I put my hair in a braid because of the wind and went downstairs to set the table.

When Daddy brought our plates to the dining-room table, my piece of chicken had a toothpick standing in it with a little tag that said "Allegra the Brave." He showed me the worst page turn. It was in a quartet by Dvořák. He said I should probably turn three measures early.

In Pioneer Square, the audience sits up above the players. It's like a Greek theater. Daddy said in the car on the way to the square, "Did I tell you I pay my page turners?"

"Nope," I said. For some reason, I felt all happy and not bothered by anything much. The competition was months away. It was summer, and it was windy but nice, with pretty evening light that happens in Portland. Maybe it was doing the Kreutzer no. 34 that made me feel good. "How much?"

"It depends. For you, I'd say a quarter for every easy turn, and a dollar for the hard ones. You have to keep track of the wind. That's your job, not mine."

"Okay," I said. Portland is built on both sides of a river, the Willamette, that flows north into the Columbia. We were going over one of the bridges. "Daddy?" I said, "will you not tell anybody about the competition?"

He looked at me and then back at the bridge he was driving over. "No, I won't tell anybody. Why not?"

"I don't know. I just don't want people to know."

We left the bridge and were on the west side of the city. "That's fair, Allegra. It's understandable," he said.

We parked the car and went to the square. Everybody else had adult page turners. They were their students or their husbands or something. Only one other page turner had a chin-rest bruise. Daddy and everyone else in the quartet were wearing their usual black stuff, but with white jackets for the men. Those are for summer concerts. A string quartet has two violinists, a violist, and a cellist. Daddy's quartet has three men and a woman; she's the violist. You hold a viola almost the same way you hold a violin, but it's a little bit bigger and has a lower voice. A violist usually has a chin-rest bruise, too.

I looked at the program. It was the Dvořák and Mozart and Gershwin and Glazounov, he was a Russian composer. I sat back and got ready to turn pages.

And that's how I found the dancing man.

2

Portland is supposed to be one of America's most livable cities. It has lots of free outdoor concerts in the summer. Some people bring picnics to the concerts; others wander in and listen for a couple of minutes and then leave. Sometimes in the square people roller-skate around while the concert is going on. At the jazz concerts lots of people dance, especially little kids.

Mommy got there late. The quartet was already playing the first piece. I'd have to wait till after the concert to talk to her. I couldn't tell from looking at her face if she knew I'd found out about the Bloch Competition. She waved to me and made this big, silly hello-thing she does with her hands. It's what people did in the Charleston dance a long time ago. She puts her hands up at the sides of her head and wiggles them and opens her mouth wide and grins. Even though it's perfectly silent it feels very loud. It's embarrassing. I looked up at her and made a very little smile, and I abruptly remembered the strange singer Bro David had meant. Her name is Deirdre, and she's beautiful.

While I was watching the first violinist and thinking about judges watching me, I saw somebody dancing in front of the audience, just a few feet to my left. He had his elbows held out to the sides, as if he had sore armpits. His head was going up and down, and he was taking steps in rhythm with his head, sort of in syncopation to the music. He went forward and back, forward and back, kind of in an oval. He was stiff, the way old men get stiff when their bones get creaky.

He was just dancing. A dancing man.

He had on old clothes. His pants were too big; he was kind of skinny, and his belt made them fold all around. They were brown and so was his shirt. It had short sleeves so you could see how bony and blistery his elbows were. One of his shoes was torn, down at the place where you start to lace them up. I could see it when his foot danced forward. Even though he looked as if he had arthritis or one of those creaky diseases, his dancing was kind of musical. It was formal dancing, the kind they do in old-fashioned movies.

His face was a little bit like another face I saw when I was little. When somebody's father came to pick up his kid from a rehearsal—it was the Oregon Prep Orchestra—he had little holes in his face. On his forehead and everyplace.

The dancing man had them. It must be a sorrowful thing to go through your whole life with holes in your face. People probably stare at you; they can't help it. He wasn't exactly smiling, but he looked happy.

He reminded me of something, or of somebody. I couldn't figure out what it was.

Some of the Stem People were staring at him. Those are the people who bring picnics to concerts and wine or champagne or something, and they bring real glasses from their cupboards, ones that have stems. They pay a lot of attention to their glasses not falling; they're very careful of the stems. And high up on the steps, almost in the last row, a man pointed at him and the lady beside him nodded her head and went on listening to the music. She was an Ear Lady. Those are the ones with dangly earrings that bounce in time to the music. The Symphony where Mommy and Mr. Kaplan play used to have an Ear Lady, but she took them off.

I made another page turn. You have to take off both bottom clothespins, then reach across and under the music to do the pin on the right, stand up, take off the top two pins, turn the page with your left hand at just exactly the right instant—two or three measures before the end of the page or sometimes the player nods at you exactly when to do it—then attach the top two pins, sit down, attach the bottom left one first because that's the page he's on, and then reach under and across again and attach the bottom right one. While you're standing up you're holding two clothespins in each hand. And while you're doing all that you can't get between the player and the music; he has to see the notes.

After I sat down I turned to watch the man dancing again. He was facing the quartet, and he looked at me watching him and he smiled at me. It was the way my mother smiled at some sheep one time in a field when we were driving along in the Columbia Gorge. My dad saw her do it and said we weren't taking a sheep home for a pet. My mother said she didn't want to take one home: they were perfectly fine where they were; she just liked to know they were there and she was smiling at them.

That was the way the man smiled at me, I think. I was surprised. I smiled back at him. He kept dancing. He seemed to have hardly any teeth. It looked like one tooth in a whole lot of darkness.

The last movement ended and everybody clapped. The Stem People usually put their stem glasses down to clap; sometimes they hold them in one hand and clap the other against the glass. Some people lean over and talk to their friends while they clap. Some people don't clap at all. They just watch the quartet standing up and bowing; they just stare.

The man danced right to the end of the Glazounov. He left when everybody else did. The quartet packed up their stuff and people came around to talk to them, and Mommy met us. I rode home with her.

"I get paid for turning tonight. I think I'll do it again," I said when we were in the car. My mother has short, very curly, kind of medium brownish hair. It vibrates when she moves her head fast.

"You did really well, honey. I watched you," she said.

"Thanks. Did you see the dancing man?"

"Of course. I've seen him at concerts before."

"Dancing?"

"I've never seen him not dancing," she said. We were stopped at a traffic light, and lots of people were leaving the square. I watched her thinking. "You know," she said, "it's a joy to see him dancing as spontaneously as the little children always do."

"What do you mean, 'always'?"

"Oh, I'm remembering you and Bro David, dancing your little hearts out one summer. You both had blue T-shirts. I think they said 'Symphony Kid' on them. You were tiny."

I tried to remember doing that; all I could see was bare feet in grass, moving up and down.

"That dancing man reminds me of somebody. Or something," I said.

"Maybe you've seen him before."

"I don't think so. Maybe I dreamed him?"

"I don't know."

What we really had to talk about was the competition. Mommy was purposely not talking about it. She knew I'd been to my lesson that morning, and since it was the first lesson after the end of school, it was probably all planned that Mr. Kaplan would pick that day to tell me. Evidently I was supposed to bring it up.

We were on the bridge crossing the river. Portland has its bridges lit up at night. My mother's orchestra played in the park for the lighting ceremony of one of them. "Mr. Kaplan told me about the Bloch finals," I said.

She didn't say anything. I listened to the hum of the steel grating. "And what do you think about it?" she finally asked.

"I think somebody could've told me about it before."

"Why?"

"So I'd be ready."

"Ready for what?"

"Why did everybody wait so long to tell me?"

"So you could concentrate on finishing the school year, get your projects and things finished. So you could give your energy to the softball play-offs. How much readier would you be if somebody'd told you before? How long before?"

"I don't know. But I wouldn't've ignored the concerto for so long."

She kind of sighed. A Mother Sigh. "Hurry up and study for your spelling test, hurry up and practice the Kreutzer, hurry up and make your bed. . . ." she said. She looked at me and then back at the road.

"What's that supposed to mean?" I said.

"What kind of hurry-ups are those?" she asked.

"Mother Hurry-ups," I said.

"Exactly. And what're they really for?"

I knew what she was getting at. When we went to see my friend in a horse show when I was about eight years old, we saw some parents leaning on the rail yelling at their kids: "Wrong lead, Sally, wrong lead!" and "Heels down!" and other things. It's called getting Parents' Trophies.

"Do you want me to play the finals?" I asked.

"I won't touch that one," she said, not looking at me.

Nobody said anything for another couple of minutes. "How scary will it get, Mommy?"

She looked hard at the road. "Well, darling, if you want to know, it'll get very, very scary. That's all I can say."

"I'm going to do it anyway," I said.

She nodded her head at the road ahead. "I thought you would."

My cat, Heavenly Days, was on my bed. Cats spend eighty percent of their lives sleeping. She's called Heavenly Days because that's what my mother said when she saw her in the shoe box I brought her home in. Some people in front of a fruit stand were giving away kittens, and they had shoe boxes for them. They were a huge fat lady and a little girl; they were both wearing shorts. They had the kittens in a big cardboard carton. Daddy and I looked at the kittens, all cluttering each other and reaching with their big feet, and squeaking and blinking. There were two gray-striped ones and a calico and a completely black one. On the cardboard box there was a Magic Marker sign: Do You Need Somebody To Love? Kittens Free.

Daddy and I just stood there looking down into the carton. The completely black one looked at me and yawned and its eyes looked surprised at the yawn, as if it were sending an SOS. I reached down into the carton and put my hand on its back. The lady said, "That one's a male. Had his shots, they all had their shots. See? He likes you."

I picked him up, and he felt very warm and good to hold. I looked at him up close. He was absolutely, completely black. And his eyes were very big and blue. I put him against my chest, and he tried to climb up me; I could feel his heart beating very fast.

I looked at Daddy. He looked at the cat. He laughed. The fat lady, who had extremely fat fingers, put the kitten in one of the shoe boxes and we all came home together.

Heavenly turned out to be a girl. We had her spayed because my mother wouldn't let her have kittens. And her eyes turned yellow; they look like moons.

When I got into bed with Heavenly after the concert, there was a note on the clipboard on the floor:

> *Do I have to rent a tux if you win?*
> *You spelled* annihilate *wrong. I fixed it.*

Two *n*'s. He'd corrected it on the clipboard.

I opened my window about six inches. There's a nice sound that comes in. It's tree frogs, and little mutters of bushes settling down. Heavenly settled herself between my feet.

It's always hard to go to sleep after a concert. It's your adrenaline. I kept seeing the dancing man with his torn shoe, moving slowly around and around, the brownness of all of him, and the music making him smile. Maybe such a man was a little bit crazy. But you couldn't be too crazy if you liked to dance to string quartet music.

That morning, all I'd had in my head was having a fun lesson and learning new words for September and missing my friends who'd gone away to do things for the summer. A few hours later, along had come the competition and the strange dancing man, and I'd turned the pages in public for money, and I'd learned "tenacity" and "annihilate." In South Africa they annihilate people. You could let nervousness annihilate your chances of playing Mozart the way you wanted to. Hitler tried to annihilate the Jews.

On our dining-room wall we have a photograph from Poland of a little girl standing in a field of flowers, holding a purse in her hand. There's a white goose standing beside her, and she's holding a homemade straw broom; it was what she used to tend her flock of geese with. The purse is velvet with some embroidery on it. She was my great-grandmother, and she was Jewish, and her name was Leah. My middle name.

My mother's grandmother was going to be a dancer. She was in Kansas, and she wasn't at all Jewish. She kept a diary of the things she did on the farm, milking goats and churning butter and rubbing medicine on the cow's udder. And she didn't get smallpox when it came. She didn't turn out to be a dancer, she turned out to be a farmer with her husband. Her diary went on for sixty-six years, and then she got senile and lay in bed asking for horses. She kept waving her arms in the air and asking for horses and then she died with her whole family looking at her in her bed with the quilt she made on top of it.

My mother came from Kansas. The same quilt my great-grandmother died under was on my mother's bed when she was my age, and now it's on my bed. They lived so far out in the country, they had several people on the same telephone line. It was called a party line. My mother and her girlfriend Alice, who lived two miles away, could pick up the phone and listen to the neighbors' conversations. In fact, on the day my mother knew she'd find out if Juilliard had accepted her, she was sixty-five miles away at her violin lesson, and the postmistress called to say it was a thick envelope from Juilliard, not a thin one. But nobody was home, and Alice picked up the phone when she heard the three rings for my mother's house, and she took the message. So Alice found out before my mother did that she was going to go to New York to go to music school. My mother and Alice were each other's answering machines. They still phone each other on New Year's Day every single year and talk for a long time. Alice still lives in Kansas. My mother can cook both Kansas food and Jewish food. She makes Kansas corn cakes and eggplant pudding, and she also makes latkes and pecan haroset the way Bubbe Raisa taught her.

The reason why Bro David got to go to New York was that Bubbe Raisa gave him that trip because my parents weren't giving him a bar mitzvah. She thought it was a shame he wouldn't have any ceremony of his Jewishness for his thirteenth birthday, she said. And she sent him the airplane tickets. My parents were surprised but there wasn't anything they could do when he had the tickets in his hand except let him go. Besides the eleven museums, they went to see the Yankees play and he got to eat anything he wanted. He came back wanting latkes and blintzes all the time.

We had to do family trees last year at school. John Muir

Middle School in Portland, Oregon. Jessica's tree had to reach from Chicago to Hong Kong, and she couldn't find the slavery parts. Maybe her father's ancestors weren't even slaves. It's a whole unknown part of her. You had to say something about yourself when you did your oral presentation of your family tree, and Jessica did hers with mirrors. She told everybody the day before that they had to have mirrors for her presentation. So she had us look in the mirrors we'd brought from home, and she had us imagine a place several generations back, to see ourselves in some place completely different. Her point was that maybe a great-grandparent who looked a little bit like us, maybe in the jaw structure or around the eyes, looked out on a river or lived near a mountain or maybe drove a horse and carriage. She explained that she knows about the Chinese side of her family—they came from Hunan—but her black side is a mystery before her father's grandparents.

Sarah's family tree went all the way back to when Leningrad was called St. Petersburg, in Russia. Sarah said Russia was where she got the beginnings of her dancing, even though she's never been there and it was six generations back that somebody was a dancer. She said she dances for all the dead people in her past. Some kids thought that was stupid. It made Sarah feel terrible.

Mine was three countries. Poland and Finland and the United States. I was supposed to include everything I could find, every name and every date in my family history. I'd always seen the girl with the goose and the broom in the dining room, but there was something that made me not ask questions about her. For school I had to ask.

"It's when. That's part of it," my father said. We were at

the dinner table. Dinner was over, and I had my notebook and pencil out. "I can't tell you *when* she died. Somewhere in Poland, sometime after 1939. Isn't that enough?"

I remember the way Daddy looked at the pencil in my hand and then away from me. He was making a miniature pile of crumbs on the tablecloth with his thumbnails.

"But was it one of the death camps?" I asked.

He looked at the pile of crumbs on the tablecloth, little brown fragments of bread on white cloth, then up at me and then back down at the pile. "Yes." He got up and left the table.

My mother said, very softly, "T-R-E-B-L-I-N-K-A. And her husband's name was Herschel." I wrote down the words.

That was what had made me never ask before. The way my father turned away from the pencil in my hand.

When I did my oral presentation I said I was half Jewish and half Gentile, and that has advantages and disadvantages. One, if you're half-and-half, you're lucky because each kind has some really good things about it. Gentiles are good at building things, cathedrals and huge barns and things. Jews have courage, to wander all around the world getting abused and killed and still go on having the Torah. It must be a terrible courage. Two, if you're half-and-half, you're the thing that can't be. You can't be half Jewish. So you go through your life being something that can't be.

And now I was still the thing that can't be, and I was going to play a competition with people all older, and they probably knew everything Mozart ever wrote down. It would get very, very scary, Mommy said.

Play the concerto one thousand times by September. My friend Sarah would probably do more than one thousand pliés by September. She changed ballet teachers last year, and all of a sudden she had a boyfriend in her ballet class. Still, a plié isn't a whole concerto.

Would that be what might make me end up like Deirdre, as Bro David had warned me? How could I end up like her? She's a very famous singer. She and my mother sometimes stay on the phone for hours; she times her phone calls for when Mommy gets home from playing a concert, and by then it's after 2:00 A.M. in New York, where Deirdre lives.

My mother told me once that when she got to New York from Kansas and met the other students at Juilliard and heard them play, she wanted to turn around and go home. "I felt like Dorothy in Oz," she said. "Take me back to Kansas, *please*."

On our dining-room wall, on the opposite side from the photograph of Leah and her goose and her broom and her purse, there are two embroidered linen pictures in frames. Bubbe Raisa in New York made one when Bro David was born and one when I was born. They have our names in Hebrew, and pomegranates, figs, dates, wheat, barley, grapes, and olives all in colored thread. Those are the seven fruits in the Bible. Bubbe Raisa met my grandfather Jacob when they were both standing in line to get standing-room tickets to the Metropolitan Opera in New York. They went inside and stood together to see *La Bohème*. It was very sad, and he gave her his handkerchief when she cried. She forgot to return it to him and she ended up with it at home. She washed it and starched it and ironed it and carried it with her to the standing-room lines of four more operas before she saw him again. When she finally saw him and returned the handkerchief to him, he bought her a glass of tea after the opera and they ended up getting married and having my father.

Zayde Jacob is dead now. They always listened to the Metropolitan Opera on Saturdays on the radio. Bubbe Raisa still dusts the living room every Friday afternoon for the Saturday opera. "You wouldn't want to be slovenly when people are falling in love and dying with their hearts broken; you can dust up a little," she used to say. My father can do a perfect imitation of her saying it.

When I was in kindergarten I had a boyfriend, I think. Teddy. We could both fit on one swing on the playground. He shared his graham crackers with me, and he taught me how to put my parka on upside down. You lay your parka on the floor with the collar toward you and the lining facing up. You lean over and put your arms in the armholes and then you straighten up and flip the parka over your back. It's good for little kids because then they don't get their arms all mixed up in the sleeves and wonder where the other side of the parka is. Sometimes I still put on my parka that way.

Teddy built a castle of blocks one day and said I could live in it. Another kid came and knocked it down, and Teddy hit him. They had a fight right there on the floor until one of the teachers got hold of them and started chanting a peace song over and over again. They calmed down.

On Valentine's Day, Teddy made me a big, red, gooey Valentine; the glue oozed out all around the edges. He and I held hands at story time. Then he moved away, while one of the teachers was reading *The Trumpet of the Swan* to us. He never even found out how it ended, I guess.

Teddy was the first and last boyfriend I'd ever had.

Heavenly paced up the bed and curled up on my pillow, leaning her back against my head.

I listened to the crickets and tree frogs outside in their little breeze and started fingering the *Allegro ma non troppo* part of the last movement of the Mozart concerto on my chest. It's in six-eight, and it's a cheerful thing to play. It's the part that comes back at the very end of the concerto, but then it's played pianissimo.

3

It was very important for nobody to tell the whole world I was going to play the Bloch Competition finals in September. I wasn't sure why; I just knew I didn't want it broadcast. And I didn't want to know who the other finalists were either. It was bad enough imagining these very tall people with computer memories and fingers like willow branches walking in and playing the Mozart as if they were brushing their teeth. I didn't want to know what they looked like.

I told everybody in my family that was the way I wanted it. They said okay. My mother was standing at the kitchen sink when I told her, early on the morning after the day I'd found out. She'd just found a fly struggling in the soapsuds and was scooping it up to take it outside and saying to it, "Oh, you poor dear . . ." I'd already practiced two hours that morning.

"I understand, dear. We wouldn't dream of telling people. You're supposed to call Charley Horner this morning."

"Charley Horner who?"

"Charley Horner the horn player. He called late last night. Woke us up, in fact. His number's by the phone." I looked at her. "Daddy's friend," she said.

"Why am I supposed to call him?"

"I don't know. Why don't you find out?"

He had a recording on his phone. "Do you know the one about Ravel and the pianist who played the 'Pavane' too slowly? He told her, 'I wrote a "Pavane for a Dead Princess," not a "Dead Pavane for a Princess." ' He said it in French, of course. Leave your name and number at the beep and I'll call you back." It was a musicians' joke.

"This is Allegra Shapiro," I said. "I think you know my number. I don't know what you want to talk—"

"Hi, Allegra. I don't pick up the phone for just anybody. Listen, Allegra, I saw you turning pages for your pop last night. I want to reserve you for next Sunday in Laurelhurst Park. We've got a blowing date, my wind quintet. I don't know what you charge. Will you save the date—if you're not busy? I don't know what the weather'll be. Maybe we'll turn out to be a windy quintet."

"You mean you want me to turn pages for you?"

"That's exactly what I want you to do. Can you be there by one forty-five? How much do you charge?"

"I don't know," I said.

"You'll never get rich that way, Allegra. Let me know when you find out. You'll schlep your own clothespins, or shall I?"

"I can bring mine," I said.

"We're partners, then," he said. "You'll put the date in your little black book?"

"I don't have a little black book," I said.

"You'll want to get one," he said.

And he hung up.

Mommy was listening. I looked at her. She laughed. "Mommy, I think he's strange," I said.

"You're a businesswoman suddenly," she said.

"I *said* I think he's *strange*."

"Honey, he's no stranger than the rest of the human race. He's a good musician. When's this page-turning event?"

"Sunday afternoon. Laurelhurst." That's near where we live. It's kind of our neighborhood park. It has great tall evergreen trees and holly trees and rhododendron and camelia bushes all over the place. People walk their dogs there; it's a friendly place.

She rolled her eyes up toward the place where the wall and the ceiling come together. "That's right. Glad you reminded me. I promised him long ago I'd be there. We'll go together, all right?"

"I have to take clothespins," I said. She was putting some plates away. "Mommy, why should I have a little black book?"

"That's the way men talk," she said. "Don't worry about it."

"Daddy doesn't talk that way."

"Right. And I'm married to him, not to Charley. Did you eat breakfast?"

"Yep." I'd eaten an oatmeal recipe I'd made up. I suppose it's called Oatmeal Shapiro. Here's how I make it:

⅓ cup rolled oats	a sprinkling of cinnamon
⅔ + cup water	a smaller sprinkling of nutmeg
about 2 dozen raisins	
a small handful of nuts (almonds or walnuts)	½ + cup plain yogurt
1 apple	a very small spoonful of honey

Cut the apple into very small bits, but don't peel it. Put the apple bits, raisins, and water in a saucepan on medium heat. Cover the pan, bring it to a boil, and then boil it for a minute or two. Poke some of the apple pieces with a sharp knife; when the knife goes through them easily, add the rolled oats. Follow the stirring and timing instructions on the rolled-oats box. When they're almost cooked, add the cinnamon, nutmeg, and nuts. Cover the pan and set it aside for the time the instructions say to. Then put the whole thing in a bowl, add the honey and the yogurt. Mix it all up and enjoy.

You can use a pear or a peach instead of the apple; the cooking time will be less. You can use a big spoonful of honey, or even brown sugar, if you want to. You can use any flavor of yogurt you want.

The music room is at the back of our house, like Mr. Kaplan's, but it's different. It has French doors to the outside, and lots of plants in pots because it faces south, and it's cluttered. It's got eight shelves of music, and a piano, and three music stands, and paintings of people playing music. And some photographs. There's room for people to play quartets or quintets here. There's even a sofa. And people are always leaving things when they take lessons from my dad. There's a Lost & Found Chair. That morning it had a green rain slicker on it, and a tan sweater, a cello sonata by Fauré with "Hoyt" scrawled on it, a pair of sunglasses, and a blue comb.

I was looking at the third movement of the concerto, the Rondeau. It's kind of like a body with all its different parts, and if you took the arms and legs and everything apart you could still match them up, because they really do all go together, kind of parallel parts. I was thinking that when you play the third *Andante grazioso* it feels as if you're at the heart of the movement.

"Playing Mozart isn't hard, but to play him well is what you can die trying to do." That's what people always say.

My mother came in with her spritzing watering can. "Allegra, how would you feel about sleeping in here for a few nights?"

"When?"

"Deirdre's coming. Chamber Music Northwest. She gets here next Tuesday." She climbed on a chair and spritzed some water on a Swedish ivy that hangs down from the ceiling. "She suddenly decided she couldn't stand to stay in a hotel."

My mother looked down at me with the spritzing can hanging in the air. "Well, she has more than her share of ambivalences about her life." I looked up at my mother in a question mark. " 'Ambivalence' means you could go either one way or the other and you're not sure which. She thought she'd stay in a hotel, but she's just gotten rave reviews in both Boston and New York and they've unsettled her. Well, scared her, really. She doesn't want to be alone. So," my mother stepped down off the chair, "she'll stay with us. All right?"

I looked at my mother and tried to imagine being scared by rave reviews.

"Besides, she keeps an eye on Bubbe Raisa, visits her. They go to lunch together," my mother said.

I didn't remember Deirdre clearly. She hadn't stayed with us when she came to Portland to sing the year before; she just came for dinner and we went to her concert. She travels around singing all over the place. She was the first person to see Bro David's cartoon about the starving Africans in the magazine. He'd signed it "B. David Shapiro" and she called him on the telephone to congratulate him. He didn't remember to tell Mommy and Daddy about her phone call for about three weeks, and Mommy got very upset.

"I don't know what kind of mood she'll be in. She may want to sleep in here herself. Sometimes she gets frightened of everyday things."

"Everyday things?"

"Yes, sometimes. She got frightened of staying in a hotel. Maybe she'll be frightened about being selfish if she takes your room, I don't know."

"Is she weird?"

Mommy walked over to a plant called Bro David's Plant, I don't know its other name, and she walked around it, bending down to look under its leaves. "Deirdre's had a troubled life, sweetheart. And she's our friend."

"Is she weird?" I asked.

She straightened up and went to an auralia. She turned its pot clockwise a bit and spritzed. "I don't know, honey. What is weird? If she feels all right about sleeping in your room, do you feel all right about it?"

"I guess so." Actually, sleeping in the music room is kind of fun. All the paintings and photographs are right there, it's a kind of social feeling. Heavenly and I sleep on the sofa.

My mother picked up a dead daddy longlegs from a table and held it in her hand, the way you'd hold an egg that fell from a birds' nest. She took it out of the room. She'd add it to the little collection of bugs that have died in the house.

She keeps them on a table in the living room, in an antique dish, with a magnifying lens beside it. She thinks it's interesting to look at all their parts. She says they're Splendid Creatures, So Magnificently Made. When the bugs get dusty and fall apart, she takes the little pile outside, and then she starts a new collection.

The first thing to do was get the concerto clearly and completely memorized, so it would be loud and clear in my mind. I'd lost some parts in the back of my mind since February. When we'd made the tape, I hadn't imagined making the finals. For a tape, the concerto didn't have to be memorized. For the finals, it had to be played from memory.

In fact, when Mr. Kaplan had given me both the third and fourth concertos and I'd played through them and then spun my bow to decide, I'd been completely ambivalent. If my bow had landed the other way, I wouldn't have ended up playing the Bloch Competition at all. The competition concerto was Number Four.

When the great cellist Yo-Yo Ma was little, he memorized two measures of a Bach cello suite each day. The suites are unaccompanied, no piano. In a year he knew three of them, how they were built, how the notes worked in patterns. Not everybody works that way. You have to find the way you work best. That's your method.

Different violinists play differently, of course. Anne-Sophie Mutter, who's German, plays the third movement of this concerto in seven minutes and twenty-one seconds. She was invited to play a solo with Herbert von Karajan and the Berlin Philharmonic when she was fourteen. David Oistrakh took seven minutes and fifty-four seconds to play the same movement. He was Russian. And Itzhak Perlman plays it in seven minutes flat. And he wrote his own cadenzas. He's American. Those were the only three recordings of it we had in our house. I didn't know which one was what you'd call Best; I don't know how you even decide those things. What's Best? Faster isn't necessarily better. All I know is that I listened to all three of them quite a bit for several weeks.

I played the recordings in my room, on the old stereo that my parents had given me when their CD player arrived. They won the CD player from the radio by sending in a question to the opera quiz that happens between the acts of the Metropolitan Opera radio broadcast on Saturdays. If the Met quiz uses your question on the radio, you get prizes. My parents had sat at the dining-room table for a lot of nights thinking up questions and throwing them away; it took them a long time to come up with a good one. The one that got used was "How many operas can you name that take place on islands? And which of these islands are real and which are imaginary?" And for that we got a CD player. It almost didn't seem fair.

Now, we all have our own sound systems. Bro David had already bought his with Safeway money, so he didn't need the one my parents were giving away. He plays mostly African music on his. My father was right when he said, "Anybody who didn't like music would go berserk in this house."

Summer was turning out to be a whole lot of practicing and not very much else. One day I got three postcards: one from Jessica with Chinese characters on it, one from Sarah saying that dance camp was harder than the year before, and one from my stand partner in the Youth Orchestra who was suddenly moving to Los Angeles. It felt as if everybody was going away.

My stand partner was seventeen years old, her name was Lois, and her parents got transferred and she had to go along. "They want me to go to UCLA next year anyway," her postcard said.

A stand partner is very important. In the string sections of an orchestra, two people share a music stand. Usually the outside person is the better player. Christine, the concertmaster of the Youth Orchestra, says, "It's important how you occupy your space." The outside player can't just let the scroll of her violin hang out in the middle of the space and get in the way of the inside player's line of vision. The one on the inside, away from the audience, turns pages while the outside player keeps on playing. Of course you have to turn at just the right moment. You also have to listen to instructions together, and once Lois explained something I didn't understand.

Stand partners also have to agree on what things they want written in pencil on the pages, and who's going to write them. Lois and I'd agreed that we could use my music, with my writing, things like "Don't drag," and with difficult sections circled.

At the bottom of the postcard she wrote, "Don't forget me, Little Buddy. Remember the time we played the wrong note together in the Shostakovich?"

I tried to imagine somebody else sitting in her chair. I missed her already. Just remembering the way she called me "Little Buddy" made me lonely.

When I turned pages for Charley Horner at Laurelhurst Park, there was just a little breeze, so I didn't need the clothespins on every turn. And my mother let me borrow these very long clamps that she uses for outdoor concerts. She wasn't going to need them until Labor Day, for the

Oregon Symphony concert in Waterfront Park. Mostly, I got to listen to the wind quintet. Daddy and Mommy and Mr. Kaplan and everybody were willing not to tell about the competition, so I didn't have to hear people wishing me luck, or looking at me and deciding whether I was going to win or lose it.

The quintet had a flute, oboe, clarinet, French horn, and bassoon. Charley Horner announced all the pieces. During the second song, a horn honked loudly and burst into the music. At the end of the song, he said, "That was our sixth member. He always comes in late."

They were just beginning the second half of the concert, and the sun was streaming through the trees, making the bushes and everything gorgeous, and people were sitting around on their blankets with their food, when the dancing man got there.

He was wearing his same clothes. And he danced the same dance. If the music got faster or slower, he didn't change his dance. I watched him a lot. He was holding his arms out in sideways *v*'s like crescendo markings, the same way he'd done in the square, and he moved his feet in a sort of oval; it was his dancing method. He still had his torn shoe.

At the end of the concert, the dancing man made a little bow to Charley Horner's quintet. He did it while they were bowing to the audience and everybody was clapping.

I earned $3.75 that day.

Daddy stayed to talk to some friends, and my mother and I walked home together, through the park and up the hill and along the sidewalk where some little kids were jumping rope. Mommy was swinging the canvas shoulder bag she carries, and I was holding my plastic bag of music clamps and jingling my money in my skirt pocket. It was a nice summer afternoon, and you could smell people's gardens.

"I love Portland," Mommy said. "If you have a little bit of ground, you can have roses. Anybody in the city can— if they have dirt."

Portland is called the City of Roses. It's because of the long growing season. Roses bloom from early spring to late fall. We have eight rosebushes. In a park there's a huge Rose Garden on a hill where you can see thousands of roses and look down on the city. The squirrels there are so tame they come and grab food from your hand.

"I wonder if the dancing man has any," I said.

She reached in my pocket and took my hand out. We walked along holding hands. My money jingled. "Honey, I don't know."

We walked along. You could hear our sandals flapping. Then she said again, "I don't know." We walked along some more. "He's a victim. Probably," she said.

"Of what? What do you think a victim of?" We were on our block, and you could hear sprinklers on people's lawns.

"I don't know. It could be a hundred different things," she said.

⁓

From Charley Horner's concert I got two more page-turning jobs in the same week. Turning for pianists makes the most money by far; they have the most page turns.

"Only two more days till we get Deirdre's Doldrums," Daddy said a few mornings later when everybody was home for breakfast.

"Deirdre's Delirium is more like it," Bro David said.

·45·

Mommy said, "I think you're both being stinkers. I don't want this to turn into Women versus Boys. Listen, she has to sing, and it'd be inhuman for us to do anything even slightly . . ."

Nobody said anything.

"And besides, if it gets cold or rainy or something, she could get sick, and it's our responsibility to . . ." She didn't finish that sentence either.

It's kind of a sad joke how singers get sick when they come to Portland from other places. In summer it's not so bad, but mostly, Oregon weather is hard on them. Lots of rain. Once a baritone lost his voice for an opera and he had to stand on the stage acting out the singing while another man stood way down in the orchestra pit, right where Daddy plays, doing the voice part. If you were there watching, it looked ridiculous.

"Fleur, word of honor. I won't do anything even slightly. Promise," Daddy said.

Mommy laughed. "You, David?" she said. "Be a sweetheart."

"How do you be that?" he said.

"For one thing, you could try not imitating her when she practices," Daddy said.

"She's gonna practice here?" I asked.

Mommy looked at me. "Where else? Do you think it'd be better if she *didn't* practice here? What if somebody told you you couldn't—"

"Okay," I said. I was looking forward to having her come to stay. It would bring some variety into the house.

"Well, enjoy your nearly last French toast for a while," Daddy said.

·46·

"Why?" I asked.

"No fried foods when Deirdre's in the house," Mommy said.

"Why not?" I said.

"Her voice," David said. "She can't do her *eeee-eeee-eeee* if there's any residual fat in the air." He made loud, high sounds, like a giant mouse.

"David, that's exactly what your father meant," Mommy said. She looked at me, partly as if she wanted me to help, and partly as if she wanted to prevent something from coming loose.

◦◦◦

Mr. Kaplan was pleased with the way the concerto was going. He got out his violin a few times and we played parts of the concerto together. We listened to the copy he'd kept of the tape we'd made in the winter. "Already in February you were in teamwork with the music," he said. "That was wonderful. For the preliminaries. Now we're ready to begin the hard part. It's no longer just the right notes in the right dynamics at the right time, Allegra," he said. He turned sideways on the piano bench. "It's time to start making the concerto your own song."

I looked at him. I didn't even have all the notes exactly memorized.

"It's like this, Allegra," he said. He held up both hands, about a foot apart. "Here's Mozart, over here. He has his concerto with him. And here you are, over here. See the distance between you? It's a fact. There are more than two hundred years. And there's all that ocean. And his mind and your mind. We're going to start moving them closer

·47·

together. See?" He started moving his hands very, very slowly through the air. "We're going to bring them as close together as we can." He put his hands down on his knees. "That's what we're gonna do."

I looked at the places where his hands had been. Music poured out of Mozart. It wasn't automatic or anything, nobody's mind does it automatically. He had to find the notes in his mind and put them in order, but he just poured them out.

Mr. Kaplan put his hands up again. This time he brought them so close there wasn't even an inch between them. "We're going to get to the point where there's just an edge. The place where you and Mozart and his concerto meet. That's the edge we want. As little air space as we can manage. We're gonna try to close the distance." He looked at the little space between his hands. Then he put them down again and looked up at me. "How're you holding up?"

"I'm holding up fine," I said. Joel Smirnoff was smiling in the photograph on the desk.

"Good. Because we've just begun. Do you like this concerto?"

I decided to come right out with the question that had bothered me. "Mr. Kaplan, why didn't you tell me sooner that I'd made the finals?" I was maybe even angry. "In fact, when you first gave me the concerto. At the very beginning. You knew there was this competition. I want to know why I was the last person to find out."

"So. You have been concerned, haven't you?"

I nodded my head. "When did you find out I was a finalist?"

He looked at me over his half-glasses and waited for a little while. "Not so long before I told you. Not so very long, Allegra."

Not so very long. It was getting through to me. "My parents knew and everything, then. A long time before I found out."

"Allegra, you had school to finish up. The softball team . . . Those play-offs you were in . . ."

For the whole last six weeks of school I'd been mostly a walking softball uniform. The school was counting on us, and in the mornings the intercom kept reciting the results of our games into all the rooms, and they made it seem like the most important thing in the world. And there were final exams. Jessica and Sarah and I had very hard ones in our classes. "But even at the beginning. You didn't say, 'If you choose the Fourth Concerto you'll be entering the Bloch Competition—but if you choose the Third, you won't, because the Competition concerto is Number Four.' "

"Indeed. Yes." He folded his hands together, then spread them out flat on his lap. "I didn't tell you you might make the Bloch play-offs." He waited for me to laugh, and I did, just a little bit. "My dear, it's this way. First, I know too much about what happens when young musicians are forced into competition. Imagine how you'd have felt, trying to prepare this concerto for the finals if you were all the time wishing you were playing a different concerto. And second, once you selected this concerto, if I'd told you right then about the competition, you'd have learned it differently. Don't you think so?"

"I don't know," I said.

"I want you first to love the music. *Then* compete."

"But it's the same concerto."

"No. If I'd given it to you and said, 'Listen, Allegra, you will play this concerto in competition in exactly so-and-so months,' it would not be the same concerto in your hands."

I looked at him and thumbed the strings of my violin with my right hand. It's a sort of nervous habit I have.

"And your softball is very important to you, too, is it not?"

I glimpsed myself a few weeks before, running to practice, running from practice, studying geography and English and math and everything else for finals, and my parents making me sit down and eat dinner with the whole family almost every single night "because we are a family, we're not just four random people running in and out of the same house," as my father said. And I glimpsed myself stretching to catch a fly in one game that made the winning out and hearing everybody yelling "Shapiro!" over and over again, and I remembered half the time having dust everywhere on me, in my ears and my hair, and the other half taking showers and hearing my whole body getting squeaky clean, and always being so tired. Tired. All the time. "It was important. It was important then."

"Indeed. And Mozart was resting then. Now he's getting his turn. Things in their seasons, Allegra." His eyebrows arched. "This is the Mozart season."

I nodded my head a little bit.

"I want you and the concerto to be in partnership first. Only then can we bring you close to Mozart. A general partnership of good feeling first. Then we close the distance. Is that clear?"

"I guess so."

"Well," he laughed, "good. Because I'm not convinced it's clear to me. These things are hard to explain, you know."

"I know." I laughed.

"Remember what somebody said: Talking about music is like dancing about architecture. Let's play. Which movement?"

"Let's do the first," I said. I wanted to try this Closing the Distance from the beginning.

He stopped me at letter E. "Allegra, I want you to try something this week. I want you to play this whole movement just as boldly as you can. I want you to say, 'ME: Allegra Shapiro. I'M playing this concerto.' I want you to jump right into it. Let's see what that accomplishes."

"Okay," I said. We started it again.

At the end of my lesson, Mrs. Kaplan brought in chocolate-chip cookies. She calls the treats Endorphin Therapy. "These are to give you the strength to get home, dear," she said. She has gray hair and a soft double chin. The Endorphin Therapy was a joke, of course, but I was glad to have the extra strength, even if it would just be for the cadenzas.

∽

I changed the sheets on my bed for Deirdre. I put on the ones with the music notation. You can read parts of *The Magic Flute* on them. Mommy and Daddy gave them to me for my eleventh birthday, last year. I dusted everything I could reach, the lampshades and everything, because Deirdre is allergic. Jessica had brought me a Chinese doll all the way from Hong Kong when we were nine years old, and I even dusted that. And I took a box of things to the music room. My pajamas and my clipboard and things.

Deirdre's airplane was late. She was coming from Aspen, Colorado. She was singing there at a festival. While we waited, Daddy kept us occupied by making us guess things he already knew. How many daily newspapers are published in New York? Twenty-three. How many of them aren't in English? Thirteen. Both Mommy and I guessed way wrong. What Tibetan product does the British army use in its helmets? Yak hair. We both guessed way wrong again. What species has nerve fiber a thousand times wider than humans'? The squid. My mother got hilarious and said Daddy could ask everybody in the entire airport and nobody would know that one.

I went to the bathroom. In the Portland airport, you have to step on a button on the floor to turn on any water at all. There was a middle-aged lady standing in front of a washbasin, feeling around. She had a white cane with a red tip hanging on her arm, and she was wearing sunglasses. She obviously wanted to turn the water on. There was nobody else in the bathroom. I said, "You have to step on a button."

She felt around with her right foot. Water spurted out of the faucet. "Oh—thanks," she said. It's always kind of surprising when you hit the button for the first time.

"It's the same with the toilet," I said. "To get it to flush." I didn't know if I was doing the right thing or not.

She turned sideways toward me but I knew she couldn't see me. "What an interesting system," she said. Then she laughed. "It's a secret code."

"Yep," I said. I laughed, too.

I pretended to be washing my hands but I was just running the water and watching her. How would you know how to turn on the water if somebody didn't tell you, if you couldn't see it? It could take you hours to figure it out. You'd be feeling around in your brain for the right question to ask, and you'd be wondering why the water wouldn't go on. You'd hear it going on at the other basins. You wouldn't have the information you need.

It was a little bit—very much—like trying to get over the gap to the Mozart concerto. I could hear it played beautifully on the records, and I was feeling around in my brain for the information I had to have to play it the way I needed to play it.

Deirdre was carrying about six bags, and she had a huge suitcase checked. She has a whole lot of big blond hair all around in curls, and she has great big loopy earrings. An Ear Lady. And she has big lips that look almost strange when she sings. It's a very dramatic mouth.

"Allegra. I knew you when you were an ovary. Let me look at you." She and I were squinched in the backseat of Daddy's car, with some of her bags, and the rest of her luggage was behind us, in the place where his cello rides. She has huge dark brown eyes that stare. "Ah, the gene pool," she said, and laughed. "You're so much like your mommy when she was younger. And there's that black, black hair! Fleur, did anybody in your family ever have black hair?"

Mommy laughed. "No. I don't think so."

"It's not really black," I said. "Just very dark brown."

"Do you know what I mean when I say 'gene pool'?" she said.

"Yep. It's the way you get things from both parents. In your genes."

"And from their parents, and their grandparents. Oh— Raisa sends hugs and kisses to everybody. She was going to send a cake—but I couldn't keep it in a bag for five days. How's the violin going?" she asked me.

"Fine," I said.

"What're you playing now?"

I shuffled music around in my mind, avoiding Mozart. I wasn't ready to tell her about the competition.

"She's playing page turner this summer," Daddy said.

"Earning money. By the way, Allegra, can you turn for a pianist on Saturday? Two o'clock?"

"Yep," I said.

"Ah, blessed are the Oregon breezes," Deirdre said. "What've you turned?"

I told her all the pieces I could think of.

We put all Deirdre's bags and things in my room. She said she just wanted to be alone for a few minutes "to try to find some coherence."

෴

With Deirdre staying with us, arranging practice times could get complicated. Bro David hung a sign-up sheet on the music-room door. It was divided into half-hour blocks, and you could sign up for as many as you wanted, as long as you weren't selfish about it. The sign-up sheet had a picture on it that he drew. It was somebody with lots of arms, like that Hindu god Siva, and the person was playing two violins and a cello and singing at the same time.

I was just about asleep in the music room that first night and I was watching this painting we have. It's by Marc Chagall and it's called *The Green Violinist*. The man has a green face, and he's playing a violin. He's wearing a purple hat and coat, and things are flying through the painting. The violinist is up in the air above some buildings, and there's a small gray man flying in the sky and another man, even smaller, holding up his arms to catch the flying one. I've always liked that painting. You can think that the man playing the violin is sending flying music into the air and that's why everything flies, or you can think there's some other reason why they fly. We don't have the real painting, we have a print of it. We saw the real one in New York once when we went to visit my grandmother Raisa.

There's a streetlight near the corner of our house, and it shines through the windows of the music room at night, so you can see things kind of in a gray color. And there are sort of trapezoids of light on the carpet from the French doors.

Somebody knocked on the door. "Am I bothering you, Allegra?" It was Deirdre.

I told her she wasn't.

"I won't stay long." She was in a balloony white nightgown with lace, and bare feet, the nightgown made a cottony sound when she walked. Her hair was hanging all down her back. She still had long, dangly earrings on, and you could hear them tinkling when she walked. She had a big glass of milk in one hand.

"Want me to turn on the lamp?" I asked.

"No, I just want to sit here with you in the half-light."

She sat down in the chair the second violinist uses when there are quartets. She put the glass of milk on the floor and stretched both arms above her head and then out to the sides, the way you do in the breaststroke. Then she folded her hands in her lap. "I'm stupid with exhaustion. And I can't sleep. Does that ever happen to you?" she said.

"I think so," I said. I was thinking of the final exams we had to take at the end of school. Jessica and Sarah and I spent the whole night just sitting in front of the TV set, watching old movies. We were at Sarah's house. We'd taken the history exam that day. All on Egypt and ancient China.

"It was Aspen that did it to me. The altitude. And rehearsal's at nine tomorrow morning. This is terrible."

I hunched up on my left elbow and bunched up the pillows. "Do you get nervous when you sing?" I asked her.

"Do I get nervous?" She didn't say anything for about a minute. "Allegra, I throw up before I go onstage."

"Deirdre, that's awful," I said.

"I know. It is awful. The first thing I find when I'm singing anyplace new is the bathroom. That's more important than where the stage is or who's accompanying me or anything else. It's ghastly."

"But once you get started singing it's all right?"

"Yes. It gets all right. I could take a beta blocker, but I don't like drugs."

"What's a beta blocker?"

"It's a drug. It slows your heart, makes it less excitable. It helps keep you steady. Great for stage fright. Juilliard kids take them all the time. They walk in and play their hearts out. It's crazy."

"It doesn't sound crazy to me." I was thinking about the competition, of course. I didn't know there was a drug for stage fright.

"Oh, I know somebody who hallucinated when she took it. Very good flutist. She won a prize and she saw donkeys in the auditorium. I don't think it's a very good trade-off."

She got up and walked over to the photograph of Einstein as an old man playing the violin. He has that white hair you always see in pictures of him. She hummed around the photographs of Fritz Kreisler, Pablo Casals, and the other musicians on the wall. She walked over to the French doors and looked out. "Your roses are wonderful. Do you know that?"

"Yep," I said. I thought of the dancing man, without any roses. We probably have more than our share.

She walked back to the chair and sat down. She almost didn't make any noise when she moved. "What are the big things in your life these days, Allegra?" she said. "Now that school's out and everything."

I moved a little bit and pushed the pillows around and sat up straighter. I didn't say anything. I hadn't told anybody in person, except my parents and Bro David, about the competition. I'd told Sarah and Jessica by postcard.

She hit her forehead with her fist. "Oh—I completely forgot. This guy your mommy and I used to know is coming here. It's a guy we knew at school. In fact, he's already here. Teaching at some college. Or university. He's a biologist. He's got a son, a violinist. Older than you. I haven't seen the kid since he was tiny. I heard about him in Aspen, though; he's supposed to be very good. Somebody who knows somebody who knows him told me. I wrote it all down on an envelope. He'll probably turn up in your orchestra—what's it called?"

"The Portland Youth Orchestra," I said.

"He'll probably turn up here. Do you like playing in it?" she asked.

"Sure. I like it a lot."

"Are you the youngest?"

"No. There are a couple of really little kids."

"But you're one of the youngest?"

"I guess so. Yep. I am. You know what somebody did once?"

"What?" She took a big swig of milk.

"This guy, he's a cellist, he had the repeat section memorized, and he didn't turn the page back, so the girl playing on the outside just went ahead and didn't play the repeat. It was only in rehearsal, but still."

Deirdre laughed, just a little bit. "That's a very dirty trick, Allegra."

"I know it. He got in trouble for it."

"What kind of trouble?"

"He didn't get to play the whole next concert. Not even rehearsals. He was kicked out for the whole time. Three months."

She was laughing again. "Good for him, he deserved it. I get the impression you really love the violin, Allegra. Am I right?"

"Yep. I do."

"Do you know why?"

"No. I don't *think* I know. It feels good."

"Can you imagine not playing it?"

"No!" It came out surprisingly loud.

Deirdre nodded her head. "Then you're stuck with it, aren't you?"

"I guess so. I guess I am."

She looked at me for quite a while with her intense eyes. "Allegra, here's something about doing music—or painting a picture or anything. When you're doing it, you have to remember everything you've ever learned, and simultaneously forget all of it and do something totally new." She was silent for a while more. "Because if you do the first part and not the second, you're making music or art just like everybody else's. It's not your own."

I was asking myself silently if I could ever do that, remember and forget at the same time.

"When I lived in Boston, I used to watch the Celtics a lot. They do the same exact thing—when they're at their best. It's the same with your Trail Blazers in Portland. You watch one of those beautiful shots go exploding down through the basket and that's what's going on. That guy has in his memory every basket he's ever shot—and at the same instant he's making up a new one. The divine inspiration of the NBA."

"Deirdre, I never heard anybody say that before."

"Well, that's the way it is."

"Is that what you do?"

"Yes, that's part of it. When I'm at my best."

I imagined her bent over throwing up. "And you still throw up?"

"Sure. That's why, in fact. Or that's part of it. I'm afraid I won't be able to get that simultaneity." She clenched and unclenched both her hands on the lap of her white night-gown. "There are all kinds of static just waiting up there," she pointed to her head, "to sabotage things."

I reached for the clipboard. "How do you spell those?"

"What? 'Sabotage'?" She spelled it for me. "It means 'to ruin completely.' You have to learn new words for school, or for yourself?"

"Well, both, I guess. A list for school, but I'll need them anyway. And simultan—"

She spelled "simultaneity." I wrote them down.

"You could wear a raincoat," I said. "For throwing up."

She was stretching her arms again. "That's exactly what I do."

"Good," I said. "What's this violinist like, this boy?"

"Oh, Steve? I don't know. When he was a little kid, he was darling. He had a sixteenth-size violin. Curly hair and huge eyes. Long eyelashes. And Lego blocks. He built the most amazing things, he must've been three years old. Big towers. He had phenomenal concentration." I was watching Deirdre take her long, dangly earrings out of her ears. They tinkled when she had them both out and was holding them in her hand. "He'll probably end up being your boyfriend, Allegra."

"I don't think so. You said he's old."

"Oh, not so old. Probably about Bro David's age, I should think. That's not old. I can tell you lots about old." She got up and went over to a photograph of Ernest Bloch. It's kind of low on the wall, and you have to bend over to look at it. I kept not telling her about the Bloch Competition.

I heard a clinking of metal on wood. Two clinkings. She knelt down, her balloony nightgown spreading kind of like a white swan around her.

"I dropped an earring." She was bending over Daddy's cello, which he'd left out of the case, lying on its side. "I can't find it. Turn on the light, will you?" she said.

I got up and turned it on. It was too bright; my eyes hurt. She was feeling around. Then she took hold of the cello by the neck. You could hear something rattle inside.

She looked at me. She looked panicked. "Allegra. It fell through the f-hole," she said in a frightened voice. She put the cello back on its side. "Oh, Allegra. What have I *done?*" She was whispering.

"It's okay," I whispered back, as I walked over to where she was squatting on the floor. "We'll shake it out. Look. You pick up the neck, I'll pick up this end, we'll just turn it over—" I started to pick up the body.

"No! I couldn't pick up a thing. I'm shattered. Allegra, it's always like this. Every single place I go I do something hideous. . . ." She put both hands up over her face, one fisted up with the other earring in it. Her hands were shaking.

I squatted down beside her and put my hand on her shoulder. I whispered, "No, really, Daddy won't be mad. It's all right. We'll just let it fall out the f-hole where it went in. . . . Or the other one . . ."

She was letting out very strange sounds, part sighing and part crying, I couldn't tell which was the main part. And she was shaking all over.

"Well, we can do it in the morning then. Really, it's gonna be all right. Daddy won't be upset. Do you want me to do it by myself?"

She shook her head hard. "No. Don't—don't do anything. . . ." She still had both hands over her face. Her hair was hanging down partly covering her face, too. I couldn't see her eyes; her teeth were clenched tight and even her feet were shaking. Seeing her so almost paralyzed was getting me shaky, too. I kept wishing for a first-aid kit, even though I knew it wouldn't have anything in it that would help.

"Maybe we'd better go to sleep, Deirdre. Maybe you're just tired. From Aspen . . . It's late. . . ."

She just stayed there squatted on the floor, shaking. I brought the rest of the glass of milk to her. I nudged the sleeve of her nightgown with it. She pushed the milk away without looking at it.

"Deirdre," I whispered, "do you want an aspirin?" I put my hand on her shoulder again.

"No! No drugs!" She was almost shouting but still in a whisper.

"Do you want to lie here on the sofa then? Just till you feel better?"

"Oh, Allegra, I can't believe I've done this terrible thing—"

I started to laugh. "It's not so terrible. Just an earring in a cello—"

"Stop it! I've ruined everything—" She let her hands slide down her face and looked up at me, almost like a little tiny kid playing peekaboo. Her eyes looked terrified.

"You haven't either. Come on, stand up, come over and sit on the sofa. Tell me what you're gonna sing at the concert. Please?"

She let her hands slide down to the floor and looked at me. Her face got smoother. She pushed herself up and stood looking around the music room. Suddenly she was talking in her normal voice. "Oh, Allegra, it's beautiful. It's an all-French program, and—just beautiful. Lovely songs . . ."

She opened her hand and looked at the earring in it. It had three gold circles and inside the smallest one were three tiny bells. She bounced it in her hand and walked over to the sofa and sat down on the down sleeping bag I was using for covers. Her nightgown looked as beautiful as a wedding dress. She stared at the earring in her hand and didn't say anything for a long time. Then she whispered, "Allegra, I am a disaster."

I didn't know what to say. I could say, No you're not, but she was being quite strange, and I didn't think I could convince her.

"What time is it?" she asked.

I looked at the clock. It was after midnight. I told her.

"Oooooohhhhh," she said in a long sigh.

"Let's get some sleep, Deirdre?"

She stared at me the way she'd been staring at the earring in her hand.

·62·

"Daddy won't be mad. Promise."

"How can you say that when men are so unpredictable?" she asked.

"He's my father," I said.

She walked over to the metronome and turned it on at a slow tempo. Then she walked around the room, staying far away from Daddy's cello. The metronome was ticking, she was walking, almost like dancing, very slowly, but not exactly with the metronome's rhythm. "I love coming here. To Portland. Your house. It's so peaceful," she said. Then she picked up the glass of milk, drank what was left in it, said good night to me and walked out, pulling the back of her long white nightgown to her when she closed the door. I turned off the metronome and the light and lay down under the down sleeping bag. I knew I should be writing a word or two on my clipboard. I didn't know what the words were, though.

4

I woke up in the middle of the night and remembered Daddy's cello. I turned on the light and wrote him a note on the clipboard paper: *Talk to me before you do anything else in the morning.* I went upstairs in the dark and slipped the note under my parents' bedroom door. The whole house was quiet; I could see the windows and chairs and things just standing there in their shapes, like something waiting to begin.

Mommy came into the music room early in the morning to water the plants. Daddy came along with her. I was just waking up and thinking about practicing. I'd signed up for the 7:00 A.M. practice slot, but I was worried about waking Deirdre.

"What's this note about, honey?" Daddy said. He stood at the end of the sofa in front of my feet. Mommy was humming around the Swedish ivy with her watering spritzer.

I looked at him. "Deirdre's all upset." I sat up.

Mommy stopped spritzing and Daddy gave her a look— just a look, no real expression on his face—as if he were listening to her, except that she wasn't talking.

"Well, last night she came to talk to me, she couldn't go

to sleep, she was wearing this gorgeous, long white nightgown—and she accidentally dropped one of her earrings and it fell through the f-hole in your cello."

Daddy kind of smiled. "The things that have fallen through f-holes could fill a small museum," he said.

"And then she had a sort of fit. She—she said she'd ruined things, and she always does this. . . . I couldn't even talk to her." Looking back on it, I realized I'd actually been afraid.

Daddy looked at me and then over at Mommy. "Fleur, you decide."

Mommy stood with the spritzing can in her hand. "Decide what?"

He kept looking at her. "Decide what's to be done about Deirdre. What time was all this, Allegra?"

"Kind of midnight," I said.

Mommy took a big breath and said, "What's going to be done is get her fed, get her to rehearsal, make sure she takes a nap, give her all the love and safety we can, get her to the Commons, and hear her sing. That shouldn't be so difficult for reasonable human beings to accomplish."

"Mommy, do you know she throws up before she sings?"

"Yes, sweetheart, I know," Mommy said. "Do you want breakfast?"

I watched my mother. She picked up a bug from a begonia leaf and closed her hand lightly over it, carried it to the French doors and opened one of them with the hand that was holding the watering can, and sent the bug out into the air. "What a lovely morning," she said to the yard. "Is it all right if I leave the door partly open? The air smells beautiful," she said.

If she left the door open, more bugs would come in, and

if she saw them she'd pick them up and put them outdoors again. When they're bees, she talks to them, nudging them toward an open door with her voice until they leave. That's the way to get bees to go away, she says.

"Sure," I said.

"Do you think Deirdre had a right to get strange with Allegra?" Daddy said.

She turned around. "The world is so full of a number of things . . ." She didn't finish it. The rest of it says, We should be happy as kings. She kissed him on the neck and went out of the room.

Daddy was trying to protect me. And Mommy was pretending everything was normal. Both of them were being kind of unrealistic.

Daddy went over to the cello. "Allegra, lift the neck, will you? Let's get this thing out and minimize the trauma around here."

"Okay," I said. I climbed out from under the sleeping bag. My blue pajamas were really dull, compared to Deirdre's nightgown. We shook the cello gently and in a few minutes the earring dropped out. Daddy spelled "trauma" for me and I wrote it on the clipboard. He said it means something terrible happening and getting whatever it happens to all upset. When people get in car accidents they have traumas. Being born is a trauma, he said. It takes you out of what you're used to and puts you somewhere else, and you don't understand anything that's going on.

Daddy put his cello in its case, "where it should've been, anyway," as he said. "Peace of Mind requires eternal vigilance," he said. We laughed. Daddy's big on Peace of Mind, and that thing about eternal vigilance is sort of his slogan.

It was past seven, and I hadn't even picked up my violin

yet. I took it out, put rosin on the bow, and did some nasty Kreutzer for a few minutes.

Everybody except Bro David was at breakfast. He had to work early at Safeway; they kept changing his shifts. The breakfast conversation was about the concert, and old friends, and Deirdre was just fine. She spilled cream when she poured it on the peaches and cereal, and she just laughed. She was wearing shorts and a huge sweater. Her hair was up on her head, in a scarf, with some long, curly hairs hanging down out of it. She said she couldn't get over the luxury of eating breakfast in an authentic dining room. "Breakfast in a dining room—can you imagine that in New York?" she said. "With trees and birds outside?" Mommy and Daddy laughed. I was thinking about her throwing up peaches and cereal that night before she sang.

"What about that friend of yours, the one coming to Portland—with the son?" I asked her. "You were gonna tell Mommy."

Her eyes got big. "Fleur! Remember Sam Landauer?"

Mommy laughed. "Sure. With his thick glasses. I wonder what he looks like now."

"You're about to find out. He's got an appointment to do research here, I don't know. He has wife number four now. His little tiny son is a great big son, plays violin."

"Number four. Number four?" my mother said.

Deirdre nodded her head and held up four fingers.

"How'd you find out?"

"In Aspen. Some people were talking about this kid who'd been studying there, and his name was Landauer, and I just asked. It turns out to be little Stevie Landauer who used to build towers with Lego blocks."

Mommy looked at the ceiling. "Little Stevie Landauer

is . . . I think he's—something like fifteen now? Seven-teen?"

"Probably. And I have a rehearsal."

"I'll drive you. It's only about ten minutes. We'll leave at eight-thirty, do you want the practice room?" Mommy said.

Nobody mentioned anything about the earring in the cello. Daddy was gathering his briefcase and things, getting ready to teach his class across the Willamette River from where we live, on the same side of the city with Pioneer Square. It's a music theory class, even in the summer.

Everybody left and I practiced. I was working on "ME: Allegra Shapiro. I'M playing this concerto." It wasn't com-pletely a matter of playing it louder. In some places, it was a matter of playing it softer. Like this part, the fifth and sixth measures after letter B in the second movement:

Right there, between the third and fourth notes, I decided I could get so soft you could hear a bunny rabbit sleeping, as Mr. Kaplan said once, a long time ago, when I was a little kid and he was trying to teach me what pianissimo really was. And this ME: Allegra Shapiro–thing was a matter some-times of landing on a note and staying there almost too long, so if you were listening, you'd almost wonder if I was ever going to leave that note.

Mommy and Deirdre got back from the rehearsal and Deirdre wanted to be on the move. Mommy had to wait for the piano tuner to arrive. The piano tuner is a very hard-faced old lady, and she won't tune our piano any other time than exactly noon, and she'd made the appointment two months ago, and she won't change her schedule for anybody. She used to scare me when I was a little kid. I was afraid of the noise her teeth made, a clack-clacking sound.

"I want to go to that place, that rose garden, the one way high up on the hill. You'll go with me, Allegra?" Deirdre said.

Mommy thought the Rose Garden was a great idea; Deirdre could drive Mommy's car, and I'd guide her there. We'd be back in time for Deirdre to take a nap before the concert. She wanted to have lunch at our house first so she could eat in a real dining room again, so we did. We made tuna fish and tomato sandwiches. Deirdre changed from her sweater to a big white shirt and she took the scarf off and let her hair hang down. I already had shorts on. The day was getting hot. We took some old bread to feed the Rose Garden squirrels.

"I never drive a car in New York," Deirdre said as she backed Mommy's car out of the garage. "In fact, I haven't driven in a year or so." She laughed. I made sure I gave her directions way ahead of time, so she could change lanes and things without getting upset.

We parked Mommy's car by the tennis courts, where some very old people were playing tennis on one court and some younger ones were playing on the other, and we walked down the stone steps. Deirdre kept saying how wonderful Portland was. "People here just park their cars and play tennis on a summer afternoon. They just do it. It's so simple. Do you have any idea what you'd have to go through in New York just to play a game of tennis? Allegra, it's absurd."

"No," I said.

"Subways. Sports club membership fees. Crowds. Reserved courts. It takes more effort than it's worth, sometimes. Everything in that whole city does."

"Then why do you live there?" I asked.

"Allegra, there are more concerts in New York every year than a single person could go to in a lifetime. An embarrassment of riches. Come visit me there, will you?" She reached down and held my hand. I looked sideways at her. "I'll take you to hear such music. Such music."

We were kind of bouncing along down the steps into the roses, holding hands.

"Look at this—millions of roses. Millions." She stood still and looked very slowly all the way to the left and then all the way to the right. "Millions," she said again. The sun was really bright and she was squinting. "Allegra, smell that smell!"

We walked around. The roses are in more different colors than you can believe at first. After you've been there a lot of times you just go along with it, but if it's your first time there, it's hard to imagine so many different kinds of roses.

"Crimson, fire engine, fuchsia, peach, sunshine, sunset, sunrise, cream, ivory, milk, blood, pearl, mustard, canary, saffron, lemon . . ." she said. I laughed. "You could spend your life here, couldn't you?" she said, and let my hand go.

"I guess so," I said. I took her over to the hill on one side of the Rose Garden where they have concerts sometimes. There's a big concrete stage, and the audience sits on steps carved into the hill.

We went down to the stone wall at the bottom of the garden. It's where you look out over the city, and where the squirrels live. They grabbed the bread right out of our hands. I watched her feeding them. They looked intensely at her hand and she looked intensely back at them.

We went up the hill to the place where the sculpture is. It's made of silvery aluminum, and it has three tall columns, connected with thick arches at the top. There are two smaller columns; they're not connected to the rest of the sculpture. They come up to about my chin and they have water coming down them. Under the sculpture is shallow water in a squared-off pool, and over it there are walkways, little bridges, in a kind of cross. People drop coins in the water, and you can jump across parts of the pool if you get a good start.

Deirdre knocked with her knuckles on one of the big thick columns and it made a nice drummy sound, echoing in the hollowness. Then she went to another one and did the same thing. The tone was different. She hit the third one, and I hit one of the small columns and then ran across to the other one and hit it. We had five different tones. It was like metal kettle drums with splashing added. Then we walked on the bridges around the columns, hitting each side, and the tones were all different. We had twenty different tones, and that didn't even include what you'd have if you played them as high as you could reach and then way down to the level of your feet.

It was Deirdre who started the song.

She began slowly, *BONG bong Bong bong* with her knuckles on the three big columns, walking between them. Then she reached up high and down low, faster, and I hit one of the two small columns when she left a silent spot. The rhythm was slow, we were just bonging around. Pretty soon,

I started moving back and forth across the little bridge between the two small columns; I had eight different sides to bong on. Deirdre accelerated the tempo, and I had to start running. Then she changed the rhythm to groups of threes, and moved into my small-column territory. I moved into hers, the big columns. We were getting a little bit faster, and a little girl in a yellow dress started bonging with us. She couldn't reach very high, so her tones were different. Now there were six hands bonging and six legs traveling across the bridges.

Then two little boys came to play tunes. They stayed on one of the watery columns for a few beats before they started to move around. One had brown shorts and one had jeans. They were a little taller than the girl in the yellow dress, so their tones were between hers and ours.

Deirdre began to hit harder, and pretty soon everyone else did, too. A teenage boy and girl in sunglasses joined in, running around the outside of the sculpture. Some other people appeared. It was getting really loud, with slow beats and fast beats and lots of different rhythms, and drops of water flying. BONG. BONG. BONG. And *Bong-bong, Bong-bong, Bong-bong.* And *Bonnnnnggggg, Bonnnnnggggg, Bonnnnnggggg.* And *Bongbongbong, Bongbongbong, Bongbongbong.* And *ping ping ping ping ping ping ping ping ping.* And *pingBONG ping-BONG.* Somebody, I don't know who, found a way to go *Bommmmmphphph.* And I kept hearing a little *plink plink plink.* I think it was the lady with the long fingernails and the big sun hat. I don't know where she came from. Maybe she came with the man in the Trail Blazers T-shirt.

A strange symphony was going on, all made of drumbeats and water.

We all had to go carefully when we wanted to move to a different column, because the little boys kept moving all the time and everybody else had to be careful not to run into them.

We couldn't see each other when we were playing; the columns were in the way, or we had our backs to the others if we were on the inside of the sculpture. We just played. Once when I turned around, I saw that an old man had joined in, *bonging* on one of the columns and checking a big gold pocket watch each time, staying out of the way of the water drops.

I never figured out how everybody stopped almost at the same time. Maybe we all just got tired. All I remember is stopping and looking around and finding out that there was no more music going on except that the old man *bonged* twice more and checked his watch. There was just a very soft hum in the air for a few seconds, and then it faded away.

Everybody started to walk away, but a lady with a camera put her arm out right in front of the teenage girl's face and said, "No, wait. Just one. Just wait for one?"

The girl and her friend laughed and shook water out of their hair. The man in the Trail Blazers T-shirt grinned and made the "okay" sign with his thumb and index finger. Deirdre started gathering everybody else together, bringing the little girl in the yellow dress along by the hand. A lady, the little girl's mother, I guess, motioned to her to stay with Deirdre, and she pulled a camera out of her shoulder bag. The two little boys had taken off their shoes to wade in the water under the sculpture and some grown-ups made them get out and stand with the rest of us to have their picture taken. The lady with the big sun hat ran after the old man, who was walking away, and brought him back. He had a big white mustache, and he was wearing a vest and a black hat. He stood still and stared at the camera.

Four more picture takers lined up. We just stood there crowded together and waited. Somebody said, "What's the name of your group?"

The teenage boy said, "Very Heavy Metal."

The girl with him said, "No, it's Knock Knock Who's There."

"How about Good Vibrations?" somebody said.

The lady with the big sun hat said, in a foreign accent, "A Curious Group of the People?" Cameras were clicking.

"Musical Anarchy?" Deirdre asked. She bent down and asked the little girl in the yellow dress what she thought. "That's a good idea," she said to the little girl. "Say it louder. Get quiet, everybody. Listen."

There were eleven of us to get quiet. "Rose Music," the little girl said.

She had a little chirpy voice and several people nodded their heads, and the teenage boy said, "Yeah, that's our name." More cameras clicked, and then everybody drifted off in different directions.

A crumpled old lady in a wheelchair, being pushed by somebody, said in a creaky little voice as she went past me, "Wonderful. Wonderful . . ." She had on a green sun visor and her head was shaking. She and her pusher wheeled on to look at more roses.

Deirdre leaned into my ear and said in a soft voice, "She's right. That's why we're here. On this planet. To make music. It's probably the oldest art form. You know, people hopping around in caves, singing their stories, singing their prayers, banging on things, making rhythm . . . It's all the same thing. Sending messages."

We stood there, staring down the slope of roses for a while, not saying anything. The smell of millions of roses was so great, a crowded smell, of almost too many roses, if there is such a thing. I squatted down and watched a big ant pushing a grain of dirt along through the grass. It went around a giant blade of grass, made a turn, kept pushing the grain of dirt, came to another giant blade of grass, made another turn, and kept pushing. I watched it move about an inch before Deirdre squatted down beside me. Her blond hair hung down to the top of the grass.

"Look at that. All that work," she said.

"It's gone about an inch," I said.

"So have we all," she said. A drop of water slid off her elbow onto the grass.

I didn't say anything. We watched the ant move about another two inches. Then Deirdre said, "I have to take a nap. You ready, Allegra?"

"Sure. Let's go." We went up the steps to Mommy's car.

"Life, my little friend, is a terrible, terrible thing sometimes," she said. I didn't say anything.

As we were on the bridge going across the Willamette River, Deirdre said, "Did you notice the way the music was happening, back there in the Rose Garden? That percussion symphony?"

"What do you mean?"

"In a way, nobody was *making* any music. Really, it was just a matter of letting the music out. Out of the sculpture."

"You mean it's in there all the time?"

"Sure. Same with your violin. Same with my body. Whatever your instrument is."

I'd never heard anybody actually say it. I looked at her, driving along across a bridge, just like anybody else. "Deirdre?" I said.

"What, Allegra?"

Even knowing that Deirdre wasn't a normal, stable, regular person, I told her a private thing from my childhood. "That's what I thought when I was a little tiny kid. I thought Mommy had music inside her violin—and Daddy had it inside his cello—and they moved their bows and it just came out. When I first picked up a violin, I was so shocked that there was no music coming out of it, I hid under their bed and cried and cried. There were just these screeches."

Deirdre looked across the car at me. Nobody said anything the rest of the way home.

5

I practiced with the mute on while Deirdre took her nap. A violin mute is a little black thing you hook on the bridge to make the sound softer.

Mr. Kaplan, of course, didn't know anything about the music living inside a thing and waiting to be let out; I wasn't sure I wanted him or anybody else to know what Deirdre and I'd said about it. And I didn't know what he'd think about simultaneously remembering and forgetting everything you know. But just three days before, he'd said more about closing the distance between Mozart and me. "The concerto is already there. It's not static—look at all the different ways people can play it. But it's there. It exists. On these paper pages." He put his hand flat on the first page of the third movement. "This concerto is what it is. You're the one doing the moving. Moving toward the center of it." He patted his stomach. "That's what you're doing. Everybody has a different relationship with it. Everybody moves into the center of it differently. You can't have Perlman's relationship with it, or Mutter's, or mine. You have your own. *You* have this concerto in your own way." He looked hard at me. "It's a very fragile thing, Allegra," he said, his eyes not blinking, staring straight into my face, "almost dangerous, getting to know something *that intimately*." Then he laughed. "Talking about it is ridiculous, isn't it?"

Mozart composed so much music, and he did it so fast, and when he died the pieces weren't in any order. Somebody named Köchel came along after Mozart had died and made a list of all his compositions. Every Mozart piece has a Köchel number. The Fourth Concerto is K. 218, and the highest Köchel number is 626.

I was spending my summer with a Köchel number.

Deirdre didn't want dinner. She did warm-up exercises in the music room for about fifteen minutes before we went to the college for her concert. She did sound kind of like the way David did when he was imitating her. I put on a yellow-and-white striped skirt and blouse and put my hair in a braid down my back.

Her hair was all down and golden, her dress was pale blue, long and swishy, with balloony sleeves, and the material was kind of gold-flecked. She was wearing skinny gold sandals with little heels. And long dangly gold earrings with little blue stones in them. She had her raincoat on.

Mommy drove her to the college early and I went along. It's called Reed College. Daddy was coming later. We usually sit on the cushions they have all over the floor for front seating. People sit in chairs behind. The concert was going to be in the Commons, the dining hall of the college, not a real concert hall.

While we were in the car, Deirdre stared straight ahead, saying something over and over again. I didn't hear exactly what it was. I was sitting in the backseat on the other side of the car, behind Mommy, so I could look at Deirdre. It sounded like "Horrible wonderful horrible wonderful horrible horrible horrible wonderful horrible . . ." Mommy reached over while she was driving and held Deirdre's hand; I saw her do it in the space between the seats. Then she let it go when she had to shift gears to go into the parking lot.

We walked around the Stem People having their picnics on the lawn outside the Commons. They eat first and then go to the concert. Deirdre whispered, "I love being in plaid-shirt country again. Fleur, this is a wonderful place."

I looked around. There were several men in plaid shirts. Mommy was laughing and doing that big embarrassing wave at some people she knew, the one where she puts her hands up to her ears and grins. Some people were staring at Deirdre.

"Remember where the bathroom is, it's around the corner on the right," I whispered and pointed for Deirdre on our way in.

She gave me a sideways hug. "Thanks. Wish me love," she said.

"Love," I said back to her.

Mommy said "Love," too, and Deirdre walked to the place they use as backstage in the Commons.

"Didn't she mean 'Wish me luck'?" I asked Mommy.

"We used to say 'Wish me love' when we were in school." She took hold of my hand for just a second and then let it go.

We walked around, picked up programs, and put sweaters across three cushions to save them, including one for Daddy when he got there. You almost always take a sweater or jacket when you go to a summer concert in Oregon, because the nights usually get cold.

We walked outside again, and somebody came dashing

over to us. It was a red-haired lady Mommy and Daddy know. "Allegra," she said, "would you consider turning pages for me next Thursday? I've seen you with your dad, and with Charley Horner? I need a page turner badly?"

I couldn't even remember what instrument she played. I just remembered her face and her hair, and I remembered she talked in questions.

Mommy looked at me. I looked at her and then back at the lady. "Sure. I can do it," I said. "Where?"

"The Community Music Center? Can you be there by six-thirty? I'll show you the fast turns?" She looked at Mommy and said, "It's the Mendelssohn C minor?" and rolled her eyes.

I looked at my mother again. "We'll have her there," she said.

"Thanks, Allegra. You've bailed me out?" the lady said, and walked away.

"My daughter the rich woman," Mommy whispered, and then did that big ear-hello thing to some more people.

I wasn't rich, and I was trying to picture Deirdre throwing up on that beautiful blue dress while people ate their food and drank their drinks on the lawn getting ready to hear her sing. Daddy got there and we went inside to our cushions. I sat between him and Mommy. He sat down on his with a thud. He has a back problem; he says ninety percent of American men have some kind of back problem. He opened his program and said, "Let's see what's on the menu," and started reading it.

Mommy explained that the red-haired lady was a pianist with a trio. The other two instruments are violin and cello. I wanted her to explain about Deirdre in the car, but I didn't actually ask.

Daddy was muttering, "Oh. The Queen of the Night's going to sing all in French." Mommy reached behind me and put her hand on his elbow and said, "Alan, please." He was making fun of Deirdre for what she'd done in the music room the night before. The Queen of the Night is a character in Mozart's *Magic Flute*, the opera on my bed sheets. It's a soprano part that goes very high and gets very dramatic.

Deirdre sang songs by Saint-Saëns and Chausson and Debussy, and a string quartet and pianist played with her. I don't know much about soprano singing, and I didn't know any of the songs before, and I didn't know enough French to understand many of her words, but several times I had goose bumps on my legs, all the way up to the top.

While we were clapping, Daddy said to me, "That's what's really inside her—Deirdre. Not all this strangeness. That wonderful voice is what's really in her."

Mommy looked across me at him and shook her head slowly and smiled kind of sadly and said, "Men." We all kept clapping. She leaned over to me and said, "You had to know her before. Before she got afraid of things." We went on clapping.

After the concert, lots of people came around to stare at Deirdre and some of them shook her hand and a few people kissed her. People kept handing her their programs and pens for her to sign autographs. Then she put on her raincoat. It looked just fine and it didn't smell bad, so she must have made it to the bathroom in time.

At home, Bro David had bought a whole bunch of fruit at Safeway. It was on the kitchen table. A honeydew melon and peaches and cherries and plums and things. He handed a note to Deirdre that said she'd sung for her supper; it had fruit-shaped notes dancing up and down the treble clef. She threw her arms around him and he looked as if he wanted to disappear. He pulled backward and asked her how the concert had gone, and she said, "All right, I think. I think. Oh, I don't know . . ."

He looked at her and said, "Then how can I congratulate you—or what?"

"It was a wonderful concert," my mother said. She put her arm around Deirdre. "She was fabulous."

"Then congratulations," Bro David said.

"Thank you," said Deirdre.

Daddy went to bed and Mommy and Deirdre and I took some fruit and plates and a whole pile of paper napkins into the music room. Deirdre flopped on the sofa and spread her arms and legs out like an x. Mommy laughed. "Well, Deirdre, what's cooking?" she said. Then she sat down on the piano bench.

"Rule number one, Allegra my girl," Deirdre said. "Talk *after* the concert. Never before." She breathed out hard and took off her shoes. She was in bare feet.

I sat on the floor in front of the platter of fruit and looked at her. "Do you want the long, grimy version or the short, grimy version?" she asked.

"Whichever one you want to tell," Mommy said.

"Let's begin with the basics," Deirdre said. "Allegra, you know what happens when you fall in love, don't you?"

I looked at her. I thought the world ought to turn into one big red heart, but I wasn't going to say so. "What happens?" I said.

"Well, you go to dirty little restaurants and you love the awful food, and you ride on carousels and you hold hands when his horse goes up and yours goes down. And you feed sea gulls together and you go *ooh-ooh-ooh* over dewy spiderwebs on bushes. It empties your brain. Those are the basics."

I picked up a peach and about four napkins.

"So," she said to Mommy, "this one was the same exact thing, of course; different exercises. Penobscot Bay—that's in Maine, Allegra. Lobster and seaweed, and sand in the toasted marshmallows. And *ooh-ooh* over the beautiful mussel shells. The whole google-eyed thing."

"What happened?" Mommy asked.

"Well. He suddenly remembered another Ph.D. he wanted to get and took off for somewhere. Geneva or somewhere. I don't know." Deirdre slid down from the sofa onto the floor across from me. She picked up a bunch of grapes. Her shiny blue dress was getting all crinkled. She stared with her great big eyes at the grapes in her hand.

My mother folded her hands like somebody in an old-fashioned painting and said, "Well, so much for romantic love."

"Chapter dozen," Deirdre said. She ate some grapes. Nobody said anything. Then she said, "Well? Fleur?"

My mother got up and picked up a piece of honeydew and a napkin and went back to the piano bench. "What do you mean, 'Well? Fleur?' " she said.

"You know exactly what. You. And Alan. The floor doesn't keep sliding out from under you without warning. What is it?"

"You mean what holds us together?" Mommy said.

"Of course. I mean, I know: you fell in love that day in Morningside Heights, and you have David and Allegra, and here you are. But what is it?" Mommy was chewing melon.

She was just a mother sitting on a piano bench chewing her food. "What would happen if Alan refused to go to a concert of yours?"

Mommy looked at her. "Deirdre, he hasn't gone to lots of them. The season is terribly long. He doesn't always have time, he . . ."

"Would you care to hear this one? 'Bruce, I'm singing a concert on Sunday, I have a ticket for you. . . .' " Her voice went baritone: " 'Deirdre, I can't imagine how that could possibly benefit me.' " Her natural voice came back. "Did you ever hear one like that?"

Nobody said anything. Then Mommy said, "Possibly *benefit* me?" She said it again. "Deirdre, was that a human being talking?"

"No, it was Bruce in Rochester. But *I'm* a human being, and I had to listen to it."

I was thinking about how my friends Sarah and Jessica come to my orchestra's concerts. They like them. I don't even play solos or anything, I just play. And Jessica and I go to Sarah's dance recitals. We clap like mad. And when Jessica gets to be an architect, Sarah and I are going to stand outside her buildings and applaud; we've already agreed on that.

Deirdre was braiding the fringe on the rug.

Mommy said, kind of slowly, "What is it about Alan and me? Hmmm. It's hard to put in words. You know. Well, there was that handed-down instrument thing in both our childhoods."

"Right," Deirdre said. "I love that part. I tell it to lots of people."

It's a funny coincidence. When Mommy was a little kid

in Kansas, somebody died and left a violin to her parents. Nobody knew what to do with it and Mommy picked it up. She wanted to play it, but it was too big. At the school where she went, some teacher arranged to get her a half-size. Then they found her a violin teacher, and she had to go on a Greyhound bus to her lessons sixty-five miles away every Saturday. She kept playing and she grew into the full-size. That was how she started.

And when Daddy was a little kid in New York, somebody died and left a cello to his parents. Same thing: nobody knew what to do with it and Daddy tried to play it. Same thing at his school: somebody found him a smaller cello and he started that way. He took a subway to his lessons. His teacher was a really old man who used to play in the New York Philharmonic but he was too old to do it anymore. Daddy started playing klezmer music in high school, that's a Jewish kind of jazz, and he just kept playing.

Then Daddy and Mommy met each other when they went to Juilliard and they told each other about the dead people and the instruments and they fell in love.

Deirdre stopped braiding and looked up from the floor at Mommy. They looked at each other for a long time, a look of trying to figure something out. Deirdre had her big long skirt hunched up above her knees and she was sitting cross-legged on the floor. She got a peach from the platter and spread napkins all over her lap. "You've got it all, Fleur. House, symphony job, kids, flowers. Parking places. A husband who's not a jerk."

"Well, it's hard work sometimes," Mommy said. "I mean, what's a jerk? Everybody's a jerk sometimes." I wondered if she was thinking about Daddy calling Deirdre the Queen of the Night. But he was right, in a way: this was the second late night in a row that Deirdre was sitting in the music room where I was supposed to be asleep.

Suddenly Deirdre screamed: "YYEEAAAGGGHHEEE!" Like that. Everybody jumped. She had her hands over her head the same way she'd had them the night before. Mommy flew down off the piano bench and I felt my arms fly up and out, and we were both making surprised noises and Deirdre's hair was hanging down the front of her face and she was moaning the way she'd done the night before.

Somehow, Mommy got inside Deirdre's hair and put her arms around her and held her. She just held her and rocked her. She was on her knees, holding Deirdre and rocking her back and forth, and I stared at them. I couldn't see any faces, just hair and shoulders and arms. And Deirdre was making that moaning-sighing sound.

"It's done, it's over," Mommy kept saying. She was almost humming it. I stared at them. They were like a dance, just there on the floor, rocking, with their faces in each other's hair. You could have set a metronome by them, rocking back and forth. I didn't know if I should leave the room, or sit there, or what. I ate some grapes.

They stayed like that for a long time. Deirdre gradually stopped making the strange sound, and Mommy still kept holding her and rocking her and sort of humming. I looked at the braided rug fringe. In a few minutes they stopped hugging and pulled back and looked at each other for a long time. Mommy said, "Want to go to bed now?" in a very soft voice. Deirdre nodded her head. She picked up her shoes and Mommy leaned over and kissed me good night on my forehead and they went out and closed the door. I took the fruit stuff back to the kitchen and put it in the refrigerator and went to bed on the sofa.

I watched the leafy shadows on the wall while I tried to fall asleep. I couldn't get rid of the sight of my mother and Deirdre hugging on the floor and rocking back and forth. Forward and back. Forward and back. A steady rhythm. Not even scary. In fact, the opposite. My mother humming and the sound of both of them breathing.

Of course I wanted to know what it was about. But at the same time I didn't. It was like a secret ritual, where they both knew exactly what to do.

∽

At breakfast, everybody had closed faces about the night before. They were reading the review of the concert in *The Oregonian*. Daddy was repeating, "Ms. Moreau's melt-in-the-mouth vowels" and Deirdre and Mommy were laughing. I read the review. It said, "Deirdre Moreau exerted formidable control and enchanting lyricism. . . . She wrapped herself around the Saint-Saëns with a bold intimacy that made one humbly grateful to have ears. . . . She is a genius."

I wasn't sure about the "bold intimacy" part, but it had something to do with the music coming up from inside, and it also had something to do with Mr. Kaplan and Mozart and closing the gap. I said it over several times in my mind. It was connected with what Mr. Kaplan said about danger, but I didn't know how.

Deirdre smiled at me. "We haven't told them about the Rose Music, Allegra. How many people were there in our band?"

We told them about the people coming to play on the

sculpture with us, and Deirdre imitated the accent of the lady with the big hat. I told them about the old lady in the green visor being wheeled away and saying, "Wonderful . . . Wonderful . . ." in her little craggly voice.

Then Daddy got a phone call to fill in for a missing cellist the next night at Waterfront Park, a concert by the West Coast Chamber Orchestra, and Mommy and Deirdre went off to pick raspberries in the country, and I practiced. Deirdre would sing her next concert, the same program as before but at a different place with a different bathroom, and she'd stay another day and we'd take a picnic and go to the concert and hear Daddy play music.

I went to Deirdre's second concert, too. She was perfectly fine; she didn't get strange at all. Just before she went upstairs to bed that night, she said, "Do you know what Martin Luther said he'd do if he thought the end of the world was coming soon? He said he'd plant apple trees."

I looked at her, standing on the bottom step with her hand on the banister, holding both tiny sandals by their straps. Her big eyes were all shiny from the adrenaline of the concert.

Bro David was standing at the top of the stairs looking down at us. "Deirdre, if the end of the world was coming, how would there be time for any apples to grow?" he said. He said it in a voice that showed he wasn't expecting an answer.

Deirdre looked up at him. "Just to have them there, you see? Not for them to be of any use—there wouldn't be time. Just to have apple trees. Just growing up out of the earth . . ." She leaned down and kissed me on the forehead and we said good night. Her dress floated up the stairs behind her.

I listened up the stairs. Bro David said, "That was in the fourteenth century. What did he know?"

"Well, sixteenth, actually," Deirdre said. "But it's a pretty idea. . . ."

"Doesn't sound too bright to me," he said.

Deirdre said exasperatedly, "Bro David, you are such a *realist*."

Immediately the family was laughing. Daddy and Mommy from their bedroom, me from the bottom of the stairs. I think we were all laughing at different things, though.

∾

At the Waterfront Concerts, thousands of people come and sit on the grass to hear the music. Charley Horner was playing in the orchestra, and I saw him walk over to Daddy's chair and say something that made Daddy laugh. Daddy has a nice reasonable laugh, where his face breaks open and then shuts itself up again.

The park has food booths all lined up along the sides. Somebody on the radio called the Waterfront Concerts "the best-smelling concerts west of the Hudson."

When the orchestra started to play the second half of the concert, the same dancing man from before started dancing. He had his same clothes on. He danced the same dance, forward and back and around, and he had the same concentrating look on his face. Some people just watched him, some people pointed at him, some people didn't pay any attention to him at all. Just like before.

Deirdre stared at him and let out a loud whisper, "Aaaahhhh." Then she whispered, "Why on earth doesn't somebody dance with that man?"

Nobody said anything. My mother and two of her friends and I just sat there.

"Well, why doesn't somebody?" she said.

I shrugged my shoulders. "I don't know," I said. I looked across Deirdre at Mommy, who was just listening to the music.

Deirdre stood up and started walking around people. She had raspberry stains on her big, swingy blue-and-white-striped skirt, at the side. Everybody had blankets or sleeping bags spread out, and she had to be careful not to step right on them. I watched her stepping around people, almost doing a kind of dance in her skinny sandals. She had to go around about six blankets covered with people to get to the open space in front of the stage.

When she got to the bare grass, she stopped for just a beat of the music, and then went right over to the dancing man and started dancing with him. I think she caught him by surprise. He sort of stopped for a moment, then he bowed a little and smiled a little smile, like How do you do, and went on dancing. She danced, following his steps, keeping about three feet of space between them. When he turned, she turned. When he kicked his foot out to the side, she did the same thing. They danced.

The music was by Handel.

I'd seen an old-fashioned music box in Kansas once when I went with my mother to visit an old lady who lived with a lot of doilies. The lady was somebody we're related to in some way. Her house smelled like dried-up flowers. When the old lady wound the music-box key, the two little dolls on top, a man and a lady, went around in a circle, and you could imagine a whole ballroom full of people watching them turning and turning. They had smiles painted on their faces and the smiles just kept turning around as the music played. The lady doll was built with a long pink dress on, and the man was built wearing a black suit. While Mommy and the old lady talked, I sat on the floor and watched the dancers on the music box, which was on a little table. The dancers were just at the level where I could see their faces. The old lady showed me how to wind the key when the music ran down; you had to be very careful because it was very old. The lady said I could touch the dancers if I'd "be careful like you would with eggs, the little bitty things could break."

Watching Deirdre and the dancing man, I thought of the music box and being a little kid sitting on the floor watching the pink dress and the black suit and the painted smiles go round and round, and listening to the music run down, and then winding the key to make them dance again. I could almost get the dried-flower smell back again.

Deirdre and the dancing man just danced, the whole last half of the concert. It was a pretty sight.

At the end, they made little bows to each other. Deirdre curtsied, the dancing man moved off into the crowd, Daddy put his cello in its case, and we got the car and went home.

"Portland, Oregon, land of parking places," Deirdre said in the car. "Nice concert, Alan. Really, more people ought to be dancing to Handel and Brahms and Mozart. Don't you think so, Fleur?" My mother smiled and ran her hand through her hair. "Well, Allegra, don't you think so?"

I was thinking about the little music box. The music was inside, and you had to wind the key just right and it came out, and the dancing man and lady went round and round, smiling. How to get close enough to the Mozart concerto so that— How to move so close to it that there would be just that edge Mr. Kaplan talked about— How to get something strung just right in me so I'd be balancing right exactly on that edge— How to remember everything I know and forget it at the same time and invent a new thing. And that would be the way to let the music out of me. ME: Allegra Shapiro. I'M playing this concerto.

"Yes, I think so, Deirdre."

But that still didn't explain *how*.

Practice.

Listen for the feel of getting closer to it. Would I recognize it?

I went to sleep looking at the Green Violin man. His green face is distorted; his nose is twisted downhill to the left, his smiling mouth twists uphill to the right. Something is happening to make the music lift out of his instrument. I wondered if there was any word for it.

6

I was the one to run with Deirdre to her plane, because she'd forgotten one of her bags in my bedroom and we had to go back for it when we were almost halfway to the airport. Already when we got there, they were announcing that the plane was ready for takeoff.

"You're wonderful, Allegra," Deirdre said while we were running. "Promise you'll come see me in New York?" She's a very fast runner, even with luggage.

I was carrying two of her bags and trying to keep up with her. People were scooting aside to let us by. "I'll try," I said. "Hey, Deirdre?"

"Yes, my sweet one?"

"I'm gonna play a competition in September. That Mozart you've kept hearing me practicing." I was huffing.

Her head swung toward me, her earrings flashing. "Allegra! Really!"

"It's the Ernest Bloch. I'm a finalist," I said. I had to stop and change the bags to opposite sides and then run to catch up with her.

"I've heard of that one—Allegra, I'm so excited—why didn't you—"

"I just couldn't find the right time—"

"Here's the gate— Hey, wait, here I am—don't leave—" She flung her ticket envelope at the uniformed woman standing at the doorway. "Allegra!" She burst down on me and put her arms and bags around me.

"It's on Labor Day," I said. The woman at the doorway was taking the two bags from me. "I wish you love," Deirdre whispered into my hair, and she was gone to Boston to sing two concerts.

I watched her running down the ramp, with bags flying out from her sides. Even in her fluster and haste, she was beautiful.

I moved back into my bedroom. It still smelled like her, perfumy.

The concert review had said she was a genius.

The weather was getting so much hotter that I'd gotten used to beginning to practice before 7:00 A.M. That way, I could work for three hours before it got really hot, and I'd save the rest of the practicing for later.

Jessica was due back from Hong Kong in a few days, and Sarah was due back from ballet camp in a week.

I took breaks from the Mozart project to play the Vitali now and then, and some Dancla études. And the awful, nasty, torturing Kreutzer. Sometimes even Kreutzer felt like a break. I couldn't do Mozart forever.

When I was a really little kid, Mr. Kaplan used to have me walk and play at the same time. You take four steps to the measure if the piece is in four, or three steps if it's in three. Or eight steps if it's in very slow four, six steps if it's in very slow three. It helps little kids learn to count and be regular. I suppose it looks hilarious: this little kid, marching around a room playing a violin. Because when you make a mistake, your feet get mixed up and you can end up standing off-balance with one foot hanging in the air while you find the right note. I used to back up to the place on the rug where I'd been a few measures before I got lost, and start again from there. I think it was a way of getting my little brain organized.

It's kind of like the way little kids always know the first few measures of a piece really well, because they're always starting over again from the beginning.

I went back to pacing sometimes with Mozart. It was about nine thirty one morning when Mommy came in and said Mr. Kaplan was on the phone and wanted to talk to me. She smiled at me pacing.

"I feel like a little kid," I said, and put my violin in the open violin case.

She laughed. "It works, doesn't it?"

I looked at her and nodded my head.

"Then pace your heart out, sweetheart," she said.

I went to the kitchen phone.

"Good morning, Allegra. How would you like to play the Mozart in public next week?" Mr. Kaplan asked.

"What do you mean, in public?" I said.

"I mean there's a little town up the Columbia Gorge, and the little town has a little orchestra, and their soloist has broken two fingers of her right hand windsurfing on the river, and they need somebody to come and play it. Outdoors. In their park."

"This concerto?" I asked.

"This very one. The orchestra's spent two months learning the accompaniment. I owe the conductor a favor, and you'd have fun doing it. Are you interested?"

I didn't say anything. Next week. In public. Mozart and

Mr. Kaplan and an actual orchestra and a whole bunch of people in a park. And me.

"I hear your wheels turning, Allegra. The concert's on Thursday night in Trout Creek Ridge. One rehearsal, Tuesday at seven, indoors. I'll drive you there."

"*One* rehearsal?"

"That's all. If she'd broken her fingers two weeks earlier, there would've been more. What do you think?"

I looked around the kitchen. Mommy wasn't in sight. Nine weeks until the competition. "Is it a kids' orchestra?"

"No. A community orchestra. Pharmacists, Sunday school teachers, farmers, some kids. You know, amateur. A woman conductor. She's very good," he said. He wasn't actually pleading.

Why not? Why in the world not do it?

"Can you think of a good reason not to do it, Allegra?"

I laughed. He was looking right into my head over the phone. "No. I think I will."

"Good girl, Allegra. We'll talk about it tomorrow morning. You'll tell your parents?"

"Of course."

Of course I knew from records how the orchestral accompaniment sounded. Of course I knew I could close my eyes if looking out at the audience began to scare me. Of course I knew this would be a concert for practice. Of course I knew I wouldn't have to throw up the way Deirdre does.

What I had never in my life done was perform three movements and three cadenzas completely from memory with a conductor and a whole bunch of players following me. I was supposed to lead them and entertain the audience and bring Mozart into a park somewhere. With one rehearsal.

Oh. Oh. Oh.

Mommy and Daddy were "surprised and very much delighted." That was what Mommy said. And "profoundly proud too," said Daddy. Bro David said, "Maybe the other one broke her fingers on purpose so she wouldn't have to play with that bunch; maybe there's something you don't know yet."

By the next morning, at my lesson, Mr. Kaplan had his one-rehearsal rules and advice to give me.

One: First time through, if you feel something wrong in the tempo or in the dynamics, play to the end of the movement and *then* stop and tell the conductor the problem. The conductor's name is Margaret, and she'll listen to you. If the same thing is still wrong when you're playing it the second time, stop exactly where it begins to be wrong. Don't wait. You may get to play the concerto through three times, or you may not. It depends on how much time the conductor has allotted for your part of the rehearsal.

Two: With amateur orchestras, one big problem is usually that they rush the sixteenth-notes. They see a lot of black on the page and they get urgent about it. They tend to try to pull the conductor along with them; they don't know they're doing it, they just do it. You may have to make a choice on the instant: follow Mozart or follow the orchestra behind you.

Three: There'll be some out-of-tune playing in the orchestra. You can't do anything about that, and, as a guest, it's not your place to say anything about it. The conductor has ears, and she deals with it as well as she can. You know a good conductor can make you play better than you can play sometimes—right? Well, she can't do that *all* the time.

Four: All these people are genuine amateurs. They play because of that thing inside them, that impulse telling them to—as it's inside you. Where they're different from you is that they spend most of their lives not being musicians. Many of them studied as children and then put their instruments aside—and then they try to begin playing again after—after maybe twenty years. They're very humble, usually. They don't have to be told they're not perfect; they know it all too well.

Five: They'll be thrilled to play with you.

I listened. I didn't know why in Number Five they'd be so thrilled, and I just looked at Mr. Kaplan.

"Because you're twelve years old. Especially the older ones in the orchestra; they'll feel very sentimental, Allegra."

I doubled my practice time, I took the printed music out of the music room and put it in the kitchen so I couldn't even peek at it, I played the recordings of David Oistrakh and Anne-Sophie Mutter, alternating, while I waited to go to sleep. Among us, we had three different sets of cadenzas. In Mozart's time, composers didn't write actual cadenzas. The violinist was supposed to improvise. Other people came along later and wrote cadenzas to fit in the concertos. Oistrakh's were by David, Mutter's were by Joachim, and mine were by Herrmann. Heavenly Days lay curled up between my feet.

Mr. Kaplan and I went to the rehearsal. We had to go about seventy miles up the Columbia River. The hills on both sides of the river looked like velvet heaps of land in the early evening sun, and we kept seeing sailboats and windsurfers. Trout Creek Ridge is built on the riverbank, so the streets are sloping. Indians used to live there. When we got off the freeway and into the town, it smelled like hay. We saw two hay mowers in fields. "Farmers and musicians work at night," Mr. Kaplan said. The town is smack in the middle between two mountains, Mount Hood in Oregon and Mount Adams in Washington.

When we walked in the door of the rehearsal room, a school music room in a sort of shed, the orchestra was already playing. Mr. Kaplan had said out of tune. But he hadn't said how much. We sat down in chairs.

I counted thirty-four people in the orchestra. One lady had a waitress costume on, with "Kitty" written on the pocket of her shirt. Three people were wearing cowboy boots. Scattered among the adults were nine kids, about high school age. I saw people squinting at the notes on the page and looking down at their instruments as if the instruments were trying to outsmart them. Out of thirty-four people, probably half of them were tapping their feet, in lots of different rhythms. They finished the piece by holding the last note very loud and long.

Mr. Kaplan whispered to me to stand where I could see Margaret's baton out of the corner of my left eye. That was all he said.

Then he introduced me to her, and she introduced me to the orchestra. She said, "This is Allegra Shapiro, from Portland, who's come to play the Mozart with us." People kind of moved around in their chairs, and the brass players emptied their spit valves. The concertmaster said, "Welcome to Trout Creek Ridge." He had very rosy cheeks and glasses. I said thanks and looked at Margaret. She was middle-aged, and quite tall, with big glasses.

Margaret wanted me to give her my tempos for all three

movements first. I gave them to her as well as I could, by going *Da da-da da* in the air. She said my tempos were fine. "Well, then, let's do it," she said to everybody. The orchestra began the introduction.

In forty-one measures I heard a lot of wrong notes. Mr. Kaplan was sitting on the other side of the room with my music in his lap. His face didn't have any expression on it at all. "Think microrhythms" is one of the best pieces of tempo advice he's ever given me. He said it when I was a little kid, and it makes everything easier. If a piece is in four, you divide every beat into four so you're automatically thinking in sixteen counts. You can subdivide again into thirty-two if you need to. If you keep that rhythm in your mind, your fast notes won't be ragged.

The instant I started my part, I was a different player, not the player I'd been that morning. It was a very, very strange feeling, playing a solo with an orchestra behind my back. It was a sudden huge responsibility. Margaret's baton was supposed to follow me. I discovered that this concerto was bigger than I'd had any idea of. Closing the gap between Mozart and me was all of a sudden terrifying.

I got back to playing my familiar way in the first-movement cadenza because it was just me—no accompaniment.

At the end of the first movement, I turned around to see what Margaret wanted to do. She was looking down at her conductor's score and frowning. I glanced out at the orchestra and my eyes landed on one of the thin-haired old ladies. She was crying and wiping her nose with a handkerchief. I looked back at Margaret. "Let's go on," she said.

The second movement can be so sweet and slow that you can get carried away. It has that place where I was leaning on the eighth-notes for a long time, but I didn't play them that way with the orchestra because they wouldn't have known what I was doing. Margaret was taking a tempo that was faster than I was used to, but I went along with it. The cadenza is a pretty song, as Mr. Kaplan would say, and I love playing it, and I sort of forgot there were all those people listening.

At the end of that movement, I turned around again. Margaret was smiling, and I quickly looked across the top of the orchestra. I realized all of a sudden that I was almost embarrassed. I'd played the cadenza as if it were just me in the room, just a private song. Something had come up out of me. Like Deirdre said. And there they all were: all those people sitting there holding instruments. It was a moment of astonishment. I was just turning back around, because I didn't want to see the faces, when I noticed the old lady wiping her nose again.

I looked quickly at Mr. Kaplan. He was smiling at me, then he closed his face. I looked up at Margaret. On to the third movement.

In the last movement, Margaret had to stop us and begin again four times because the orchestra got separated.

I hadn't even taken my violin down when there was a very loud clapping. For a moment, it was as if I were at the end of a telescope, looking at the orchestra from far away, and then they got close again, in normal vision. An optical illusion. They were clapping the way orchestras always clap for a soloist. I smiled at them, and a little laugh came out of my mouth. I don't know why. Then I scrunched my bow back in my hand and clapped for them. Because we'd gotten through the concerto together.

I told Margaret about the different tempo I'd been using in the second movement. She nodded her head, and we did the whole movement again. Then we did the whole concerto again. Then the orchestra took its break and Mr. Kaplan and Margaret wanted to talk to me.

Mr. Kaplan stood with his head leaned to the side watching Margaret as she talked. "Your stability is particularly important in the last movement, I'll be counting on you there," she said to me. I nodded my head. "And the dynamics will be different in the park—you may find you'll want to rev up your pianissimos somewhat." I nodded. "We'll see you Thursday," she said. "You'll be just fine, Allegra."

"Thank you," I said. There was so much going on in my head, and that was all I said.

Just as I walked out the door, I heard somebody saying, "But Karen took the cadenza faster, too." "And besides that . . ." somebody else said, and then I was out of the rehearsal room.

Mr. Kaplan and I got in his car and drove home. The sun hadn't set yet, and we followed it down the river, going west. The hills are in layers of blue as you look downstream, going from very dark to very light. It's a beautiful place. Mr. Kaplan was wearing sunglasses for driving.

He asked me how I'd liked the hour we'd just spent. I told him about how I felt surprised to have all that responsibility. He nodded his head. And I told him about the optical illusion and he said, "Hmmm. Indeed." I told him I was nervous about the concert, and he said, "Of course. Of course you are. It goes with the territory."

And he said, "In Europe you find many little orchestras like this one, in little towns. Not so many in America . . ."

I looked at him. He said, "The sounds aren't ever perfect. But the spirit is often quite wonderful. For some of those players, the orchestra is the only thing they have."

I couldn't get the faster cadenza and the "and besides that" out of my mind. There were long silences as Mr. Kaplan drove back from Trout Creek Ridge to Portland. It was like trying not to think about elephants, of course. Which cadenza did the lady mean Karen took faster? "And besides that," what? It was as if somebody was looking over my shoulder and having opinions about me but wasn't telling me what they were.

"What's the problem, Allegra?" Mr. Kaplan asked.

"I don't know," I said.

"You'd better say it," he said.

I wanted to and at the same time I wanted to say anything else but it.

"Beware the boomerang," he said.

"I know," I said. I squirmed a little in the seat and folded my arms in front of me. I knew I was folding them to keep things inside me, like protection. He meant the boomerang you throw in Australia and it comes back and hits you in the head if you're not paying attention. He meant that if you throw your problems away somewhere so you won't have to think about them, they'll come back and hit you in the head.

"Is Karen very, very good?" I looked away from him the minute I'd said it. I looked at the Columbia River. You can't even tell if it's moving.

"Karen who?" he said.

"Karen Karen. With the broken fingers."

He drove along without talking for a while. Two huge

crows were sitting on the guardrail above the river, staring at us as we drove past. "Yes," he said. "Karen's good."

She was probably going to play the competition. When her fingers healed. She'd be one of the tall ones who'd never had a Waterloo in their lives. No: she'd had lots of Waterloos and won every single one of them with her magic fingers.

Broken magic fingers now.

Allegra, I said to myself, you are being evil and cruel. If you're glad even for one second about her broken fingers, you're a nasty fiend. I looked at my face in the side-view mirror of Mr. Kaplan's car. I was looking at a nasty fiend. Clean up your act, Allegra, I said to myself.

"How old is she?" I asked.

"Oh, I think Karen must be nineteen by now."

Remember, I said to myself, when you first heard about the finals you didn't even want to try. Then you thought it would be better to lose. You only decided to play because you saw that picture of Joel Smirnoff. *Then* you got all excited about it. Did you think there wasn't going to be anybody else playing the competition? Did you think you were going to march in there and play and have all the judges clap their hands and forget about hearing anybody else? Act your age and don't be a nincompoop.

"Does she go to college?"

"Yes. Yes, she goes to college," he said.

That night I dreamed about the competition. It was in an auditorium. I was waiting to play and I had a raincoat on, all buttoned up. My turn was coming and I couldn't get the buttons unbuttoned, and then I saw that everybody else was wearing bibs, the kind ski racers wear. I looked around and the bibs all said "Karen" on them. I couldn't tell how many there were, but they were all tuning their violins and they were all very tall and beautiful. They looked like sisters. They had the same faces, all with stage makeup on. I kept trying to unbutton the raincoat so I could see what my racing bib said. I hadn't even taken my violin out of the case yet. One of the Karens said, "It's too slow." She had sharp, plucked eyebrows. I couldn't find Mr. Kaplan. He was supposed to meet me backstage. An usher was saying, "Put the elephants in here," and pointing to a big closet with mops and buckets and brooms in it.

I woke up and saw the little green stereo light still on. The needle was going round and round at the end of Anne-Sophie Mutter's third movement. I turned the stereo off and took Heavenly Days under the covers with me to wait for morning to come. I had an extra lesson scheduled.

At 6:00 A.M., I was in the music room, playing all three cadenzas faster. I sounded horrible.

I was a grouch at breakfast, so I took my oatmeal and stuff to my room and listened to Miles Davis, and Heavenly Days drank the leftover milk from my bowl. Miles Davis is a jazz trumpeter. It's an old record called *Kind of Blue,* and my parents let me have it in my room. There's a house rule that says you don't have the right to make everybody else miserable just because you are. The rule is Don't Try to Make Your Misery Contagious. Of course it's a hard rule not to break.

Miles Davis makes the music sound as if he's just doing it, not even working at it. I yelled, "You stink, Miles," and stuck my tongue out at the record on my way to the bathroom. The door was open.

Bro David was shaving, getting water all over everything.

If we had water rationing, David would be put in jail the first day. I sat down on the toilet cover.

"Hear that sound?" David said.

"Which sound?" I said.

"That crowd on the lawn."

"What crowd?"

"It's the Jazz Society of America, coming to draw and quarter you."

I kicked him in the left shin.

He held the razor up like a microphone. "Ladies and gentlemen, welcome to 'Lifestyles of the Weird and Crazy.' . . ." Then he went on shaving.

"David, you are a creep," I said.

He didn't say anything. He looked down sideways at me, then looked back at the mirror. He went on shaving and dripping and splashing. "How'd you like the hinterland?" he asked.

"What's that?"

"The remote countryside. Up the river."

"It was okay." I walked out of the bathroom, wrote "hinterland" on the clipboard, turned Miles Davis off, ignored my unmade bed, and went to my lesson.

Mr. Kaplan had "only a few things to say. First, you handled the job very well, Allegra. Margaret was struck by your confidence and your technique. Second, you have some adjustments to make. In the pianissimo sections—the seven-note sequences before letter I in the first movement, and the *da-da-da-da-duh* sections in the second movement—and some other places—you just can't play *as* pianissimo as you've been playing. The audience won't hear you. The orchestra doesn't have enough control over its own dynamics to let

·106·

your sound come through. And of course the end, the end of the concerto. And third—what was third?" He looked at me over his glasses.

"I don't know," I said.

He sat staring into space. "Ah. I know. The second movement cadenza. The first time you played it last night. I don't know what you did, but it was unusually beautiful. It had a magic I didn't teach you. Do you know what you did?"

I'd forgotten there was anybody else there. I told him.

He leaned way back on the piano bench and then leaned forward again. "Allegra. What a thing. You did that. Indeed."

"Yep," I said.

"How awfully difficult. And you did it. You're remarkable." He stared at me for several seconds, and then he said, "Now, let's play."

I felt better after my lesson. There was a note on the kitchen table in Mommy's writing that said to call Jessica. I put my violin and stuff down and called her.

"I just got back last night. I'm still on Hong Kong time; it's weird. What's going on?"

"Strange stuff. How was Hong Kong? Can you come over?"

"Crowded. I ate so much I'm fat. What kind of strange stuff? Bad strange or good strange?"

"Both, I think," I said. "Ask your mom if you can come over. Not for the night. I'll explain. Can you come?"

Jessica had been to Hong Kong and I'd been to Trout Creek Ridge.

She showed up wearing a chopstick in her hair. She looked beautiful.

We went to the lawn behind our house. My mother said

we had to clip roses. You have to clip them at an angle, and the pianist I turned for had said they have to be cut just above a stem with seven leaves so they'll bloom again. We took turns with the rose clippers and gloves, and Jessica told me about eating steamed frogs and fungus and coral, and about sailing her uncle's boat, and the lights on Hong Kong harbor at night, and about going to places called Cheung Chau and Sok Kwu Wan, and about her little cousin who was impossible.

"You know, I feel more Chinese than I did before we went," she said. "I talked it all the time, I wrote notes to my uncles telling them where I was going, all in characters— I ended up even walking Chinese."

She was excited about the Bloch Competition, and I told her about Trout Creek Ridge. "It must be scary to think about," she said. "I mean, at night. In bed. With your heavenly cat."

"Yep. It is. Tomorrow night is just for practice, but it's— I think it's like the feeling you probably get if you're in the Olympics or something. I mean, Trout Creek Ridge isn't the Olympics. But it's in public. And. And you only get one chance."

I told her about the faster cadenza, but I didn't know which one, and I told her about the dream with all the Karens. We were cutting a huge bouquet, and we had a pile of dead roses to put in the compost heap.

She said, "That's why I'm going to be an architect. You can make sketches and do plans and think about them before you actually build the building in front of God and everybody. It's not just a one-chance thing. You can make mistakes and fix them so you don't build a crooked wall and knock everybody down." She looked straight down into a rosebush. It's hard to tell when Jessica is thinking about her father. She doesn't let it show very often. Pretty soon she said, "Is there anything about this competition that's fun?"

"Sure," I said. "The adrenaline, when I'm playing well."

I looked at her, standing up to her armpits in the garden, and remembered the flower fight we had once, Jessica and Sarah and I, right in this same place, when we were very little. It was a hot summer day like this one. We were having a little-kid picnic and suddenly somebody started throwing flowers, and pretty soon we were covered with them. Flowers stuck to our socks, inside our shirts, they floated in the red Kool-Aid.

"Remember the flower fight?" I said.

We burst out laughing.

And I remembered that after the flower fight my father came out in the garden and gave us each a swing-around, holding us at arm's length and twirling us off the ground. I told Jessica she could share my father because hers was dead.

"What little kids we were," she said.

My mother made Jessica take a big bouquet of roses to her mother. Before she went home, she helped me decide what to wear to play the concerto in the hinterland and showed me how to draw the Chinese character for elephant.

I went to the music room to practice.

7

To play in Trout Creek Ridge, I wore a flowered dress and white flats. And I had my hair in one braid hanging down. Mr. Kaplan reminded me that the sun might be in my eyes or it might be down behind the trees in the park by the time I began the third movement. I'd have to deal with it the best way I could.

He and I went early for the short run-through that Margaret wanted; my parents were coming later and bringing Jessica. Mr. Kaplan had his taping stuff in the car. "I think it'll help us to have a tape. Don't you? We'll compare this one with the February one," he said as we started out.

"I don't know," I said.

"Yes, you do know. Your softball coach made videotapes, didn't he?"

"Yes. She did," I said.

"Well, listening to the performance is going to give us some new ideas, and it'll give us a chance to check on our old ideas. Right?"

"Okay," I said.

He reminded me that people would probably applaud between movements. "And that's all right," he said. "There's nothing wrong with people liking music enough to clap for it. They don't have to know all the concert-hall customs. It'll be very informal, very homey."

But not informal or homey for me.

"You'll be fine, Allegra. Just do it the way you love to do it."

"I'll try." Easy to say, hard to do. Play it the way I love to do it—in front of a whole bunch of people. I kept saying to myself, as we rode along, This concert is for practice, This concert is for building courage.

"Nobody's immune to the fear, Allegra. Even Horowitz. Vladimir Horowitz. He used to stand in the wings—paralyzed with fear—and somebody had to push him onstage. *Then* he'd sit down at the piano."

The park was spread out on a little hill with swings and slides at the top and a stage at the bottom. The stage was a concrete platform, with a backdrop made of concrete too. Kids were swinging and sliding at the top of the hill, and people were already sitting on blankets on the grass when we were doing the run-through. We played just a few measures of each movement. The orchestra players were in black and white, and Margaret was wearing a long black dress. It looked almost like the West Coast Chamber Orchestra at Waterfront Park.

The orchestra was bigger than it had been at rehearsal. Two more cellos, a double bass, a percussion player, and there seemed to be more violins. Margaret explained that she could never get the whole orchestra in one place at one time except in concert. She shrugged her shoulders. "This week it was the county fair. Some of them had to work in booths. A nurse and two doctors were on call. And the Port

Commission had an extra meeting this week. That's the percussion section."

The concert wouldn't have an intermission, she said. "If we stop playing, people will go home, so we just keep on. You're third on the program."

Mr. Kaplan sat on the grass and set his taping stuff out on the blanket he'd brought. My parents showed up. A whole carload: Bro David and Jessica and Mrs. Kaplan.

One, I still wasn't used to having an entire orchestra behind me. Two, some of the people hadn't been at the rehearsal. Three, the orchestra players weren't full-time musicians. Four, the cello section was staring into the setting sun and they couldn't see Margaret's baton clearly and they came in wrong three times. Five, outdoors does very strange things to music. It's physics. The way air moves. Strings get out of tune almost instantly, and people on one side of the stage can't hear people on the other side.

I was very sure I wasn't playing with the simultaneous remembering and forgetting, the divine inspiration of the NBA.

So. The concerto sounded like one Mozart might have written, but not exactly like the one I'd been practicing. The people gathered in the park on their blankets eating picnics really seemed to like it, though. They clapped every time they got a chance. Between movements, at the end of the first cadenza, everywhere. Some people whistled at the end.

I'd gotten through it. I remembered to bow.

And the next thing I knew, a little girl came up on the stage and put a big bouquet in front of my face. It was full of daisies and delphiniums. I scrunched my bow into my left hand and took the bouquet and remembered to bow again. And I turned around to shake Margaret's hand and she put her hands on my shoulders and kissed me on the cheek. She whispered, "Marvelous." Or maybe it was "Harvest." Or "Horriblest." Or "Barfelous." I remembered to shake the concertmaster's hand. He grinned at me. The orchestra was clapping, and people on the grass were clapping, and I walked off the stage and went down onto the ground.

I sat down next to Jessica on one of the three blankets they had spread out. I put my violin in the case and laid the bouquet in my lap. Mr. Kaplan smiled and nodded his head at me. My mother and father both leaned over to me and patted me on my shoulders or arms or whatever they could reach. Bro David pushed a plate of brownies at me and I took three.

Jessica whispered, "You must really be good. Just at the end of the second movement, I heard some girl go, 'Oh, Mozart . . .' It was like he was her boyfriend and he was kissing her or something." We ate brownies and got ready for the orchestra's last piece.

And out of the crowd came the dancing man. Deirdre's dancing man. We were seventy miles from Portland, and there he was. He started dancing. His same dance. His same clothes. And the shoes.

Mommy was explaining to Jessica about him. I heard her whispering that somebody said he'd been dancing at concerts for three summers, and something about our friend Deirdre who'd slept in my room. Jessica looked at me. "He just comes and dances?" she whispered. I nodded my head. "I bet he's lonely," she said.

"He must be," I whispered back.

A baby started crying just behind us. "Would it be okay if I dance with him?" Jessica was asking my mother. Mommy spread out her hands, saying, "Okay." Jessica looked at me, shrugged her shoulders, and got up, walked forward on the grass and began dancing. Just the way Deirdre had done, but keeping a little bit farther away from him.

He did the same thing he'd done with Deirdre. Smiled and danced. The sun was going behind the hills and shining on Jessica's long black hair and the dancing man's pocked face. When the piece was over, she shook his hand. Then when she saw him bowing, she bowed to him. They said something to each other. She came back and sat down and the concert was over.

"His name is Trouble," she said.

I looked at her.

"That's what he said," she said. "I didn't make it up." People were standing up, getting ready to leave the park.

Bro David leaned over while I was zipping up the violin-case cover and said, "It was good, Legs."

I looked at him. He meant it. I stood up and picked up the bouquet. Several people were coming over to say they liked it and I kept saying Thank-you, and some people told me their names, and a couple of people knew Mr. and Mrs. Kaplan and they were all talking together and introducing me, and Daddy and Mommy were talking to Mr. and Mrs. Kaplan's friends and I couldn't see over the people to find out where the dancing man was. He just disappeared. He just wasn't there.

I was looking around some people's shoulders hunting for him when I saw a girl standing in front of me, with thick glasses held together at the left earpiece with adhesive tape.

I didn't see her appear; she was just there. She said, "I really liked hearing you play the concerto." I looked at her face. It had some giant pimples on it. Her hair was sort of light brown and hanging straight. She put her right hand up to brush her hair out of the way. Her arm was round, almost fat, and two of the fingers on her right hand were splinted together.

"Thanks," I said. I had to change pictures in my mind very fast. Out went the tall, beautiful Karens with the ski-racing bibs. In came this Karen, with one button of her plaid shirt popped out of its buttonhole, just above her jeans. "It's too bad about your fingers. You should've been playing it—" I took a deep breath and said her name. "—Karen."

She looked at her hand and laughed. "Your name's Allegra?"

"Yep," I said.

"Well, Allegra, never go windsurfing when you have to play a concerto, that's my advice."

"It's really too bad," I said. "I mean it's unlucky."

"Yeah," she said. She looked at me. "You're really good. I loved the second movement. Makes me feel like going home and practicing."

I didn't know what to say. She was nineteen years old and in college.

"You know what I love about Mozart?" she said.

"What?" I said.

"He can make you forget everything else. All your problems. You know?" She sort of laughed.

"I don't know. I mean—I don't know. . . ."

"You played it really well. Nice meeting you, Allegra." She walked off. I stood there in my flowered dress holding my violin case in one hand and the bright bouquet of flowers in the other, and watched her big hips waddle away, bumping into people. She was holding her right hand up out of the way.

"Nice meeting you," I called to her, but I don't think she heard me.

I felt selfish. I wanted to erase the last three minutes from my life. I looked down at the flowers and their big yellow ribbon. Karen should have had the bouquet. I felt guilty holding it in my hand. I felt guilty about my dream. I felt guilty that people had clapped when I played. I even felt guilty for not being fat.

Jessica came scooting through the crowd. "I looked all over for him. He's vanished," she said. "That girl—the chunky one in the jeans. The one you were talking to? She's the one that said, 'Oh, Mozart!' "

"That's Karen Karen," I said.

Jessica made a silent O with her mouth. She said, "Broken Fingers Karen Karen."

"Right," I said.

"I wonder where the dancing man went," she said. "He dematerialized. How can somebody do that?"

"Allegra," somebody said, a man's voice. I turned around. It was concertmaster of the orchestra. "We liked playing the concerto with you," he said. "You kind of inspired us." He had two little kids with him, a boy and a girl. They stared at me, and the little girl put her hand on the big yellow ribbon on the bouquet and stroked it.

"Oh, I liked it, too. It was scary. But fun." He was wearing one of those hats people wear when they drive tractors. It said, "If you ate today, thank a farmer." "Thank you," I said. I meant his hat. "I mean, I ate today. Are you a farmer?"

"Yeah," he said. "Part-time apple farmer, part-time fiddler. I bet you'll be a full-time fiddler someday. You really made us practice." He laughed and took the little girl's hand off the ribbon.

"Really?" I watched the little girl's hand make a fist and go behind her back.

"You sure did. Most of us went home Tuesday night and did some woodshedding."

Woodshedding is hard practicing. "I did, too," I said. The little girl hooked her hand in his pants pocket and started swinging back and forth in an arc.

"Well, thanks for coming. We were kind of up a creek. . . ."

"I know," I said. "Unlucky for Karen, lucky for me."

"Yeah. She'll be okay, though. She's tough. She'll play again, better than ever." The little boy tugged on the man's violin case. "Well, these kids oughta be home in bed. So long, Allegra."

"So long," I said.

The crowd was separating. People were getting little kids off the slides and pulling them along down the slope and into cars. Our bunch broke into two groups, part of us to ride back with my parents and Jessica to ride with Mr. and Mrs. Kaplan because she lives near them and Daddy's car was crowded. "I just don't know where he went," Jessica said to me.

"I don't even know where he came from," I said.

"Miss Shapiro?" somebody said. I looked. It was the old lady who'd cried at rehearsal. She was very short, and her violin case looked too heavy for her. In the white blouse and long black skirt she looked sort of like a rabbit. "It was wonderful, Miss Shapiro," she said in a quaky voice. She reached her hand up to her collar. It was shaking. An elderly shaking hand.

"So were you," I said. "The orchestra was fun to play with."

"*I* like it," she said. "It's my home away from home. We're amateurs."

"So am I," I said.

For a little moment it was just the little old white-haired lady and me both bursting out laughing. Maybe she knew what we were laughing at, but I didn't. Her laughing was old and crackly and mine was probably childish. There was just a set of sounds coming out of both of us, and we stood there looking straight at each other and laughed and laughed. What was strange about it was that I didn't feel weird laughing with a total stranger probably six times my age. In fact, it felt wonderful. Then we both stopped laughing, almost at the same time.

"Go well, my dear," she said, and she put her hand on my arm. I looked at her hand. It was veiny and spotty and it had gullies along the back between the bones. I looked at my arm and her hand together, at the place where her hand stopped and my arm began, and I felt the borderline, the little gaps of air under her fingers. I thought of all the notes she'd played with that hand and all the notes I'd played with that arm. I was still looking at my arm and her hand together when she lifted her hand away and turned around and walked off across the grass.

Night was coming. People were hustling instruments and picnics into cars and turning on headlights.

Mr. Kaplan hadn't said anything to me. Now he said, "See you tomorrow, Allegra," and got into his car with his wife and Jessica. I put my bouquet in the back of the car where Daddy's cello rides, and kept my violin between my legs. David was driving, and if we made a sudden stop my violin would get broken. Daddy was beside him, and my mother and I were in the back.

"Well, one down," Daddy said.

"And goal to go," David said.

We drove past three churches and a service station on our way out of Trout Creek Ridge and onto the freeway.

"How did you really like it?" my mother asked me.

"Very strange," I said. I wished Jessica was riding with us.

"How strange?" she asked.

"Strange from beginning to end," I said.

"All that sound," Mommy said.

"Right," I said. "It just kept jumping out at me. Like pushing me from behind."

She nodded her head and said, "Right."

"Everybody has a first time," Daddy said.

"I guess so," I said.

"And those rushed sixteenth-notes. You stayed steady, that was great," Mommy said.

"My brain didn't," I said.

Daddy said, "I couldn't tell that from listening."

I don't remember the rest of the trip home. Daddy and Bro David were arguing over whether the horizon is 2.8 or 2.6 miles away if you're standing on flatland and your eyes are five feet above the ground, and I fell asleep. I woke up with my head on my mother's lap and David was driving into the garage.

But when I got into bed I couldn't sleep. I played with Heavenly Days for a while, swinging the end of the sash from my nightgown back and forth like a pendulum for her to catch. She moves her head like a metronome when you do that, and you can change the tempo whenever you want. Cats don't get tired of doing the same thing over and over again. They have a good attention span.

I tried going to sleep. It was a hot night. Portland has a few of those in the summer, not too many. I kicked all the covers off. Heavenly went to the foot of the bed and started to study the wall. Usually she sleeps curled against me. I turned over. And over. And over.

It's always hard to sleep after a concert, or even after a big rehearsal. Your adrenaline is going too fast. You have all these tunes going around in your ears. I don't know why I slept in the car.

Did I play well? Or were those people just saying those things? The four wrong notes—didn't anybody notice them? Well, what would people say—"You played really well, except for that part in the first movement, which was awful"? If I'd known Karen Karen was in the audience, would I have played differently? I wondered what her last name was. I didn't want to know.

I looked at the bouquet, in a pitcher on my desk. If only she hadn't turned out to look that way. I wouldn't have felt so bad. I turned over and tried not to look at the flowers. And she could stand there and say Mozart makes you forget your problems. I put my head under my pillow. It was too hot under there. I kept listening to my own breath. I sat up.

The clock said 12:22 A.M. I didn't want to read. I didn't want to go over my list of words, starting with "tenacity," all over again. Heavenly and I were tired of playing. What do people do? Jessica knits. She's knitted six sweaters in her life. And Sarah gets up and does exercises beside her bed.

I put on some shorts and sneaked down into the garage and got my bike and went out bike riding.

I hadn't ridden my bike for a long time. I couldn't ride to my lessons because I might drop the violin case; Jessica and I hadn't had time that one afternoon; and I'd been busy practicing; and I don't know what the other reasons were. I rode down our street to the corner and took a left turn. The streetlights were on, but I used my bike light anyway. I rode around three blocks twice. The air felt so good, just nice air. Nice air, I kept saying to myself, in rhythm with the pedals. I stopped and unbraided my hair.

I felt my hair blowing straight back. I felt bugs hitting my legs and bouncing off; the handlebars were shiny under the streetlights and then gray and then shiny again. I rode past an all-night doughnut shop and saw three men laughing inside. One of them was holding a doughnut high in the air and they were all shaking with laughter.

I went into the dark again and rode in a straight line for a while. A bat or something swooped down in front of me. Maybe it was a swallow. We had a nest of swallows once when I was a little kid, and I saw the babies getting fed when they were brand new. I think seven or eight years had passed. Where would those baby birds be now?

I rode into Laurelhurst Park, where I'd turned pages for Charley Horner. The bushes were shadowy, clustered in bunches, and the air was cooler. Some kids were sitting on a bench, smoking cigarettes. I had a tune in my head: I tried to remember what it was; it was from somebody I'd turned pages for. It kept on playing in my head and it was so beautiful and sad; it's a tune about love. I mean it's about love for everything: stars, hills, bushes, trees, and it was about being in love, too. It kept going around in my head, as if it were on a tape, just that one part of something I'd turned pages for. It's a melody that makes your stomach and brain and everything get all melty. I slowed down and pedaled in time to it.

Joel Smirnoff was much too old for me, and I kept hearing the tune anyway.

When I rode out of the park the tune was still in my head. I rode straight home, not around any extra blocks. I put my bike away in almost silence, not to wake anybody up. I walked around to the back door and stood between two rosebushes smelling them and hearing that melody for a couple of minutes. Then I got inside without making anything click noisily, went up the stairs very carefully, skipping the sixth step because it creaks, and I went to bed.

Exercise is good for you. It helps you sleep better. It makes peace.

8

Mr. Kaplan was wearing a sweatshirt that said, like a *National Enquirer* headline, "Dvořák alive! Terrorizes couple in Tampa!" The first thing he wanted to do was listen to the concert tape. We both sat in chairs in his studio and closed our eyes.

"Intonation problem . . . dragging on that shift . . . sixteenth-notes are beautiful. . . . Too soft right here, I can't even hear you . . . nice descending trills. . . . You landed on that second G like a dive bomber. . . . Where's the fortissimo? I thought you were supposed to be fortissimo there. . . . Mozart thought so, too. . . . Take longer on that low A. . . . Your timing here needs to be more assertive—remember, it's *your* cadenza . . . again, trills quite strong and good here. . . . Second movement wants somewhat more, I don't know, it wants some, some, some kind of quiet elegance . . . not that there isn't *any*, but. . . . Here—right here—hear that pleading tone? That's wonderful, Allegra . . . and here, where he answers the questions he's just asked in the previous section. . . . This cadenza isn't quite liquid enough. . . . Again, fine, fine trills here . . . you lost the *grazioso* a bit there, didn't you? Nice bright tone here, good for you. . . . Margaret's band sounds like a flock of geese. . . . Good fluid grace notes, they're like birdcalls ascending, aren't they?"

At the end, I opened my eyes and he said, "In short, Allegra, your violin invites you to do more with this concerto. Mozart does, too. Listen to your instrument more, hear what it's capable of doing. More, much more." He looked at me, then away, out the window. "Indeed."

He looked back at me. "I'm proud of your work last night. But. But. In the first movement, you can run like an athlete. In the second, you're capable of melting snow. In the third, everyone should feel like dancing." He smiled. "But it's not happening yet. Are we ready to go to work?"

"Yes," I said, and opened my violin case. There's a music teacher saying: Did you come here to be praised or appraised? I thought of the voice my softball coach used when she said, "Pretty good isn't good enough. Let's go to work." While I was rubbing rosin on my bow, I glanced at the *A teacher is someone who makes you believe you can do it* pillow. We went to work. I hadn't had much sleep, and there was a lot to remember, everything he'd said about the tape. It wasn't very much fun at times that morning, but I didn't say so. And I didn't ask how many minutes and seconds the performance had been. It didn't seem so important anymore.

As we played that morning, in the first movement my sixteenth-notes were too muddy; in the second movement, I wasn't melting any snow; and in the third, I didn't feel anyone dancing.

"If you can do in performance what you did with the second-movement cadenza the first time in rehearsal with Margaret's group—ah, Allegra. . . ." he said. "Isn't it strange—how difficult it is to do the perfectly natural thing?"

I nodded my head. "Something got into me and made me forget people were listening," I said.

"Almost but not quite, Allegra. *Let* you forget, not made you. Shall I tell you a funny story about Menuhin? A genius at relaxation. He once woke up in a concert in Boston and realized he'd played an entire movement asleep. And he'd played it beautifully. The Beethoven concerto. Koussevitzky was conducting. This is a true story, Allegra."

I laughed. I'd heard the story before, but it was still funny.

"This sleeping performance is not our objective for the competition, however. . . ."

As I left my lesson, he put his hand under my chin and said, "No reason for you to be a 'fraidy cat, Allegra. Mozart didn't want you to be one."

And he also said, "Have you been doing anything for just plain fun this summer? Anything irresponsible?"

I thought about banging on the metal sculpture in the Rose Garden with Deirdre and all those people. And messing around with Heavenly Days. And going bike riding last night. "A little," I said.

"Well, why don't you do more than a little?" he said. "Give yourself a day off—do something different? Tomorrow."

"You mean not practice?"

"Indeed. I mean not practice. Do something away from your violin."

"Okay," I said. I didn't really know what to do.

When I got home, Heavenly had a mouse on the lawn and I stuck my tongue out at her for doing it. I used to get berserk when she killed things. But I've gotten myself under control and don't do that anymore. I made myself think of it differently: Heavenly was doing what nature taught her to do. She wasn't a maniac being made happy by murder. Nature didn't plan on a whole species running to the sound of electric can openers; cats were designed to get their own food, and they kill things because that's their law.

But that mouse had had such a short life.

I went upstairs to my room to take a nap.

I was supposed to run like an athlete and make snow melt and make everybody want to dance. Menuhin could play the violin while he was asleep, and I was supposed to be as divinely inspired as the Boston Celtics, and I was supposed to take a day off and not practice, and Mozart didn't want me to be a 'fraidy cat, and I was supposed to take longer on that low A and have more quiet elegance, and I was supposed to be ME: Allegra Shapiro—I'M playing this concerto, and there was a mouse being chewed up on the lawn that just thought it was going out for a walk. I think I was bewildered.

Sarah called and woke me up. She was back from her ballet camp in California. We should celebrate.

The concert that night in the park was another orchestra that both my father and mother play in in the summertime, called the Festival Orchestra. It's not against their union rules to play in it. People, including Daddy, had been kidding Mommy about how she might never play again after this concert so she'd better enjoy it. In fact, if the Oregon Symphony players didn't get their contract for the next season, they'd be "locked out" and the Youth Orchestra might have to play the concert in Waterfront Park that my mother's orchestra was supposed to play on Labor Day weekend.

The calendar dates suddenly hit me. The Bloch Competition would be on Labor Day. The Oregon Symphony was scheduled to play in the park on Labor Day night. If my mother's orchestra got locked out, I'd be playing the competition in the afternoon and playing a concert that night. I braided my hair and said to myself that it wasn't fair to have everything crowded together that way and then have to start school the next morning. And I'd have a completely new stand partner; I wouldn't be anybody's Little Buddy anymore.

And I wondered: When do you stop being a seventh-grader and turn into an eighth-grader? Is it on the day when you get your report card in June, or the day after Labor Day, when you start in a new grade? Or is it on Midsummer Night or some other time?

I met Sarah and Jessica where we usually meet, by the violin side of backstage in the park. My parents weren't as strict this summer about where we could sit, because we were twelve. Last summer we'd had to put our blanket exactly beside at least one other symphony family if we didn't have our own grown-up along. This time they said we could sit anywhere if there were only three rows of blankets between us and the stage.

Sarah said, "Parents lie in bed at night and think these things up, the same way teachers do. You really have to work to think up that three-rows-of-blankets rule." It was great seeing her again. She thought the Bloch Competition was nifty. "Nifty. Sure. How many people in the whole world are finalists for something like that?" She put on her little kid pose and said, "Totally awesome."

We walked up one side of the park and down the other, smelling the food. You can get a whole meal if you want to spend a lot of money. Chinese food ("very un-Chinese," Jessica says), and shish kebab, all kinds of pastries, pasta salads, grilled sausages, bagels, ice cream. We had to walk around the long lines of people waiting to get into the bathrooms, and every once in a while we saw somebody we knew and said hi, and stuff stuck to our sandals, and we just walked along in the summer evening.

Sarah had her own food in a bag; she wouldn't eat any from the booths. She said, "You know what's in those things? You know what they dip the chicken in? That cooking oil has forty-one percent saturated fat. You know what a fat-filled cell looks like? The nucleus and the cytoplasm are all squinched up; there's no room for anything but fat. If you get a whole bunch of fat cells you can have a stroke and brain failure." But she still wanted to go along and smell. Sarah is an extremely healthy person. She doesn't get colds or anything and she hasn't been absent from school in three years. She gets these embarrassing Attendance Awards and has to get up in front of the school and receive them at the end of the year.

We were reading the signs on the food booths, all the various kinds of cappuccino you could buy, and all the things you could get with a plate of fried noodles, when we saw QUITE BROILED SALMON. Jessica and I decided we wanted that. "How do you 'quite broil salmon'?" I said. It smelled fabulous.

Sarah said, "It's probably a British expression. You ever hear it in Hong Kong?" she asked Jessica.

"No. Never," Jessica said. We stood and stared at the sign. Quite broiled salmon. Sarah walked up close to it and burst out laughing. "It's partly covered up." She pointed. Hooked under a board was the beginning of the sign, "Mes."

MESQUITE BROILED SALMON. We roared. Mesquite is a smoke flavor from a mesquite tree.

While Jessica and I were eating Quite Broiled Salmon and fried noodles and chicken and Greek gyros and Sarah was eating her healthy food and taking bites of the salmon because it passed her Healthy Test, we played I'm Neek. Somebody taught it to us in school in second grade, and we still spell it that childish way. It's called I'm Unique: everybody has to tell unique things about themselves. It was supposed to make us more thoughtful when we were little.

"I'm Neek because I'm the only one in this park right now who's forgotten how to write the Chinese character for old age," Jessica said.

"Not counting the ones that never knew in the first place," Sarah said. "I'm Neek by winning a pirouette contest last week."

"How do you do that?" Jessica asked.

"I didn't fall down till the fourth one. See my knee?" Sarah pulled her big lavender skirt up to show us. It was a big floor burn. "They were on pointe, too."

Sarah was dancing when she was three years old. Or not much more than three. She was a Nutcracker Victim, that's what she said in her school report last year. Nutcracker Victims are the little kids who watch the *Nutcracker* ballet every Christmas on television and get up on their feet and dance while they watch it. She said they eat and sleep *Nutcracker* and pretty soon they find out it's hard work, but by then they're addicted.

Our teachers call us the Three Weird Sisters sometimes in school, the ones in Shakespeare that say, "Double, double, toil and trouble." "I'm Neek because I played a solo in a park last night and the girl who should've been playing it wasn't beautiful the way she was in the dream I had about her and I feel guilty about that," I said.

Jessica said I was the star of the show, and then Sarah told us about her roommates at ballet camp, one from Wisconsin who shaved her head and one from Arizona who had taken a vow of silence for the entire summer and would only whistle. Then we started to tell Sarah about the dancing man. Jessica said his name was Trouble, and she said, "I bet he'll show up here. Watch. Allegra has seen him how many times?"

"I don't know," I said. "Lots."

"I've only seen him once," she said. "But I'm Neek 'cause I danced with him. You should've been doing it, not me," she said to Sarah.

"I'm Neek because Andy liked me for eight whole classes last year before he went on to somebody else. He's such a jerk he only likes somebody for three or four classes usually," Sarah said.

Jessica and I'd had to listen to how wonderful Andy was after all eight classes too. "I'm Neek 'cause I knew he was a jerk before you did," I said.

"No, you're not," Jessica said. "We both did at the same time, so you're not Neek that way. Remember when he told her he'd never look at another girl? That was when, and we both knew. He was already a jerk then."

Sarah sat quietly with her legs in a complete lotus position and said, "It sounds like you're both trying to make me feel stupid at the same time." I felt terrible. The three of us are friends because we don't usually do that. We all know which buttons not to push with each other. With Jessica, we don't push the button about her mother going to the cemetery every single day and making Jessica or one of her sisters or brothers go with her to see her dead husband's grave. With Sarah, we don't push the Nutcracker Victim button; we don't give her a hard time about how crazy and intense dancers are, especially dancing boys. And with me, they don't push the button about never having a single boyfriend since Teddy in kindergarten or the one about being a maniac for practicing. And we never ever argue about who's pretty or who's ugly on which day.

Jessica said, "We're not trying to make you feel stupid, Sarah. Nobody can tell if a guy's a jerk close up. Not at first when he's all friendly and whispery. It's only if you're away from him. Then you can tell. You have to get perspective." She looked extremely serious. I thought of Deirdre and the man who suddenly remembered another Ph.D. he wanted to get.

Sarah looked at her and thought about it and then she laughed. "Thank you, dear Abby," she said, and we all put our arms around each other and swore our friendship "in thunder, lightning, or in rain" again, from Shakespeare about the Weird Sisters.

The music started and the dancing man appeared, as usual, out of the air.

He was wearing his same brown clothes, or ones just like them. But he had a different shoe on; it didn't flap open. It didn't match his other shoe. He did his same dance from before. We watched him, and Jessica and I partly watched Sarah watching him. She was fascinated. He turned, and half turned, and moved in his sort of circles, and he looked that same stiff way but his dancing still had a nice feeling in it, and he had his same kind of part smile on his face, and his same dance went on and on until the piece was over. Then he bowed to the orchestra.

During the applause, Sarah said, "He's got no stage fright at all. Absolutely zero. That's a fox-trot he's doing. Kind of a waltz–fox-trot."

"I want to know who he is," I said.

Sure enough, Sarah wanted to dance with him. "I'm gonna do it," she said. She hopped around people's blankets just as the music was getting ready to start, and took a position right near him but not too near.

At first, it was just two people moving in a sort of parallel way, the way it had been with Deirdre and with Jessica. But pretty soon Sarah started moving around him and he started following her, and her lavender skirt was sliding back and forth in the air, and she made their dancing area bigger by slowly stepping farther to both sides. Eventually, they were using the whole front of the grass, coming very close to some Stem People and just missing stepping on people's blankets but never once doing it.

The sun was going down and the bright, almost orangy light from the stage was on them, and for a little while it was like the old lady's music box in Kansas again, and the whole world could be happy if those little minutes could go on and on, music and dancing on the grass everywhere in the world and everyone would stop fighting each other and people could just listen and watch.

It even made the concert a better one. I secretly think they gave the audience a better show.

After the concert, people were getting up to leave, and calling to little kids, "Stay right here. Don't you go one step away," while Jessica and Sarah and I grabbed our blanket and picnic stuff and followed him.

He was already slipping around to the back of the stage but Sarah caught him. She put her hand on one of his arms.

"Is your name really Trouble?" she said.

He turned around and looked at all of us. Up close, with the lights from the stage, the little holes in his face were very big. Looking at his face felt a little bit like looking close up at Heavenly's whiskers and mouth. Different and fascinating. "Yeah," he said. He really had almost no teeth that I could see, just two in the front, one up and one down. "They know me on the block."

I heard all three of us breathe in at the same time. He started to duck around the side of the stage. There was a smell of dirty laundry. Of fried food and dirty laundry together. People were coming down the steps from the stage, carrying flutes and oboes and violins and horns.

"Wait a minute," Sarah said to him. He looked back at her without turning all the way around. Part of him was in the dark where the side of the stage cut off the light. "I never had a dancing partner just disappear before," she said. He kept looking at her. His face began to open up and then it closed again. We must have looked to him like a committee.

Jessica said, "You're a very good dancer." He turned around to face us.

He looked in a strange way like the man in Chagall's *The Green Violinist* in the music room at home. It was hard to tell what he was thinking, in the same way it's hard to tell in the painting. You know the face is saying something, but it's hiding it from you.

· 133 ·

"Thank you, ma'am," he said. "Me, I like to dance."

"Me, too," Sarah said.

"I gotta get my gear," he said. Then he darted behind the stage. Sarah followed him, and Jessica and I looked at each other and then followed her.

He went around to the very back of the stage, where the grass was worn away and the ground was hard dirt. He knelt down kind of stiffly and reached underneath some broken boards in the base of the stage and pulled out a big plastic garbage bag partly full of clinking cans. He shook the bag to get the dust off, making the cans clank together inside, and stood looking around for a few seconds, as if he were alone.

"You dance at lots of concerts, don't you?" Jessica said.

I said, "You even went to Trout Creek Ridge."

"I danced with you there," Jessica said.

"I saw you at Pioneer Square. And Laurelhurst," I said.

"You must've been dancing for years," Sarah said. He was down on his knees in the dirt, reaching under the stage again. He pulled out a plastic bag with a notebook in it. He stood up. "My name's Sarah," she said.

"Pleased, Sarah," he said. He glanced very fast at Jessica and me and then off into the shadowy park. He held the notebook in its bag tight under one arm.

Horns were honking in the traffic jam that always happens after a park concert, and people were lugging blankets and picnic coolers and little kids across the grass.

Jessica was standing between Sarah and me. I was kind of behind her, and she poked me by sliding her arm around to the side and back so that her elbow went right into my stomach. I didn't know what she meant.

"You're the fiddler one," he said, looking straight at me and then looking away.

"Yes," I said.

"That there's a pretty song you played," he said. He was looking sideways, not quite at anything. "Upriver."

"Do you live there? In Trout Creek Ridge?" Jessica asked him.

He looked at her. "Me, no. Catch a train," he said. He ignored us and took the notebook out of the plastic bag and took a stubby pencil out of his pants pocket. We stood absolutely still and watched him clutch the plastic bag under one arm, open the notebook, turn the pages, move his lips as if he were reading, and then write on a clean page. Sarah was closest to him, and she stood on her tiptoes to peer very sneakily over his writing arm. It took him a long time. Then he closed the notebook, put it back in the plastic bag, picked up the bag of cans, and saw us still standing there. All three of us backed up abruptly.

"Good night, ladies," he said, and moved away across the grass, clutching the notebook and clanking his bag of cans. He just clanked away into the crowd.

Sarah turned to us and said in a soft voice, "He wrote the date in his notebook."

"That's all?" Jessica said.

Sarah nodded her head slowly, over and over again. "And he misspelled 'July.' "

We were all completely silent for a moment. Then Jessica said, "He's an American man and he keeps a diary and he can't spell 'July.' "

We just looked at each other.

"He has to pick up cans for money," Jessica said. That

was what she'd poked me about. Of course. At a nickel a can, you could easily make several dollars at a concert.

"That's the most fascinating person I've met all summer," Sarah said. "He supports his dancing habit by can refunds, and he . . ."

". . . is a good dancer," Jessica said.

"And something more than that," I said. "His face. While he dances."

"Yeah." They both agreed.

Then we were all quiet. A couple of people, friends of my parents, walked past us with instruments and said hi and we said hi back, and then we went to where my mother and father were standing with their instruments, looking impatient. "You took too long to get here," Daddy said. "This isn't the safest place in the world for three kids to go waltzing around after dark." We went to where my mother's car was parked and crowded in and my parents took us all home.

∽

The next morning I took my day off. I left my parents a note, and I rode the bus downtown and got off at the park. The sun was bright, not hot yet. I walked around feeling how it felt not to be practicing on a summer morning. I watched some kids skateboarding on the sidewalk. I watched two police cars slowly driving past the park. I watched pigeons and squirrels. Maybe I was really looking for the dancing man because there he was, with his bag of cans, going through the garbage containers.

I stood and watched him for a few minutes. Then he looked at me. He straightened up, letting the bag rest on the grass. "You play fiddle real good," he said.

"Thank you," I said. "I try hard. My name's Allegra."

"Me, I got the brain damage. I lost my song Waltz Tree, Miss Allegra," he said. He changed his grip on the bag and some of the cans rattled.

"You what?" I said. The sun was reflecting off the cans.

"Lead poison, ruint Rome. Can't remember. My song it was Waltz Tree back then. Nobody done play it a long time. Waltz in Three."

I put my hand up like a sun visor. "You had a song. It was called Waltz in Three. Right?"

"That's it. Waltz Three. In form school."

"What's form school?"

"Where they put the bad boys. Form school. I come to find the Waltz Tree."

"What did you do that was so bad?"

"Didn't set no fire. Farmer set the fire. My dad, he said I set it. The Pression. I was Trouble."

"Somebody set a fire and your dad said you set it?"

"The Pression. My dad, he had a Kodak he give me; I hid it with my valuables in them branches on the pasture edge. I didn't set no fire there. Nineteen and thirty-three, the Pression." He picked up the bag of cans and walked away. I followed along behind him.

"You had a camera, a Kodak, you hid it in a tree."

"Nope. In them branches piled. They was on the ground. Nineteen and thirty-three. Farmer set the fire; he had brush to burn. My dad's Kodak, it burned, never a sight to see of it. Whole pasture burned. Put me in form school. It was filberts and that." He was still walking. I was following him.

"Who put you in form school?"

"Them farmers. My dad's Kodak. I was Trouble. Said I et

paint, the docs. Lead poison. Same with the Roman Umpire, it fell. They was poisoned."

"The farmer thought you set the fire, but you didn't? Why didn't the farmer just say he set the fire?"

He stopped and rested his big bag beside the next garbage container. He looked at me. "He don't say nothing. They said it was my lead poison; I was Trouble. Them Romans they had it in their jugs, brain damage with their wine. Don't drink no wine, Miss Allegra."

"I won't, Mr. Trouble."

He rummaged through the trash for a few minutes, pulling out cans and putting them in the bag. I picked up three cans from the ground a few feet from the trash container. One Pepsi and two Seven-Ups. I held them out in my hands, he pointed to the bag, and I dropped them in. "They found it when they dig 'em up. Them bony remains. They had their lead stored up. It was a burden in the bones. Them Gyptians had it. Them Jews, too."

"Lead poison?"

"That's what, Miss Allegra. It makes you imbecile. Them docs said I et paint. Thought I'd kick my bucket. I'm still here. I got a life span." He went on rummaging through the trash and putting cans in the bag.

I went on scavenging with him. We moved along to another garbage container. "And your song, Waltz in Three. Did you sing it in form school?"

"Nope. It gots no words. It's a song. Them violins. Waltz Tree. You know that song? It's a record on the player." He straightened up and looked straight at me, and stayed that way, staring.

"No. I don't know a Waltz Tree song. Can you hum it?"

"Me, no. I lost it." He looked up to the right, at the trees.

"I worked sanitation, they blame me a dog gets poison. I didn't do no poison; they fired me." He set the bag down on the ground and bent over the trash container.

"Why?" I picked up some cans and put them in the bag.

"I fed them dogs. So they don't bite you. But I didn't carry no poison for no dog. They fired me, I was Trouble." He stood up straight and looked at me. "You can't play Waltz Tree?"

I looked at him. If you lose a song you can stay awake all night wanting it to come back. It's a desolate thing all inside you, a terrible empty thing. It hypnotizes you. And he'd been looking for his song for more years than I'd been alive. "I wish I could, Mr. Trouble," I said.

"Me, I don't want to never die without I find it. Waltz in Three."

"I'll try to help you find your lost song," I said.

He looked at me, then away. "Nobody done that," he said. Then he carried the bag of cans off to the other side of the park. I picked up about eight cans on the way and put them in the bag when he set it down near a dumpster.

"Me, I could use the Kodak. Wished I had it."

I looked at him. He looked away. "Put it right up there on the table. Right up there." He was looking off into space.

"What table?" I asked. My parents would have a fit if they heard me prying into his private life.

"The Gospel gots a table."

"The Gospel?"

"Mission yonder." He pointed with his thumb sideways into the air. "They don't gots no violins. No Waltz Tree." He opened the lid of the dumpster and began hunting around in it. I watched him for a while.

Two police on horses came riding toward us in that slow

walk they have, the kind of picture that makes being a cop look so easy. They were a man and a woman. They stopped near us. "Morning, Mr. T.," the man said. "Found yourself a friend?" Both horses were handsome in the sun and one of them puffed air through its nostrils.

Mr. Trouble lifted his head. "This here violin," he said, pointing me out. The police and I said hi to each other. I looked at the horses and listened to the clanking of Mr. Trouble's cans and said to myself that this might be the only time in my life I'd ever be called a violin.

"He telling you his Roman Empire story?" the man asked me.

"Yes," I said. The horse breathed heavily, and the man smiled.

"You don't want to be late for lunch, Mr. T.," said the woman cop. "Meat loaf today. Smells good."

Mr. Trouble kept his head in the dumpster.

"You have a half hour till lunch, Mr. T.," said the man.

"I be there, I be there," came from the dumpster.

The cops both said good-bye and rode on through the park.

My parents would have had a complete fit. I asked anyway, "Where's lunch, Mr. Trouble?"

"Gospel. Meat loaf Thursday. Maggie and them." He clanked some cans into his bag. "You find a Waltz Tree?" He straightened up and looked straight at me and didn't look away.

"No. Not yet." His mouth stirred itself up in a wrinkled motion. "But I'll try. I haven't had time yet. I haven't even gotten started." I sounded like someone making an excuse to a teacher. He bent his head back down into the garbage.

"I have to go now," I said. He was rummaging in the dumpster. He didn't turn his head or say anything, and I left.

Gospel. Maggie and them. I could have jumped up and down right in Waterfront Park. He wasn't homeless. He lived somewhere. Somebody fed him. Maggie and them.

I rode the bus home, back across the Willamette River, and started looking through waltz books. No Waltz Tree. No Waltz Three. No Waltz in Three.

Daddy came home from teaching his class and saw me on the floor in the music room with piles of music around me. I told him. About the police being there and everything. I especially emphasized the police, and I described their horses very carefully, the way they stood. Daddy said he didn't know how I was going to find a song that had at least three titles, but he said I should call the reference librarian at the university where he teaches. My father looked down at me with my sprawl of music all over the floor and said, "Poor old guy. Poor old guy."

The reference librarian told me she'd look it up. "But every waltz is in three, Allegra," she said. She had a tone that was like "But all cucumbers are green, Allegra."

"I know. But maybe it's about a tree. Could you look under that, too?"

"Well. I'll try," she said. She said good-bye as if she were closing a book.

I wasn't supposed to practice all day. I called Sarah and she called Jessica and we took a bus and went to the zoo. We spent the whole afternoon walking around and we saw the whole entire zoo, every kind of animal.

We stood for a long time watching Portland's famous elephants. Some of them were showering themselves. Looking at the elephants always makes us feel like such little kids. We get so happy. Just watching elephants with their skin like walls and their little tiny eyes.

"Why would the Trouble man tell you his life history?" Jessica was wondering.

"I don't know," I said. "Maybe he tells everybody. You know what I think? He was explaining himself. But I don't know why."

"It's obvious if you think about it," Sarah said, and then she waited for us to pay attention. "You're a musician. You're a connection. He's a disconnected person. That's all."

"Why wouldn't he tell you, then? You're a dancer, so is he."

She looked at me. "Allegra, it's so simple. He hasn't lost his dance. He's lost his song."

We looked at the elephants walking around in the sun. "I am *so glad* you both came back from your faraway places," I said.

"Speaking of China," Jessica said, "did I tell you bamboo is a big important symbol there?"

Sarah said, "Of what?"

"Bending without breaking. It's a symbol of that. Like Mr. Trouble," Jessica told us.

When I got home from the zoo, Heavenly had thrown up in Bro David's shoe and he was putting up signs all over the house with pictures of headless cats on them.

9

By the time I'd had my day off and had actually missed Mozart—really missed him—there were other things to practice, too. The Youth Orchestra was probably going to play the last of the Waterfront Concerts because my mother's orchestra didn't have its contract yet and the musicians would probably be locked out, and we had three rehearsals scheduled. I felt nervous about not having Lois there, calling me her Little Buddy. I'd have to get used to a whole new stand partner.

The music librarian at my father's department called me and said her staff couldn't find a Waltz Tree or Waltz Three or Waltz in Three, and asked me how soon I needed it. I didn't know what to say. It had been lost for probably more than fifty years. He didn't want to die without finding it. I didn't even know if he was sick.

I'd started depending on my midnight bike rides. I saw old people walking their dogs, once a lady pushing a sleeping baby in a stroller, and I saw a man sitting on a bench in the park flossing his teeth, all alone. I saw people coming home and putting their cars in their garages, and a couple of people coming out of their houses with lunch boxes, going to work on late shifts. And the bushes and trees with their leafy shadows in the night, and once in a while a rabbit scampering in the park. One night I saw a man and lady arguing beside a tree. She said, "You always do that, every single time. . . ." and he said "*You're* the one that always" something. Once I saw a porcupine in front of me on the trail, going along in its slow waddle. And usually there were cats crouching or springing, their lemon-shaped green eyes eerie in the dark They were little stories I was seeing; they helped me get unfolded inside. The night riding helped me go to sleep.

But somebody saw me one night and phoned my mother the next day. I heard it happen.

"*Our* Allegra? No— No. She was fast asleep in bed. You what? She *what*? Allegra, come here right now— Allegra? She— No, no, I had no idea— It was *what* time? I can't believe— Alan, come here— On her *bi*cycle? Are you sure? Thank you, thanks. Thanks. Of course. I just didn't— Thanks, good-bye.

"Alan, you won't believe— I can't believe— Allegra, where were you at seven minutes after midnight last night?"

My father and I had both come almost running. We stood in the living room listening to my mother's voice all choppy and afraid. I took a deep breath.

"In Laurelhurst Park," I said. I tried to say it as quietly as I could, and I was hoping the neighbor was wrong, that I'd actually been home in bed.

My father took a few seconds to understand. My mother put her hand over her mouth and leaned against the end of the sofa. They both stared at me. My mother's hand fell down from her face. "On your bicycle," she said.

I felt my head pull back into my neck. "Yes," I said.

"By herself," my mother said to my father.

He shook his head. My mother nodded hers. It was very quiet in the living room. My father looked at me and believed my mother. He leaned toward me with his whole body and said, "Why?" I felt terrible for both my parents, being so afraid of something.

I couldn't think of a single reason that would make any sense. I didn't dare tell them about the porcupine waddling across the trail. Watching stray cats when I could be in my room watching Heavenly wasn't logical, either. I couldn't tell them I'd seen a man sitting on a park bench all by himself flossing his teeth.

My mother said, "What reason could you have? At seven minutes after midnight?"

"No reason's good enough," my father said.

And then I was angry that I was supposed to have a good enough reason. Adults don't always have good enough reasons for what they do. I didn't say anything. I thought of a rabbit I'd seen, with its long feet kicking out behind as it scurried under a bush. I couldn't mention the rabbit.

"All the pernicious things out there," my father said, accusing me.

"I can't believe you'd do such a . . ." My mother didn't finish what she was going to say.

"It's the *most* irresponsible *thing*," my father said.

I opened my mouth. "I'm supposed to be a child and stay in my bed at night and I'm supposed to be an adult and be responsible. How can I be everything at the same time?" I heard my angry voice blowing through the room, and I thought of terrible punishments they might give me. They could ground me completely, telephone and all. Or even take my bike away.

"This is Deirdre's influence," my father said suddenly, like a verdict.

"Deirdre, who doesn't even know how to ride a bike?" my mother said very fast.

"This living on the edge. This middle-of-the-night, this wandering around. I don't know—we've got a lunatic soprano in one room and a dish full of dead bugs in the other—I just don't know." My father was exasperated. "There's something not normal going on. Normal people go to bed at night."

"Alan—that's not fair. It's not because of—"

My parents went on talking to each other. The front door opened and closed, and David walked right past us and up the stairs.

I followed David. I don't think my parents even saw me leave. He went into his room and tried to close the door but I pushed it open and went right in after him and closed it behind me. I stood in the middle of the room and just breathed.

"What started all that?" he said and sat on a chair at his desk. The last time we'd seen Daddy and Mommy this upset was a long time ago, and it was about David getting his driver's license.

"I went out and rode my bike in the middle of the night and they found out about it."

He looked at me. "Where'd you ride?" He has very intense eyes; they're almost black.

"Around. Laurelhurst. Around."

"The park?"

I nodded my head.

"You know in New York you'd last four minutes—"

"This is Portland. I was on my bike. I could go faster than anybody that wanted to— And then Daddy said normal people go to bed at night, and he called Deirdre a lunatic, and. . . . Don't you think it's normal to go bike riding?"

He swiveled on the chair, which makes an awful screeching sound. He leaned back, looking like a lawyer in a movie. "I'll tell you what isn't normal. Practicing the violin six hours a day isn't normal. Playing nursemaid to a loony soprano isn't normal." He put his hands together—he was looking more like a movie lawyer all the time. "Trying to track down a Waltzing Tree for a man who's lost his mind isn't normal."

David can be a very cruel person. I asked him, almost in my regular voice, "Is going bike riding normal?"

He swiveled in the chair again, as if he liked hearing it make that screeching sound. "In fact, Legs, you want to know what would be normal?"

I was still standing in the middle of the room. "Yes, Mr. Wonderful. Tell me."

He picked up a ballpoint pen. "You and your girlfriends could be mall babies, slinking from store to store and popping your gum—and buying useless things because if you didn't buy 'em you'd die. That'd be normal." He twirled the ballpoint pen on one finger, like a baton.

It was the first funny thing I'd heard in hours. I sat down on his bed. "Mall babies?" I said.

"Capital M, capital B. Mall Babies from the black lagoon." He tossed the pen across the desk. "Quintets of 'em, octets, battalions. They've got to be seen in every mall in the free world by the time they die, and it's—" He was bending over laughing. "It's hard work."

We sat there and laughed and laughed and shook, and his

chair squeaked little tiny squeaks, and I remembered the day he'd warned me about letting the competition make me a crazoid, and pretty soon we were both just sitting there looking at each other. I tried to imagine both of us in our little blue "Symphony Kid" T-shirts, dancing in the grass all those years ago. Mommy's and Daddy's voices downstairs were getting louder and then softer and then louder, but I couldn't hear the words. I opened David's door very quietly to hear what was going on.

"Why are you yelling at me?" Mommy said, almost yelling.

"Because I love you!" Daddy said, almost yelling.

Then there was absolute silence. I was scared and relieved at the same time. David and I weren't supposed to hear that, and I looked at him, and I had a feeling of being spies together. I tried to close the door silently and stood against it, holding the knob back so there wouldn't be a click. He whispered, "Did I tell you the world was crazy?" and picked up the ballpoint pen again. But he didn't swivel his chair; he didn't want to make a sound.

I had to keep holding the doorknob to keep it quiet. "Is all this my fault?" I whispered.

"Legs," he whispered back, "use your brain. What if your little kid went out alone in the middle of the night—you know what I saw in New York?"

"Yes, I know you saw somebody selling drugs."

"Right on the street—"

"I know it, David. You told me and told me."

"They're getting old, just try to keep 'em happy," he whispered. "You know what you are? You're an endangered species. They're just trying to keep you alive."

"What do you mean, I'm an endangered species?" We both kept on whispering.

"What I said. They could have a Mall Baby instead of you. You *care* about something, and it gets them all excited." He looked at my hand on the doorknob and went on whispering. "They probably love you so much they're terrified." He squeaked the chair again. "Besides, they've completely forgotten it's their fault you're not normal."

"They let you do anything you—"

"I'm not a child," he said. He can even be cruel when he's whispering.

"What does 'pernicious' mean?" I asked him.

"Evil," he said. He turned on his African music.

I opened the door and went downstairs. Daddy and Mommy were holding each other tight, standing right beside the table where Mommy has her dead bugs and magnifying glass. I didn't even try to be quiet. Mommy had her back to me. She was holding tight to Daddy, and she was snuffling, "Hopeth, believeth, endureth all things," and then she said in her regular voice, without even turning around, "Allegra, you will not go out in the middle of the night again ever, ever in your life."

"With or without your bicycle," Daddy said, looking around her head at me, still with his arms tight around her.

"Even when I'm forty years old?" I said.

"Allegra Leah, this is not something you can be flippant about," Daddy said. He broke his hold on Mommy.

My mother said, "It's time to tell you about Deirdre." She sounded as if she were blaming me for something.

"What's Deirdre got to do with—"

"Just listen," she said. "Deirdre had a baby once, and the baby got killed, it was a little girl, and she had a husband, too, and somebody hit the baby, in her stroller, it was a drunk driver—actually, it was drugs and alcohol both, and—" My mother looked down at the floor and shook her head fast, as if she were trying to shake out bad pictures. She looked back up at me. "And that's why she's the way she is—and—and that's why."

I saw Deirdre in my mind, crumpled on the floor in front of Daddy's cello, saying she always ruins everything, and hissing at me, "No drugs!" and then I saw her with her arm around the little girl in the Rose Garden, and I saw her mumbling in the car on the way to her concert, and I saw her singing the concert, with her eyes and her mouth wide open in those gorgeous, ringing notes, and I saw the word "genius" in the newspaper, and I saw everybody applauding while she bowed, and I saw her with her raincoat on so she could throw up before she sang.

"I didn't know anything about that," I said.

"Of course you didn't," my mother said.

I looked at my mother. That was what she was afraid of: that I'd die on my bike in the park and she'd end up like Deirdre, needing to be held and rocked and put to bed. I looked at my father. "Why do you make fun of her, then?" I said.

He rubbed his nose with his thumb and looked down at Mommy's collection of dead bugs. "No good reason," he said.

My mother looked at him quietly. "It's your father's way of pretending it never happened, pretending Deirdre never had such a tragedy," she said. Her words came out very slowly. "Because—if he admits it really happened, he'll have to admit it could happen to his children, too—" She stood there looking at him. I could hear her breathing. "A person can take only so much, Allegra."

I watched my father pick up one of Mommy's dead striped beetles and hold it in his hand and look at it and then put it back in the dish with the others. He looked as though he was wondering if Mommy was right about him.

"I want you to grow up strong and healthy and happy," he said to me in a very soft voice. "I want you to be someone who—"

"How about right now?" David's voice came from behind me, in the doorway. "Maybe you could worry a little bit less about what she's gonna be and notice she's right here, right now. Everybody's alive in this house. As of this morning. Everything doesn't have to be a matter of life or death. How about taking some of the heat off?" I kept my eyes on my father. Then I heard David walk away and out of the house. Everybody else just stood there in the living room, listening to the front door close.

"Mr. Wisdom has now been heard from," my mother said after a few seconds. "And I for one think he's wrong. Everything does have to be a matter of life or death. Everything is." She stared at the place where David had just been standing. I looked at her hands.

A sudden thought hit me. My mother saved insects' lives and then saved their carcasses for the exact same reason she rocked Deirdre in the music room, years after Deirdre's daughter was dead. It was because something is alive one minute and dead the next. Like my great-grandmother Leah. Or my other great-grandmother in Kansas, lying on her deathbed waving her arms in the air asking for horses and then she stopped breathing. Bro David was right: my parents were terrified.

And I remembered the way my mother had acted when

Bro David got off the airplane when he came back from New York, as if it was some miracle that he was alive. She even cried with happiness.

And maybe when my mother made that silly wave at people, she was saying, Hey, everybody here is alive, let's celebrate! Like a little kid, waving and looking silly, but underneath she had that terrible reason to be happy.

I looked at my father. Maybe I was his grandmother Leah in some strange way. I had her name. That wasn't so strange. And I thought of Jessica: she couldn't save her father from the eruption of the mountain. And Sarah, who thinks she dances for all those dead people.

"Daddy," I said, "is everything a matter of life or death?"

He looked at me, and he looked around the living room, at the chairs and the sofa and the lamps. "I don't know, Allegra," he said.

I went to the music room and practiced. I'd been at it for about an hour when Daddy came in. "Listen, Allegra," he said, walking across the room. "Put down your violin a minute." I put it on a table. "And your bow." I did. He put his arms around me. I was listening to his heart beating against the right side of my head. "Whether everything has to be a matter of life and death." He cleared his throat. "The evidence is right here, right now. Suffering and joy. That's all there is. There isn't anything else. And they're so close together—" He was talking very softly. "They're so close, it strikes terror into the human soul." He backed up and looked at me. I tried to imagine him as a little boy, watching his mother dust the living room before the opera came on the radio.

"Oh, Daddy," I said.

That night was the first rehearsal of the Youth Orchestra for the Waterfront Concert. I'd be on the inside chair, third stand, first violins, and somebody completely different would be on the outside; I'd be turning pages for a stranger. When I walked into the rehearsal hall, sitting in Lois's chair was a boy I'd never seen. I saw his very dark curly hair first, from across the room. I got to my chair and didn't know what to say to him. He didn't look at me. I tuned up, and he tuned up, and we sat there. I pretended I was looking at the music and the Xeroxed list. For a Waterfront Concert there isn't a whole symphony, the audience can't listen that long at a time. We play short things. We were going to play Respighi's *Fountains of Rome*, the *William Tell* Overture, and short pieces by Tchaikovsky, Sibelius, and Samuel Barber. We'd played them all before in the two years I'd been in the orchestra.

I sat in my chair and remembered how funny Lois had been about the *William Tell*, which she'd called "the Billy Tell." There's a section in it where the strings sound like buzzing insects, and she said we were the flies buzzing around the apple on Billy's son's head.

I looked at my new stand partner. He was obviously in high school. I've never gotten to sit beside anybody my own age in an orchestra. Somebody had to start the conversation. "Hi," I said.

He said hi. Under the curly hair he had a sort of roundish face, with a mole on the right side, below his mouth. And very long fingers. He looked at the music and said, "Do you always play this easy stuff?"

"No," I said. "Just for a park concert." This music wasn't

necessarily easy stuff. And in March we'd played a Shosta-kovich symphony; it was very hard. It was the one where Lois and I'd played the wrong note together. She'd said the Wrong Note Police were going to come and get us. I didn't mention it to my new stand partner.

He was very good-looking. We still had a few minutes before rehearsal began, and he said to me, "Put the *Fountains* up, will you?" I shuffled the music and put it in front. He found a place he wanted, and played it a couple of times. He played very, very well. He rested his violin on his left leg and looked at me sideways. "What's your name?" he said.

I said Allegra.

"Allegra what?"

"Allegra Shapiro."

He looked back at the music and worked on tuning his D string. "My parents know your parents. I mean my dad. I'm Landauer. Steve." That was all he said.

Little Stevie Landauer with the Lego blocks and the sixteenth-size violin and the phenomenal concentration.

"I've heard of you," I said.

"Yeah, I was at Aspen."

I didn't say that wasn't where I'd heard of him. Rehearsal began.

I love playing in the Youth Orchestra. It's more fun than the softball team, although they're both hard work. In soft-ball there's a lot of waiting around for the fun parts. In the orchestra the fun parts come more often. It also has more different kinds of people, more different ages. The little kids usually have tense mouths, and they move their eyes in quick sideways looks to see if anybody's watching them. On almost everybody in the whole band you can see a combination of the urge to play and the fear of playing badly. In the older kids, the fear isn't so obvious, of course. Christine, the concertmaster, has this little speech she makes sometimes. She says, "Make your fear work for you, not against you. Let it push those fingers into place; think of it as just one part of what you do. Let it be part of the force of your music. May the force be with you." It cracks people up, the first time they hear it.

But in both music and softball you work to be as good as you can, you get breathless with effort, you surprise yourself sometimes, and you know everybody in the whole bunch is feeling sort of the same way.

Lois and I'd been like teammates. We'd had a rhythm of sitting together: I knew just when to turn the page, and once she'd shown me a whole new way to braid my hair.

I was definitely not Steve Landauer's Little Buddy.

At intermission, I was standing with some of the wind players, listening to a girl tell about getting her driver's license and getting the braces off her teeth on the same day, and in the middle of it I heard somebody playing part of the first movement of Mozart's Fourth Violin Concerto very fast. I had a momentary shiver. My reflexes turned me around to see where it was coming from, even though I didn't want to find out. It was coming from a corner of the rehearsal hall, and it was as if a thread was pulling my ears to it. I saw Christine whirling around to look, too. Out of the corner of my eye I saw her puff her cheeks out and blow hard out of her mouth. Steve Landauer was in the corner with his back turned to everybody, and I watched his bowing, not wanting to watch at all. His arm moved smoothly and hard;

the notes were perfect. I caught Christine's face watching him closely.

Christine and Steve Landauer would both be playing the Bloch finals.

I closed my face and turned back around, and everybody was laughing at the driver's license and orthodontist story. I didn't let my face show anything. I tucked my shirt into my jeans and scratched my chin. We all went back to our places. I looked between the heads of the second-stand players at Christine's back. Christine is in college, a nice girl with very fast fingers. I knew her mainly from when she turned around to tell the section a different bowing; that's part of her job. She was listening to the conductor tell her something.

Steve Landauer came back to his chair. I didn't look at him. I got out the next music, the Sibelius, and put it in front of everything else.

"Now, ladies and gentlemen," the conductor said, "we remember, don't we, that in this piece the happiness of the dance is only one side of the music. The music ends in death. We play it knowing that. It has a double meaning, perfect for the kind of piece it is." He looked over the orchestra, stopping his eyes at some of the little kids. "We all understand 'double meaning,' don't we?" he said, and some of the big kids laughed. I noticed a little boy in the cello section looking scared; he only joined last year. "This music has a profound yearning and a profound lament—at the same time. Like life. Let's play." He raised his baton. "Be ominous," he said.

I heard Steve Landauer mutter, ". . . waste of time." We began.

We stopped just after letter C. "I'll remind you," the conductor said to everybody. "Remember—when we played this before? The pause between the second and third beats in this section—*that's* where the question of great happiness or great sadness of the heart arises. The audience doesn't have to know what you know. But they deserve to hear that pause in all its silence. We suspend *everything* for that moment. That means we have to get off the second beat precisely and together. No split-second errors. In this case, the precision of the silence will equal poetry." He raised his baton again.

Steve Landauer let out his breath in a whispered way that he maybe meant for me to hear. It was a whispered *Aaawwwfffffff*.

We began again.

At the end of rehearsal, Steve Landauer said to me, without exactly looking at me, "You're the best page turner I've ever had." And he walked off to put his violin away while I was feeling three things. One, I was a professional—a paid page turner—so I ought to be good. Two, that was a nice compliment. Three, he said it as if that was my job in the orchestra, to be his page turner.

When David picked me up from rehearsal, I said to him, "Don't ask." He hadn't even said anything yet.

"Hello, grump," he said. I put my violin case upright between my knees and we started home. "Look, Legs, I'm not gonna ask what's wrong. But just maybe you're taking yourself too seriously. Maybe."

I watched cars going past, traffic lights changing, Bro David shifting gears, a dog running along the sidewalk. Isn't that what you're supposed to do? Take yourself seriously? How else do you get anything done? "If I didn't take myself seriously, wouldn't I be just a joke?" I said.

"Everybody's a joke," he said.

When we got home, Daddy and Mommy were in the music room playing duets. I had another memory: being a little tiny kid, walking in the door and hearing Mommy and Daddy playing together. All of a sudden it was a feeling of safety, with the smell of hot chocolate and marshmallows in a little yellow mug I used to have.

The mug had gotten broken years ago.

David and I went up the stairs together. At the top, I whispered to him, "That's not a joke, is it? Mommy and Daddy playing duets after they got so upset this morning?"

He shrugged his shoulders. "No. Not really. Borderline."

I couldn't go bike riding, of course. I sat in my room and played with Heavenly Days. I went over my list of words, with "pernicious" and "flippant" and "ominous" added. I kept seeing violinists lined up at the competition. Steve Landauer, Christine the concertmaster, probably Karen Karen, if her hand was healed. Me. That made four. Some others, and I didn't want to know who they were. I just saw violins and hands, all lined up.

I put on my pajamas and brushed my hair.

Steve Landauer was very good-looking. And he played very, very well. And he'd given me that compliment. I didn't want to like him. But I did. Even his neck was good-looking. He had four mothers, one real and three step. He had good-looking eyes, too. But I didn't see them much; he didn't look straight at me. They were brown, and he had long eyelashes.

"Put up the *Fountains*, will you?" Lois never ordered me around that way. And she was probably older than Steve Landauer.

How could anybody have four mothers?

Waltz and Three. Why couldn't the music librarian find

it at the college? Waltz Tree. Probably because there were so many pieces listed under just plain Waltz. There must be thousands. And I didn't know the exact name of it. Maybe she'd call back the next day and say she'd found it.

I wondered what had happened to the husband Deirdre used to have.

I remembered the clinking of her earring going into Daddy's cello. And how she got so delirious. It must have been because she wasn't paying attention and suddenly things went wrong. Poor Deirdre.

Abruptly I realized something: It was almost like Daddy. His thing about Vigilance and Peace of Mind. Daddy and Deirdre were exactly alike in that way and they didn't even know it.

It was almost midnight. I pulled Heavenly's ear and woke her up. "Hey, Heavenly, it's midnight and I need someone to talk to." She stretched.

Why are you yelling at me? Because I love you! Maybe David was right. The world is crazy, and they were terrified.

Mall Babies from the black lagoon. I wanted to call Sarah and Jessica and tell them both. I put Miles Davis on the turntable and listened to "All Blues."

10

I was in the music room the next morning practicing the first movement before I was even very much awake. The sun was just coming up, and I still had my pajamas on. My lesson wasn't for three hours yet.

I even hit two wrong notes. And the actual notes in this concerto aren't even hard ones. When you hit a wrong note, you're likely to hit another one pretty soon because your concentration is interrupted: You can't help hearing the wrong note you've just played. It echoes in your head, and it jostles things around inside you.

ME: Allegra Shapiro. I'M playing this concerto. Maybe it was watching Steve Landauer's arm that pushed me out of bed so abnormally early in the morning. Or maybe it was that I was so glad to see yesterday end.

No matter what I did with the concerto that morning, no matter where I was in it or what kind of bowing I was using or anything, there was Steve Landauer right in my way, with his perfect bowing arm and his notes:

When I walked into the Kaplans' house, Mrs. Kaplan gave me popovers and peach jam. "We had a kitchen full of peaches from my brother, and the only thing to do was make jam. Take some home with you, Allegra. Sit down for a minute and eat one, won't you, dear?"

I like her double-chin look. I may be way off in my judgment, but I never met a double-chinned person I didn't like. I put my violin case and music case on one chair and sat on another one. She pushed everything about an inch closer to me than it already was: popovers on a plate, jam, butter knife, napkin. I spread jam on one of the popovers.

"Well, I'm on my way to work. Have a good lesson, Allegra," she said. "Oh, and by the way, dear. Remember the French composer Chausson? Your friend Deirdre sang such a lovely song of his at the concert. . . . He died of a skull fracture from riding his bicycle into a stone wall, poor man." And she walked out of the room.

Their kitchen has wallpaper on the ceiling with grapes and leaves. I ate two popovers and jam and looked up at it. It's as if the Kaplans have a permanent harvest canopy like the one religious Jews build for Succoth. I couldn't make my mother and Mrs. Kaplan not be friends, and I couldn't make them not talk about me when I wasn't looking, but I could be Very Irritated when they did. Chausson probably died way back in the nineteenth century when they hadn't invented bicycle lights yet.

I got my hands washed and went to the music room. Mr. Kaplan's sweatshirt was a really old one, and the words on it were almost faded away. They said "The *What* Quintet?"

He wanted to hear some scales first, the ones with seven sharps and seven flats. And Kreutzer no. 40, a whole page of trills. Then the concerto, start to finish. As usual, he played the piano version of the orchestra part. During the cadenzas, he turned around and watched me.

Like skiing, you're doing two things at once: the thing you're doing right that instant and the thing you'll be doing in the next instant. You look at the face of somebody who's just finished a ski race and you can see how all those instant events have been going on, overlapping each other. It's adrenaline. And other things.

It's a kind of alertness that comes on you, as if somebody has turned on all your lights inside. Sometimes it can get almost too bright in there.

At the end, he turned sideways on the piano bench. "Allegra, I'm concerned," he said. He folded his hands in his lap. Then he unfolded them and spread them on his legs. Then he scratched the back of his head where he still has lots of curly blondish-grayish hair, then he put his hand back on his knee. He was silent long enough to give me time to think, and I didn't know what to think about. I didn't know any question to ask in my mind, so I didn't know what answer I was supposed to be looking for. I'd just played the concerto without a kink, without missing a note, and I had the good tired feeling of finishing it well, and he was concerned.

"Have you any idea what I'm concerned about?" he asked,

looking up at me. And not smiling. He evidently meant he was Concerned.

I hung my violin and bow down straight in my hands. "No."

"I'm wondering if you're remembering whose concerto this is," he said, and looked at the piano keyboard, then back at me. He took a deep breath. "I'm wondering if you remember that a young boy— a teenager—in 1775 . . . Allegra, I'm wondering if you—I sense an aggressiveness—" He stopped. "Not that we don't want *any* aggressiveness—" He stopped again. "It's a fine line, Allegra, you know that. But I think I hear coming into your performance a spirit more of attack than— You're beginning to sound like a string tuned too tightly. . . ." He looked straight up in the air. "What is it I mean?" he asked the ceiling. He looked back at me for a long time. "The word is 'embrace,' " he said, finally. "In moving ever closer to Mozart—which you're doing very well—*very* well, Allegra— In moving closer, you're beginning to—I don't like saying this—" He stopped again. "You're almost on top of him." He looked at my feet, and then said in a very soft voice, almost hard to hear, "Don't upstage the nineteen-year-old boy who gave us this concerto."

He leaned his elbow on the keyboard, on G and A and B above middle C, forcing them to play together, and leaned his forehead on his hand. As if somebody'd hurt him. G and A and B hummed.

I was worse than afraid. Worse than shocked. Worse than horrified. What must Mozart have felt? There was some terrible thing I couldn't name whistling inside me. I felt my eyes bug out, and I tried to look at nothing but air in the room. I saw rosin dust in it. The tip of my bow was on the floor, holding me still.

Upstage the nineteen-year-old boy who gave us this concerto.

"Look at me, Allegra," Mr. Kaplan said.

I didn't even try to. I looked at the edge of a music stand across the room. Things that had been so arranged in me a minute ago were clashing into each other. I suddenly understood what Deirdre meant—the floor sliding out from under you without warning.

"Allegra, I think this is the first time I've ever hurt you?"

I didn't know the answer. It didn't matter.

"Come here," he said.

I stood with my eyes on the corner of the music stand. Stainless steel. There are millions like it. In China they wouldn't let anyone play Mozart or Beethoven for years when the government changed; they put people in closets and took away their instruments.

"Please come here, Allegra."

I lifted my bow tip and took two steps forward.

He took hold of my right hand, around the frog of the bow. He held it loosely. Over the top of his glasses his blue eyes were steady and serious, as if they wanted to keep me company. "The heart of the matter is . . ." He looked down at his hand around mine and the frog of my bow. "Is . . . is tenacity. We'll change our direction slightly, take what might be called a detour. We'll move in on the center of this concerto . . . in a slightly different way."

His eyes were very middle-aged. Sometimes I just trust him because he's old. "Brahms's 'Lullaby.' Any key you like.

Just play it for me. Play it exactly the way you feel right now."

I backed away from him. I closed my eyes and looked at what I saw inside my eyelids. What I saw was a little baby, sick and terrified and whimpering. It was in a corner of a room, wrapped in a dirty little blanket in a box or a basket, and the paint was chipped off the walls. I played the "Lullaby" with my eyes closed.

When I opened my eyes, Mr. Kaplan had his closed. He was nodding his head slowly. "Yes," he said. "There it is. There is what you can do when you are inside your instrument, Allegra. Indeed."

I didn't say anything. I wondered who the baby was. I was perplexed and ashamed. Doing something good with Brahms and doing something so horrible with Mozart was closing my head in. A question kept putting itself in me: How? Just that one word. How?

"We aren't going to have any more conversation with Mr. Mozart this morning," he said. "Instead, come tomorrow morning, an extra lesson—" He reached up and picked up his little brown schedule notebook from the top of the piano. He looked at it, moving his mouth around. "Yes, tomorrow morning, ten o'clock." He snapped the notebook shut. "We're not going to undo anything. We can't." He laughed. "That's a proven historical fact." I kept looking at him. "We'll—well, we'll take a detour. . . ."

❧

I stood on the Kaplans' porch. Mr. Kaplan said, "Don't punish yourself, Allegra. I mean," he looked out at the lawn in front of their house, "not any more than you have to.

You need both hands free for the work we have to do; and you won't, if you have a birch rod in one of them."

I tried to smile at him. It wasn't much of a joke, and he knew it.

He said, "And part of the fault here—a great part of it—" He looked past me, over my shoulder. "It's mine. We talk too much about 'mastering' music. Every time you turn around, someone is concerned with mastering a piece. I do it myself." He lowered his voice and looked straight at my face. "Great music isn't something we master; it's something we try all our lives to merge with. Indeed."

I didn't really see Mr. Kaplan's face. I saw Deirdre as she sang the low, soft notes in her concert, and I saw Mr. Trouble as he danced his old-fashioned dance on the grass. Then I looked out past them, and Mr. Kaplan was saying good-bye. I said good-bye and went down the steps.

I walked home. My violin case banged against my leg in regular rhythm. Some leaves were turning yellowish. My skin felt bad, all over me. Don't upstage the nineteen-year-old boy who gave us this concerto. What a horrifying thing. Unthinkable. Don't think about it. Elephants. I tried walking with my eyes closed, but I slipped off the edge of the sidewalk, so I opened them again.

Merge with. Not master. It felt so absolutely strange, because I knew that anyway. I'd always known it, in my stomach. I'd committed a crime by forgetting it.

I thought of the thing I'd told Deirdre about: crying under Daddy and Mommy's bed when I was a little kid and found out that the music wouldn't just automatically come out of the eighth-size violin.

On the kitchen table was a package addressed to me from

New York. It had all kinds of post office stickers on it, Express Mail and Insured. My grandmother Raisa gets my birthday mixed up with somebody else's. I didn't want a gift. Didn't deserve a gift. Nobody was home. I put my violin case and music case on the floor and sat down and stared at the brown wrapping paper.

Then I stared at my violin case on the floor. Then I stared out the window at a hummingbird on the feeder. Heavenly rubbed the side of her head against my leg and walked to her water dish and began drinking. I listened to her tongue going in and out and picking up water, reflexively.

When you think about how many millions of words old people have written, it's no wonder their handwriting gets a little bit jerky. I looked at my grandmother's.

Don't upstage the nineteen-year-old boy who gave us this concerto.

The package was soft, maybe she was sending me a sweater, for the birthday that was somebody else's. I didn't want a sweater; I wanted to undo my crime against Mozart. I got a pair of scissors and cut the tape on the package.

There were several layers of wrapping, then pink tissue paper with a pink envelope that said READ FIRST. The flap wasn't sealed, it was tucked in. I opened it.

> *Dear Allegra Leah,*
> *The gift I am sending you would have been for your bat mitzvah, and I hope you would carry it proudly on that occasion but you have a liberated family who have forgotten already in one generation. We are lucky to have a connection, to break such a thing is not understandable. Your mother I forgive, she wouldn't*

know. She happened on a Gentile background from Kansas, not her fault.

I am nervous for you, and your brother David too. You would have to understand such nervousness by going to synagogue. Here is your gift from my love for you so far away 3,000 miles.

Your great-grandmother Leah was born in the turn of the century, 1900, in Suprasl. This was a shtetl I saw once. There are stories from this place. Poor people, tailors, bakers, and animals all went back and forth on the roadway. Her rabbi was the son and also the grandson of a rabbi. When she was a child she had geese to tend and there is the picture of her with her straw broom and her favorite goose. You know the picture. Where her family lived the field went up on a hill and the morning light came into their house, a blessing.

Then she married and became my mother and soon my father took her to Bialystok. I was born in 1921, and my sister in 1925 who died in childhood. My father played a wooden flute and my mother sang to us. She tried to sing the fever out of my sister and was unsuccessful. I remember her voice. She could sing like leaves falling from off a tree. She also made rich breads and cakes, and even today the smell of some certain kugels makes me unable to speak.

I saw black armbands when I was 13 years old. I asked what they were and my father replied they were a tribal symbol. I didn't know from tribal symbols, I wanted a pink dress for my birthday which I did not get. There was hunger and disease and we as well as our neighbors were frightened. Punishments for being Jewish were meted, small ridicules and then larger ridicules. My father's partner in business had his beard cut off by a soldier's bayonet. It was this savagery in joking that frightened us all.

In the year 1939 I was 18 years old. My parents told me one day I was to pack my things to go on a trip to visit my father's uncle in America. Of course I did not want to go so far away on a boat all alone without the language, but they insisted. Uncle Moshe is a jolly man, they said, with luxuries, a radio, and there are movies just down his street in New York. Uncle Moshe would take me to a school to learn to typewrite while I visited him. His wife I would like, a berrieh, a live wire, and his grown-up children, my cousins, would be my friends for my visit. This would be a vacation for me from the bad life in Bialystok, and they taught me some words to use in English. "So how about it?" "Some milk in the coffee, please." "I am a nice girl."

With these words I got on the boat unwillingly. My father and my mother sent me with blessings and kisses with their arms around me, I will never forget. I believed them about my "vacation" because I wanted to believe them. In Poland we did many things for that reason.

I never heard my mama's and my papa's voice again. I never felt their hand. We believe they died at Treblinka, but one can never be sure.

My mother Leah had soft arms and her weary eyes were tender with imagination. In the photograph you sent me at my birthday, I see some sameness in your eyes, Allegra Leah. The gift I am sending you have seen in the picture you have on your wall of my mother Leah as a girl with her broom and her goose. It came in my satchel across the Atlantic Ocean in 1939. I did not know it was in my satchel; my mother tucked it inside.

Only later I understood this was her final good-bye to me.

A memory is a thing you always have. But it is about a thing you cannot get any more of.

You will be all your life this connection with Bialystok and Suprasl. This gift is only for you. You are the one with the name of the great-grandmother, the elter bubbe. I wish you the dreams and not the nightmares.

When you visit me again you will play your violin for me and we will walk in Central Park and I will tell you the stories. About the "birdseed" that Uncle Moshe put on the window ledge of the apartment and I thought he meant to grow birds. And about my little friend Broche in Bialystok, how she and I peeked at the bride on her wedding morning. And I will show you how my mother Leah made her cakes.

Now care for this tribal symbol I am sending and with it my great love across the many miles.

Kiss your mama and dada and your brother David for me.

Bubbe Raisa

I read the letter twice. Then I stared at the pink tissue paper and ran my hand over it and listened to the crinkles. I was almost frightened to look inside.

I'd spent the whole summer of my twelfth year doing the wrong thing, trying to be more important than Mozart, and I didn't even know it. And now my grandmother was trusting me to be the connection with Bialystok and Suprasl. To take care of the tribal symbol.

Maybe if I'd been all Jewish, or even all Gentile, I'd have known what to do. But I was half-and-half and I sat at the kitchen table not even able to unwrap pink tissue paper.

How hard to do the most natural thing. Heavenly could walk to her water dish and lap up the water, Mozart could write five violin concertos when he was nineteen years old, Elter Bubbe Leah could have her photograph taken with her favorite goose and her broom and her purse, these were natural things to do. I could unwrap a package if I tried.

I stared at the paper.

I saw in my mind a young girl with a satchel getting on a boat for a vacation, knowing how to say "So how about it?" in a foreign language, and I saw arms hugging her, and I saw the black of the armband and I saw something horrifying. It was a thirty-nine-year-old woman with weary eyes doing the most unnatural thing in the world. She knew she would never see her daughter again. And she sent her away on a boat, blessing her and kissing her. To save her life.

To go against everything you think you know. To do something you must do because you must do it. It's an unnatural thing, and you do it anyway.

I reached for the package. My fingers went very slowly, lifting off the layers of pink tissue.

The purse was smaller than in the picture. It was purplish velvet; it had probably once been the color of grape juice. There were places where the velvet had worn thin. It had embroidery on it. Someone had embroidered pink-and-white flowers and green leaves on the velvet. They were faded, very pale. It had a strap, to hang on a girl's arm. I held it on my lap. Then I held it against my face to feel the softness. It smelled like lavender and mothballs. I stood up and hung it on my arm. I walked around the kitchen with my arm bent, with the purse hanging. I walked into the bathroom and looked at myself in the mirror. My Jewish half and my Gentile half were standing there with a Polish purse dangling. Elter Bubbe Leah had tucked it into her daughter's satchel and sent it to America.

I looked at the purse in the mirror. "Welcome to Portland," I whispered to it. And I swung my head to the east, toward New York, and said, "Thank you, Bubbe Raisa."

I held the purse against my stomach.

My great-grandmother. Elter Bubbe Leah.

Dead at Treblinka.

I felt a homesickness. For what? Something I'd never seen. I didn't even know what it was. Bubbe Raisa was inviting me to be something—forcing me to be something nobody else had ever even mentioned. I didn't know how to be it. All I knew was that there was a homesickness. I stared at the purse on my arm in the mirror.

Then I took it back to the kitchen table and laid it on its tissue paper. I stood there looking at it. Then I picked up the whole thing, the outside wrapping and Bubbe Raisa's letter and the sticky tape and all of it, and took them upstairs to my room. I put them on top of my chest of drawers where Heavenly wouldn't sit on them. I looked at the flowers embroidered on the velvet. Eighty years ago? Somebody had used a real needle and real thread thousands of miles away in Poland, embroidering those flowers while geese waddled up the hillside.

11

Five minutes later I stood in the doorway of the music room and looked at the plants all over the place. They were Jew-Gentile plants. Or maybe just Gentile ones since they were mainly my mother's.

I looked at my violin as I took it out of the case. It's Italian. And my bow is French, but it has a new thumb guard, and that's American. The scarf I wrap around the violin inside the case has a tag that says Taiwan. The rosin is American. So are the strings.

On my father's music stand was a cello sonata written by a Japanese composer.

Ernest Bloch was Swiss. And Jewish.

The white horsehair in my bow is from Poland.

I rubbed the back of my violin against my stomach. How to unlearn my wrong Mozart? How did I get started doing it wrong? I looked down at the side view of the bridge and strings. Mozart looked at the same side view when he held his violin that way. I was ashamed.

I sat on the sofa where I'd carried on with Deirdre and I held my violin and bow on my lap. Deirdre had a dead baby she always remembered. Mr. Trouble went around looking for his lost Waltz Tree or a Waltz in Three. Somewhere I'd lost the Mozart concerto I loved and had put something else in my head instead? I saw Steve Landauer's arms moving in the corner of the rehearsal room. I saw Christine's head jerk instantly around to watch. I saw Karen in Trout Creek Ridge with her broken fingers, saying Mozart could make you forget your problems. I saw Sarah dancing with Mr. Trouble in Waterfront Park. I pictured Jessica visiting her father's grave.

I stood up, walked to the middle of the room, not near the piano, just out in the middle of the room, and I closed my eyes and looked inside for something to start me. If Deirdre was right, and the music was in there all along, maybe a better music had been waiting inside me—waiting to be played. The idea sounded ridiculous.

Elter Bubbe Leah's purse was lying on its pink tissue paper in my bedroom. I went upstairs and got it and carried it flat, on its paper, held out in front of me, downstairs and laid it on the sofa in the music room.

I went over several sections of the concerto and repeated and repeated them. I tried playing some parts with the mute. I played all three cadenzas faster and then slower. There wasn't any method in what I was doing. I was just wandering around the concerto, like a tourist, trying to make it look different to myself.

While I played the third movement, I looked now and then at the embroidered flowers on the velvet purse lying on the sofa. Peaceful little flowers, growing up the purse and bending back and forth. Little faded pink-and-white petals brushing against their pale green leaves.

There wasn't even any grave where my father would be able to put flowers for his grandmother. Not even any date when she died. She had become just a blank. A nothing.

I went to the dining room and sat down at the table. David says the world is an insane asylum, and he's absolutely right.

A-n-n-i-h-i-l-a-t-e.

My violin was made two hundred years before Elter Bubbe Leah sent her daughter away on a boat. Pieces of wood and some glue. The Portland Art Museum has a wooden Chinese horse from the third century B.C. When Jessica was in her horse period we used to go to see it all the time. Save a wooden horse for twenty-three centuries, but kill somebody who had a pet goose and straw broom and a velvet purse and two daughters, one of them dead.

There was no word for how angry I was.

Deirdre. No wonder she got strange. And Mr. Trouble. His whole life of lost things.

Losing things. That was what the whole world was about. Why bother to get born in the first place?

I went back to the music room. When Itzhak Perlman's wife was pregnant, André Previn wrote two songs for the baby. They didn't know if it would be a boy or a girl, so he wrote "Noah" and "Naava." I looked through stacks of music on the shelves and found them. I played "Naava." It's a perfect song for a little girl.

The Bloch Competition was five weeks away. I asked myself: Allegra, are you going to play it? If it had been five minutes away, of course the answer would have been no. Allegra, I said to myself, you do what you say you're going to do.

And I'd told Mr. Trouble I'd help him find his lost song. I had no idea how I was going to do it.

I looked at Elter Bubbe Leah's purse on the sofa, I closed

"Naava" and put it back on the stack of music, and I took out the Mozart. I would read the notes, like a beginner, and I would start all over again.

It would be like learning a new language. I stood in front of the music stand and read the top of the page: Mozart. Concerto no. IV in D Major. K. 218. "So how about it?" I said, out loud. Like a beginner, I felt my way up the finger-board to the first note and made myself read every single note, not letting my brain or my fingers run ahead. I tried to listen to the concerto as if I'd never heard it before, but it was impossible to forget.

Remember everything you know and forget it simultaneously, so you can invent a new thing. The divine inspiration of the NBA.

I couldn't unlearn the concerto. But I could unlearn my wrong attack on it. If I could find exactly the spots where my arm was going wrong. Those spots were in my brain. Where in my brain? I looked at Elter Bubbe's velvet purse on the sofa.

I called Sarah. She had her verdicts. Steve Landauer was a class-A jerk. He was Neek for his show-off manners; it didn't matter if he was good-looking or not. "Arrogant" was one of the words on her summer list, and Steve Landauer was arrogant. It was partly that he had four mothers, but he was still arrogant. If anybody could find Mr. Trouble's lost song it had to be me; I knew more music than anybody. His story was the saddest one she'd heard all summer. Mr. Kaplan was the one to blame for my Mozart problems. He was the one who told me to say "ME: Allegra Shapiro. I'M playing this concerto." And it was no wonder I'd played too aggressively after spending a whole rehearsal with Mr. Aspen

Celebrity Jerk Landauer; it was my anger coming out. And I was lucky to get such a symbol in the mail, and it was going to bring me good luck.

"But it's a symbol of—it's a symbol of *terrible* luck. My great-grandmother was dead at Treblinka. And I'm alive and what am I even doing to de*serve* it?" I said.

She didn't say anything for a little while. Then she said, "You're finding a lost song for a lost soul, Legs. I'm gonna call Jessica."

They both showed up in less than an hour. The velvet purse was still lying on the music-room sofa on top of its tissue paper.

"I'm afraid to touch it," Jessica said. "It's a holy thing. I'm not even a little bit Jewish." She stood very still on the spot where my mother had rocked Deirdre. Chinese people do ancestor worship, and it makes them feel different about their dead ones.

Sarah and I looked at each other and laughed. "You're everything else," Sarah said. "And I'm not Jewish, either."

"Not *everything* else," Jessica said.

They read Bubbe Raisa's letter. Jessica ran her hand very lightly over the flowers on the purse. "Holy cow," she said.

Sarah was walking around looking at my mother's plants. She said, "Legs, is this purse a burden?"

I looked at her. "Maybe if I'd gotten it when I wasn't already feeling guilty. Maybe then it wouldn't be."

She walked around some more, taking her big, long steps.

Jessica said, "That Landauer called you a page turner, didn't he?"

"Yep."

"Don't you think you played the concerto the way you did just to show him you're more than a page turner?"

"But I must've been going in the wrong direction with it all summer."

Sarah said from behind a big plant with huge leaves, "Because your teacher told you to. He's the one who said Mozart doesn't want you to be a 'fraidy cat and all that. Look: it's not your fault. And your great-grandmother with no grave isn't your fault."

೧৩

When I got to my lesson, Mr. Kaplan was wearing a sweatshirt that had Alfred E. Newman from *Mad* magazine sitting at a harpsichord and saying, "I'm into nuances."

He said, "Good morning, Allegra. My conscience tells me I was not as nice with you yesterday as I might have been. Are you angry with me?"

"No," I said. I put my violin case on the floor and started to open it. I was squatted on the floor, and I realized that wasn't true. I looked down at the latch under the handle of the case and then I looked up at him. "Yes, a little bit," I said.

And then of course I felt terrible. Mr. Kaplan stoops a little bit, his posture is kind of slumped; and his teeth aren't perfect, they have gaps between them. And I guess Mrs. Kaplan doesn't tell him he's got little hairs growing out of his ears, and he doesn't know they're there. And one long hair was coming out of his right eyebrow, almost blondish; it had been there all summer, sticking out over the top of his glasses. If you look closely at his eyes you can see a kind of old sadness; maybe it's just the way old people's eyelids come around their eyes.

From the floor, I looked up at that eyebrow with the long hair coming out of it and remembered that he probably had somebody at one of the death camps, too. Maybe a whole family.

"Tell me," he said. He was standing right above me.

I turned around and got the rosin out of the violin case. I unfolded the felt cover, looked at the ridges in the rosin, and got my bow out. I heard him moving away, and out of the side of my eye I saw his shoes walking backward. I stayed in the squatting position and rubbed my bow back and forth across the rosin.

"Beware the boomerang," he said.

I folded the rosin cover closed, put it in the violin case, and picked up my violin. I stood up. I still had my back to him. I thumbed the strings.

I turned around. He was sitting sideways on the piano bench, facing me. "Remember 'ME: Allegra Shapiro. I'M playing this concerto'?" I said.

"Indeed."

"Well." I didn't want to say the rest of it. It would be accusing him of something.

"Indeed," he said again. He nodded his head three times.

I had the urge to shrug my shoulders, and I resisted it.

"Do you feel that that—announcement of yourself—do you feel it's affected your relationship with the concerto in any way?"

"Of course. It's obvious," I said.

"Tell me what things you feel have been affected."

"My notes are clearer."

"Indeed. I would say that almost every note in your Mozart is utterly cloudless. Good, Allegra. In some cases, ruthlessly clear."

·179·

I suddenly saw the back of Steve Landauer's head in the corner of the rehearsal room, and his shoulders, and I heard the same notes again. "In fact, that's what's wrong," I said. "Probably. I was so determined to get unscared, and I went around doing what you said—announcing myself—and I went over the top. I upstaged Mozart. Like you said. And—I should've been saying, 'HIM: Wolfgang Amadeus Mozart. HE wrote this concerto.' *Not* 'ME, I'M playing it.' "

Mr. Kaplan kept looking at me. "Anything else, Allegra?"

I saw the Landauer shoulders and arms and back of the head all moving again, with the corner of the rehearsal room behind them. I saw him playing facing the cinder-block wall. "And I think somebody should've told me. I'm surrounded by musicians, and nobody tells me anything."

"Told you what?" I could almost see Mr. Kaplan's face and the Landauer bowing arm at the same time.

"Well, told me I was getting too—'ruthlessly clear,' you said. Maybe it happened as far back as the concert with Margaret in Trout Creek Ridge. Maybe even before that."

He just kept looking at me. No change on his face.

"And I think somebody should've told me about the finals long before June. If I was to have this—this huge—responsibility, somebody should've told me." A little glimpse of Elter Bubbe's embroidered flowers came into my head and then went out again.

He looked at me, still listening. He was concentrating, I could tell his mind wasn't wandering. He scratched the back of his head, the hairy part. He said, "And where would we be, today, if—one—someone had told you about the finals right in the middle of your softball season? And, two—if someone had been able to use a seventh sense or something of that sort—and told you you were getting just the smallest bit—this much"— he held up his left thumb and index finger, about a centimeter apart—"just *this much* more aggressive than was necessary—perhaps just one eyelash out of place in the portrait of the concerto . . ."

I saw in my mind the newspaper review of Deirdre's concert, "bold intimacy."

I tuned my A string and kept on looking at him. Nobody ever tells you when you're just beginning to make your mistakes. Nobody ever warns you that early.

"Do you know somebody named Steve Landauer?" I said. The words felt strange coming out of my mouth in Mr. Kaplan's house.

A little light bulb went on in his face. "New in town. Yes . . ."

Then Steve Landauer was taking lessons from Mr. Kaplan. He stood there in that same room and played for Mr. Kaplan and listened to Mr. Kaplan encourage him and analyze him and criticize him and— They made jokes together in that same room. Mrs. Kaplan fed him popovers and peach jam. He came straight from Aspen into their house, by radar. Every time I walked in, I was moving through the same air Steve Landauer had breathed out. He had the pattern on the rug memorized the same way I did. And he'd win the competition, of course.

". . . Yes, yes . . . He played for me once. . . ." Mr. Kaplan said.

Steve Landauer didn't take lessons from Mr. Kaplan. He didn't have the rug memorized. He went back out of the room, sucked right out the keyhole.

Mr. Kaplan and I stared at each other.

"Is there anything else?" he said.

Steve Landauer played for Mr. Kaplan once, auditioning for lessons. Mr. Kaplan didn't take him. I saw Steve Landauer's back and shoulders; I saw his bowing arm moving in the corner of the rehearsal room.

"And my grandmother sent me my elter bubbe's purse from Poland, she disappeared to Treblinka and her daughter, that's my grandmother, her name's Raisa—" I'd opened my mouth and it had started coming out. "She wants me to be the connection with—" It was ridiculous, the embroidered flowers on the velvet purse when Hitler was a boy trying to get into art school . . . "I'm named after her, Leah, she was a child in a shtetl and she was annihilated—and I have her name and now I have her purse and I'm supposed to be a symbol of something—" There was no earthly reason for me to tell my violin teacher my family history. "And Bubbe Raisa, that's the daughter she sent away to New York—" I saw the wind blowing on the boat dock and Leah knowing she'd never see her daughter again. "She was eighteen years old and she found the purse tucked in her satchel when she was already out to sea, her mother sent it along with her—" I saw the hands unpacking the satchel. "Maybe it was like a code symbol, maybe Raisa knew it and maybe she didn't—" I saw hands in gray mist waving at a boat leaving a dock. "And she never saw her mother again. They *think* she went to Treblinka, nobody knows for sure. Her mother. Leah." I heard my voice get very soft. "And I have her velvet purse with embroidered flowers in my bedroom. It came in the mail yesterday."

I remembered Bro David saying everything doesn't have to be a matter of life or death and my mother saying everything does have to be.

Mr. Kaplan was leaning forward on the piano bench as if he was watching a movie. "Yes," he said. "Hmmm. Indeed." He nodded his head slowly up and down.

I looked down at my violin. "And when I got the velvet purse in the mail I already felt guilty—I already felt terrible about what I'd done to the concerto, and— Now . . ."

Over the top of his glasses he looked at me with his middle-aged eyes, the strange single long hair coming out of his eyebrow. He raised both eyebrows and his bald head looked rounder, and the odd hair looked like an antenna. "Yes," he said. "This is the great horror. Indeed."

I felt my own eyebrows go up.

"The things," he said. He turned his head, looked at the piano keyboard, then looked back up at me. "A purse. A razor. Sometimes a picture. A button. A teaspoon." He nodded his head slowly. "This is what it is."

And I suddenly remembered Mr. Trouble dancing, the first time I saw him, when Daddy's quartet was playing, and the wind was blowing a little bit, and Mr. Trouble was moving in the small circles. I just saw him for an instant in my mind.

Mr. Kaplan and I looked at each other. Between us I saw Deirdre and my mother rocking back and forth on the music-room floor, my mother humming into her hair. And there was Steve Landauer in a corner, playing with his face to a wall. And Elter Bubbe Leah waving her arms at a boat in gray fog.

My mind gets too busy sometimes, and I have to put everything back in the places they came from, Deirdre and Trouble and my brother and everybody. You don't have time for everything. You just have to push things back out of the center so you can do what you're supposed to do. I switched my bow over to my right hand where my violin was and ran my left hand through the top of my hair.

"Allegra Leah Shapiro, we are going back to this concerto," Mr. Kaplan said. "And we are going to hold it in our hands and care gently for it, knowing what we know." He looked at me, breathed in and out, and turned to face the keyboard.

I wiped both hands on my skirt and got ready to play. We stopped about a dozen times and at the end Mr. Kaplan sat silent. Then he said, "Indeed. Two youngsters. Each with so much locked inside."

He looked at me for almost a minute. The last three notes were still going in my head. "Allegra, have I told you the story about the hammer and the stone?"

"No."

"One day in Italy, a man was hammering and hammering on a piece of marble. A young boy sitting on a wall asked him, 'Why do you keep hammering on that stone?' And Michelangelo said, 'There's an angel inside this stone, and I'm trying to let it out.' "

I looked at him and nodded my head, trying to keep my face partly closed. It was exactly Deirdre and the Rose Music in the Rose Garden.

"Perhaps we need to hammer a little more lightly on this concerto; perhaps the angel will come out more willingly if we use your most personal touch."

∾

Four days later I answered the phone early in the morning.

"Allegra, I'm glad you're home. I need you to turn pages? I mean tonight? I'm terribly sorry, dear—so little notice, you know? Things happened. You'll do it, I hope?"

It was the red-haired woman, the pianist who talked in questions. "Indoors this time, eight o'clock in Lincoln Hall? Will you be there by seven-fifteen?"

I said I would.

"Besides the trio, we're adding a violin and viola for a quintet? We have a new violinist, a very exciting young player. We'll do that splendid Brahms, and a Mozart and a new piece?"

I told her I'd be there.

I lay on the floor in the music room, looking at the Green Violin painting. All the people and the animals in the painting are reaching toward the music. And there's that flying man at the top, with the smaller man waiting to catch him when he falls. And the green man just keeps on playing. His feet are kind of tapping. And his shoes don't match. I hadn't noticed that before. Or maybe I'd noticed it but I hadn't thought about it. Like Mr. Trouble's shoes.

I got my bike and went out riding. Ten thirty-eight in the morning, nobody could complain that I was going to be kidnapped.

I went toward Crystal Springs Park, which has rhododendrons and ducks. Did I want to win the competition? Did I even want to play it? Steve Landauer would win it. What about Christine from the Youth Orchestra? And Karen Karen? And the other people, whoever they were? What did the judges want?

The main path in the park leads downhill and across a bridge. As you pedal over the bridge you hear the boards making a sort of low drum sound. When I was little, we used to come here for picnics. Once I rode my tricycle across the bridge and the boards said, "Tug-a-lug, tug-a-lug," and the whole family called the park Tug-a-lug Park for a long time.

That was years ago. Bro David was a beginning Boy Scout and he was wearing his uniform.

I got off my bike and stood and watched the ducks, in groups, in families, scooting across the pond, going somewhere, all of them on their way to something. Probably just more food. Maybe adventures. If you're a duck, just swimming around a log is probably an adventure. They were just going places, the same places over and over again, places on the pond. They seemed to be going so smoothly but all the time their feet were paddling hard underneath. They were going where they had to go. For who knew what reason. Just going and going places.

On the far side of the bridge, I put my bike against a tree and sat on the edge of the grass and looked at the water.

All the questions in my mind suddenly seemed like a quiz.

Do you want to win the competition?

    Yes

    No

    Maybe

    Why did you select the answer above?

Do you want to lose the competition?

    Yes

    No

    Maybe

    Why did you select the answer above?

Why did you say yes to playing the competition in the first place?

    To please Joel Smirnoff

    To please Mr. Kaplan

    To please your parents

    To prove that you're good

Other—if so, what?

Are you sure?

Do you really love Mozart enough to go through all this torture?

Is it really torture?

Are you doing it for Elter Bubbe Leah even though she's already dead?

And what's *wrong with that*?

I jumped. I'd said that last thing out loud—very loud—and a little girl ran away and hid behind somebody, maybe her mother. I saw her red socks jump across the grass and I heard my echoes in the air. I turned around. She was hanging on her mother, staring at me. I stared back at her. I could see just part of her face. She was holding a piece of torn bread for the ducks, holding it in her fist. She wasn't even three feet tall.

I said it again, inside my head: What's wrong with that? What's wrong with doing it for Elter Bubbe Leah who had a goose and a broom and a purse and went to the gas chamber? I was still staring at the little girl with the red socks. I looked at her hand with the torn bread in it. Would Elter Bubbe even care? She and I were named the same name and would she have any way of knowing about the Mozart, and if she knew, would she care?

I stopped staring at the little girl and looked down in front of me at the dirt. An ant was walking along with all its legs busy. I could smush that ant and just quietly go on sitting there. The little girl in the red socks could walk right over and put her foot down hard on the ant and kill it.

Nothing matters, I heard myself say in my head.

And I instantly saw in my head Mozart sitting down with his quill pen writing the middle part of the second movement.

And I saw Deirdre with her mouth open just slightly, singing the softest of her soft notes at the concert, her blue dress quivering, and I saw Mr. Trouble dancing with Sarah and their feet swinging and kicking on the ground.

I looked out across the pond, all dotted with ducks, like notes on a page. I said in my head, *Everything matters*.

The little kid and her mother walked on to another part of the shore. I watched the ant move about an inch before I stood up and got on my bike and rode the long way home.

On the kitchen table was a note from my mother saying station KORV had called and wanted to know if I'd be willing to be interviewed as one of the Bloch finalists on the Saturday morning of Labor Day weekend, the day before the competition. On TV. It was the show "Hello, Oregon," and the producer said all the finalists were being invited. I was supposed to call her back and tell her whether I would or not.

My mother purposely hadn't given her opinion on the message.

It would mean I'd find out who the other finalists were a whole day before I had to play.

I opened the refrigerator door, took out a peach, rolled it over and over and over in my hand, leaned over the kitchen sink, looked out the window at a hummingbird at the feeder, bit into the peach, felt the juice dribble down my left arm, and decided I would go to the TV studio and be interviewed.

I got to Lincoln Hall to turn pages just when the pianist was walking in the door. She showed me the fastest turns, and then I went backstage to wait. The cellist, a man I'd seen in the Symphony but didn't know, came in and started tuning up. We said hi to each other. And then the violinist from before came, with a violist. I'd just sat down on a wooden crate when in walked Steve Landauer all dressed in black-and-white concert costume, with a violin case.

He nodded hello at the other people, and said, "Well, Allegra." And then he bent over to put his case down and get his violin out.

The added violinist, a very exciting young player, about to play the splendid Brahms, was Steve Landauer.

The pianist said, "You know each other?"

"She's a hot page turner," Steve Landauer said, and stood up, tuning his D string as he moved.

"Oh, I know that?" she said, and laughed. "She's a professional?"

As a matter of fact, Steve Landauer didn't really know what he was talking about. He'd seen me turn with my right hand, but not with my left. You don't use your right hand in front of a pianist's face. And in an orchestra you turn from the bottom of the page; when you're only a page turner you turn from the top. All the same, it's timing. I looked at him and then turned around.

While they played, I thought about playing chamber music. Of all the fun things to do sitting down, it must be near the top of the list. Of course I'd played duets and trios and some quartets; Mr. Kaplan gets his students together with other kids to do it once in a while, and sometimes kids from the Youth Orchestra get together and play. But to do it for your whole life, like the Juilliard Quartet, to play chamber music as a career—the way somebody else might play basketball or work in a bank—I sat and wondered how that life would be.

When they got to the quintet I heard Steve Landauer play. He was better than I'd even thought before. Second violin isn't as hard a part as first, but in a quartet of all professional people it has to sound perfect. As far as I could hear, it did. The page turner isn't supposed to turn around and watch people play, so I just listened. Steve Landauer's notes came humming over my shoulder, and they sounded smooth and round and like little waves of water.

While they bowed to the audience, I tried to be invisible, of course.

When I got home, in one way I didn't want to go near my violin: I was horrified by the idea of upstaging Mozart. And in another way, I wanted to spend the whole night playing. I was in bursts of energy, and I played through two or three Dancla études, seeing pictures of my life go by in layers: going to lessons; watching rain drip on leaves outside the music-room window when I was a little kid playing little songs; seeing the hand-prints of everybody in my whole first grade on the classroom wall and laughing and splashing at a big white sink with the other kids as we washed off the paint we'd dipped our hands in. I played Kreutzer no. 38 and remembered a picnic we'd had when Bubbe Raisa visited us. I remembered skipping along a trail holding her hand.

I spent about an hour on the third-movement cadenza of the Mozart before I went to bed. When it's going well, it can sound like beads falling down a string.

While I was waiting to go to sleep, I told Elter Bubbe Leah I'd be playing the Mozart for her in a few days. Anybody walking by on the street could have told me I was doing an insane thing, lying in my bed promising a corpse I'd play a Mozart concerto for her. They could tell me the last thing this great-grandmother needed—alive or dead—was a Mozart violin concerto. They could say I was being disrespectful of the dead, and they could say I was being impractical, and they could tell me I was trying to rely on something supernatural to help me win. They could accuse me of trying to bribe the spirits.

In the incomplete dark I lay and looked at the outlined hump of the purse on top of my bureau and talked to Elter Bubbe Leah. If I kept it to myself, nobody could tell me I was crazy or impractical or immoral.

The Leah I was talking to was the one in the picture, the one with the goose and broom.

And I kept seeing Steve Landauer sitting behind me and to the right on the stage, his fingers going like hummingbirds on the strings, his sound in some places like rough silk, the kind Jessica has in her family from being partly Chinese.

And I saw, too, Mr. Trouble's feet dancing, pointed outward, away from each other, in unmatched shoes. I looked at the hump of Elter Bubbe's purse against the wall and listened to Heavenly giving herself a bath.

I set the alarm clock for 6:00 A.M. and went to sleep.

12

I woke up two minutes before the alarm was due to bleep. I was ready to talk to my grandmother. I went to the kitchen phone. It was 9:00 A.M. in New York.

"Hello." Already I missed her. Her voice has a tone that says, This Is the Way Things Should Be Done, Trust Me. "My Allegra Leah! You've had your breakfast so early?"

"No, Bubbe—"

"The strawberries are blooming already in Auragon? I saw on TV you had eighty-three degrees yesterday; it will be hot today, too."

"Strawberries are past now, Bubbe. Peaches are on. I got Elter Bubbe Leah's purse, I want to . . . I want to say thank you. . . ."

"You'll take good care?"

"Oh, yes—of course. I'm. In fact, it's— Well, it's—Oh, Bubbe—"

"You're telling me something?"

"Yes. I am. Bubbe, I'm playing a violin competition. And the purse is—Well, I'm thinking of Elter Bubbe Leah when she had her goose and her broom and her purse. In the picture. And that's the way I'll play the competition."

"Such a tragedy, there's no word. My Allegra Leah, you'll

play with other children? In a contest?" She wasn't listening completely.

"Well, not exactly children. It's a Mozart concerto."

"And there is a prize?"

"Bubbe, the others are all older than I am. I'm the youngest. Yes, there's a prize. But I'm not thinking about that. It's to get through the competition—Elter Bubbe Leah's purse. I decided to play the Mozart for her."

There wasn't any sound on the other end of the phone.

"Don't tell anybody, Bubbe?"

Another silence.

"This is your offering, Allegra Leah."

"Yes. That's what I mean."

More silence.

"This is your kaddish. Yom Hashoah."

I didn't understand. I didn't say anything.

"Such a goyishe family. Your prayer for the dead, your remembrance for her."

"Yes," I said. "Say it again?"

"Kaddish. Yom Hashoah. When will you come to see me, Allegra Leah? Such a big girl, I hardly know you."

"Are you inviting me, Bubbe?"

"We'll go to the museums, we'll go in Central Park, of course I'm inviting you. Rosh Hashanah?"

Vaguely, I thought it was sort of in October. "I'll ask my parents."

"They'll find excuses. School. 'She should be playing her Mozart.' Childhood is short, you could skip Mozart a little, tell them that, Allegra Leah. Come see your bubbe. We'll bake kugel, I'll tell you the stories—I'll tell you the stories of who you are."

"I'll ask, Bubbe. Thank you for inviting me."

"Oy, thank you for calling me and saying thanks. You made my day, Allegra Leah."

"And mine," I said.

"Keep cool, the television says it's hot where you are. Eat your breakfast."

"I will, Bubbe."

"You're being a good girl?"

"I think so. I love you, Bubbe."

"I love you. You carry her name, Allegra Leah."

"I know, Bubbe."

"Come see me. We'll do the town. We'll be grand ladies on Fifth Avenue."

"I'll do it, Bubbe."

"Such a girl. Good-bye, Allegra Leah. Kiss the others for me."

"Of course. Good-bye, Bubbe."

With most people, you end a conversation and there's something you should have said or they should have said, it's not a complete conversation, there's more, and you walk away with things left not finished. With Bubbe Raisa, there were thousands of things we both could have said, but we almost didn't have to. I had the feeling she could understand without everything being said.

I took toast and orange juice to the music room. Outside the French doors a brand-new spiderweb hung swaying on a rosebush, all glistening with water drops. I went to the living room and got my mother's magnifying lens from the dead-bug collection and looked at the web through it, moving the lens back and forth as it swayed. Suddenly I wanted to be a little kid again, just thinking a spiderweb is so pretty, just thinking about the designs of the little thready lines in it. I wanted to go back down inside my childhood and not know the things I knew now. I stood there looking at the web for a long time, watching it sway back and forth.

I had to practice the Youth Orchestra music, and I went straight through the program, then went back and worked on the parts I'd marked with x's.

My parents were almost reverent about the purse. They acted as if it were a museum piece. My father kept nodding his head, and my mother kept saying "Oh, my. Oh, my."

My mother and father said you could fill a book with stories about stand partners, and my mother mumbled something about inviting Sam Landauer and his fourth wife to dinner "sometime."

When I took Bro David into my room to show him the purse, he recognized it immediately from when he'd visited Bubbe Raisa. "She had it under glass. She kept it in a dark corner where the sun wouldn't fade it," he said. "She told me about finding it packed in her suitcase when she was already on the boat—She almost worships it. Under glass."

"Is Bubbe Raisa trying to make me all Jewish?" I asked.

"That's impossible," he said. "But if you want a yes-or-no answer, yes. She tried it with me too. You know—it's the half-and-half she doesn't like. Religious Jews feel sorry for us; Gentiles think we're Very Interesting. We're outsiders to all of them."

Maybe it's because David's so much older than I am that he can see these things I don't even get a hint of. Evidence that you can't be half Jewish. "How do you know that?" I asked.

"The way her friends looked at me. I can't explain it. But she always kept that purse under glass."

I turned pages for four more concerts, tried to unlearn the concerto and learn it again, which of course I couldn't do; and Jessica and Sarah and I started going swimming in the pool at the university where my father teaches, where it didn't cost us any money because we go in on my father's card. When we were in the pool, we played being the three Rhine Maidens from the opera by Wagner where they sing underwater, trying to protect their precious gold. We went singing and gurgling underwater being Rhine Maidens for four afternoons before we got tired of it.

I didn't tell anybody exactly about my conversation with Bubbe Raisa. I just said I'd called her to say thank-you.

My parents went away for three days, and Bro David and I were in charge of each other. I mainly practiced, and he had two of his friends over one day and they worked on the comic book they're drawing together. My parents had said I could invite Jessica and Sarah in self-defense, and everybody except Sarah ate so much pizza we felt sick.

I went to two more Youth Orchestra rehearsals, and I turned pages for people, and I practiced. I watched the days go by, and I knew I was going to honor my agreement with Elter Bubbe Leah, and I knew it might be an insane thing to do.

And most of the time, even sometimes when I was swimming with my friends, what was walking along through my mind was the terrible way I was playing the concerto.

While my mother and father were away, a thing happened. It was late afternoon after I'd practiced for hours, and I was sitting in a slanted sprawl at the dining-room table holding Heavenly on my stomach, feeling her just begin to dig me with her claws and then pull back. Dig, retreat, dig, retreat. I was sort of counting out the rhythm of her claws, and she was kind of humming along in an in-and-out purr. I was tired from practicing, and we were just hanging out on a summer afternoon not doing anything. My eyes closed.

I don't know what made me open them. In the middle of Bro David's mess on the table was a cartoon of me, playing my violin like some kind of madwoman and wearing an animal skin slung around me, and my feet were wheels. Sweat was pouring off me, and I had an insane look on my face. None of that was so strange, David is a cartoonist. What was extremely weird was that I was huge, like an Amazon, and the violin was so tiny it looked as if I'd break it any instant. And an auto mechanic was standing there with a wrench in his hand saying, "When your violin overheats, check your head gasket. You may need your whole head replaced."

It was an insulting picture. And at the same time a bell was ringing in my head. *That* was what Mr. Kaplan meant. Very slowly, I began to put some pieces together. An Amazon on wheels, wearing an animal skin—she could crush the tiny violin. She was in a frenzy.

I heard again in my mind, "Don't upstage the nineteen-year-old boy who gave us this concerto."

I stared at the cartoon. It was horrible.

I stood up, Heavenly leaped down, I went to the music room and got my violin and bow, I took them to the downstairs bathroom where there's a big mirror, and I started playing. Little sections of the concerto. Bits from the third movement, a longer bit from the second, part of the cadenza from the first. I watched myself.

And I remembered a thing that Jessica thinks is so ridiculous at school: the athletic coaches talk about how the team is going to give 110 percent. I watched my arms. Mr. Kaplan has always told me I have to be in partnership with the violin. I'd gone beyond that. Way, way beyond. David was right. *That* was what Mr. Kaplan meant. Almost on top of Mozart.

I was a combination of angry and relieved. I stood in the bathroom and let the tears spurt right out onto the counter. I'd been trying too hard. I looked at myself in the bathroom mirror, holding my violin and bow. I would play the Bloch finals for Elter Bubbe Leah, just the way I'd promised. But I'd make changes. I had to. When you think about it, it's the most obvious thing, and I should have realized it weeks before: trying too hard to play Mozart well would be like driving a car through a rose garden, or ironing a silk dress with a very hot iron, or cutting a lace doily with a chain saw, or—or like having a marching band play Brahms's "Lullaby."

After that afternoon, every time I went to the music room, I could feel the changes. The concerto didn't get any easier. The notes were still the same notes, but I gave myself permission to—this was the most surprising thing: I gave myself permission, down way deep in me, not to try to be Steve Landauer.

And I didn't tell anybody about it. Not anybody.

With the finals three weeks away, Mr. Kaplan turned sideways on the piano bench and said to me, looking in his over-the-glasses look, "I think our work together is getting somewhere. I think you're finding your way. When was the last time you listened to a recording of this concerto?"

"Maybe a week ago," I said. "I just simply stopped, I'm not sure why." I realized that I'd silently given myself permission not to try to be Anne-Sophie Mutter or David Ois-trakh too.

"Good. I wouldn't advise you to listen to anyone else until after the finals, Allegra."

"Is there ever going to be an after-the-finals?"

He laughed. "I understand. Yes, and your school will begin again, and you'll be an eighth-grader. And we'll have only one lesson each week again. And we'll do a different con-certo. . . . Indeed."

It was hard to imagine, but I knew it was true.

"And this week you should have new strings. They'll have just about the right amount of time to adjust before Labor Day."

I don't think I would have admitted to anybody that the practicing was getting easier. It would seem as if I were cheating. If it doesn't hurt, it's not doing any good: that seems to be what we're supposed to believe.

I almost laughed as I tuned and retuned and retuned my new strings, listening to them getting used to being played.

I turned pages for two more concerts, both pianists.

൭

Labor Day weekend meant I was supposed to be on TV. I watched the show a couple of times to find out what it was. A man talked to people and made jokes. It was like other shows.

Jessica and Sarah helped me decide what to wear. It in-cluded a shirt of Sarah's and Jessica's socks.

My mother took me to the studio very early in the morning and said she'd pick me up at 10:05 A.M., after it was over. "Don't worry about being on TV," she said. "It'll be all right." I gave her a look. She said, "I'm a mother. I'm supposed to tell you it'll be all right."

She got berserk when I went bike riding but a television interview in front of thousands of people was going to be all right. I got out of the car and went into the building. Somebody told me to take the elevator to the sixth floor. I pushed the button and waited for it. Then a man come rushing down the hall and said to take the other elevator, they'd had some trouble with this one. Then he said No, take this one after all. There was a tall lady in a lace collar standing just outside the elevator. I told her who I was. She shook my hand and said, "Congratulations." I didn't know what for.

She said, "You're a bit—no, I guess you're not late, we don't have everybody quite yet." We were walking down a narrow hallway. She turned left suddenly, into a doorway. I followed her. It was a big room with couches and chairs and a vending machine and bright fluorescent lights, no windows. "Just have a seat," she said, and walked out.

An Asian girl was sitting on a leather couch, and Christine was on a chair next to her, and a very freckled boy wearing serious glasses and a white shirt was across from her. Steve Landauer was sitting on the corner of a table, away from the others, flipping the pages of a magazine. I stood in the doorway. The room smelled like paint thinner.

Christine didn't look surprised to see me. She said, "Hi, Allegra. I had a feeling you'd be here." Her eyes shifted instantly to Steve Landauer and back. She almost didn't look at him at all, it was so fast.

"Hi," I said. I started to say hi to Steve Landauer, but he was staring into the magazine. I walked over and sat on the couch.

"This is Ezra," she said, pointing to the boy in the white shirt. "He's from Culver. And this is Myra Nakamura. She's from Roseburg. This is Allegra. She's from Portland."

I said hi. Out of the corner of my left eye I could see Steve Landauer's hands stop moving on top of the magazine. I turned a little bit toward him and said a part of a hi. It was just kind of an "h" hanging in the air. He nodded his head at me. Then everything went quiet. He started flipping magazine pages again.

Christine smiled and slid around on her chair, shifting her legs into a different position. Myra said, "I thought there were going to be six."

"There's one more coming," Christine said. "I think." Then she was quiet. So was everybody else. *Fp, fp, fp,* went the pages of Steve Landauer's magazine.

"They probably want us to get acquainted," Christine said. "That's probably why nobody's here."

There was more silence. I looked at the four pairs of shoes I could see.

"I mean nobody official," she said.

Steve Landauer started to swing one leg back and forth in the air. His pants moving against the table made a very slight sound. Ezra uncrossed his arms and crossed them the other way.

"Is anybody else as nervous as I am?" said Myra. Everybody laughed a little bit, nervously, except Steve Landauer. His leg made just a slight pause in the air and went on swinging.

Christine said, "I don't know. How nervous are you?" We laughed nervously again. Then nobody said anything. Mr. Kaplan was right. I was definitely the youngest.

"Very," said Myra.

"Is it about the competition or about being on TV?" Christine asked.

"I'm not sure. Maybe they're equal." She had beautiful hands.

"I'd much rather play for people than talk for people," Christine said.

"Me, too," said Ezra. What a name. Ezra. I tried to imagine him playing the violin, but it was easier to picture him mowing a lawn.

Myra Nakamura was talking. ". . . and so my teacher said I had to call every club and church in town—and it's a real little town. I had to volunteer to play for everybody till I got over my stage fright. . . ." Christine and Ezra were laughing. "And—you know—some of the groups have all the same people in them, and—" Myra stopped and held her left hand up, counting very fast on her fingers. "I can't believe some people had to listen to the same Bach sonata six times. It's embarrassing."

Everybody was laughing except Steve Landauer.

"And the last movement of the Mozart," she said.

We laughed again.

"And a lot of them didn't even like classical music to begin with. . . ." she said.

I thought of mentioning the beta-blocker drugs Deirdre had told me about. But they made you see hallucinations. And another thing: I've had quite a bit of experience being the youngest, and it teaches you to be kind of quiet.

Christine asked, "Did the project work? Are you so afraid now?"

"Not so," Myra said. "Not so afraid. My bow doesn't shake anymore. I guess you could say it worked."

"You showed up here," Ezra said. He had a slow, drawly voice. We all looked at him.

The lady in the lace collar hurried in again with a bundle of papers, and Karen Karen was behind her. "Here, fill these out," she said, kind of nudging Karen into the room and handing us each a long sheet of paper and a pencil. Then the lady left the room.

Karen came over to me all excited. Her glasses didn't have the adhesive tape holding them together anymore. "Allegra! A familiar face! Boy, am I relieved! This place is full of strange-o's. They sent me to the freight elevator—they're all these really vague types—all these people saying, 'Someone will be with you in a minute'—And I'm late to begin with because I was listening to the end of *The Magic Flute* in my car. Don't you just love that opera?" She flopped down on a chair.

"Hi," I said. She was wearing a flowered dress that made her look even dumpier than she'd looked in jeans. "How's your hand?" I asked.

"My hand. It's okay. Not perfect." She held out her right hand and flexed her fingers. "Why does it smell like paint remover in here?"

Everybody except Steve Landauer laughed.

Christine introduced herself to Karen and told her who everyone was. I looked at the paper we were supposed to fill out and tried to imagine each person in the room playing the Mozart concerto.

The paper was a questionnaire. How long have you been playing the violin? Why did you choose the violin? What are your chief interests besides music? What is your favorite subject in school? Do you have any pets? What is your advice to young people today? How do you see yourself ten years from now? Some words were crossed out and retyped. I think it was a first draft.

A very short, skinny man wearing a huge wristwatch that wobbled around on his arm hurried in and collected our papers but left the pencils. He said we'd be going to the studio in about four minutes, and said, "Just relax." He hurried out.

Karen said, "They set a terrific example around here. They're all so relaxed they're gone—till we have to do something, then they get all tense."

We laughed. "What did you say for 'advice for young people today'?" Christine asked us.

"Never play a violin sonata for a Rotary Club in a lumber town," Myra said.

"I said twenty-three hours of TV a day is too much," Christine said.

Everybody except Steve Landauer was laughing.

The skinny man walked in again and hesitated in the doorway. "Well, I see you're all having fun. That's the bottom line here at KORV, having fun. They're ready for you on the set."

In the studio we stepped over big thick camera cables. They sat us in chairs; they wanted the oldest first, and we had to sort ourselves out. I was last, of course. We were very crowded. The skinny man said to us, "Folks, meet Larry Ladley. He'll chat with each of you, it'll be fun. Just be yourselves."

Larry Ladley was wearing makeup. "We always tell you to just be yourselves with thousands of people watching," he said. He was smiling but not really looking at us. He was skimming our questionnaires, and he looked as if he was holding his breath. He had very bushy eyebrows.

Suddenly the whole studio lit up with bright lights. A man with headphones and a cord hanging from him said, "STAND BY!" Then the whole studio audience clapped, and a man shot his arm straight down through the air. Larry Ladley said, "These are the six finalists in the second annual Ernest Bloch Competition. The competition is limited to young people from Oregon. The maximum age is twenty-one, and these young people were selected from a field of eighty-five violinists. Let's get right to the music makers. I don't think I've been surrounded by so many geniuses since I flunked third grade." He laughed. A camera moved to aim at Christine.

"Christine Estler's played the violin since she was six, she teaches violin students herself, she's concertmaster of the Portland Youth Orchestra. She's nineteen years old and enjoys tennis and video games. . . . Tell us, Christine, which do you like more: video games or playing the violin?"

Christine looked surprised. "Well, the violin, of course."

"Of course. Next to Christine is Karen Coleman, also nineteen. Karen broke two fingers on her right hand wind-surfing not long ago. Karen, even a musical dunce like me knows that wasn't a very good break."

"Well, it was a pretty stupid thing to do. I had a concert to play and everything. But Allegra stepped in and played the concert for me."

Larry Ladley looked blank.

"I think Mozart helped my fingers heal," she said.

Larry Ladley laughed. "Could you explain to the folks at home just what you mean?"

She looked at him. "Could you explain just why you laughed when I said that?"

His left eye twitched. I've seen lots of people do that. It's the bottom eyelid; the skin of it jerks and you can tell it's something they can't control. He said, "People that aren't musical need to have it explained."

"Well, when you think about how he made such great music out of his pain—like the worse the pain, sometimes the better the music. Sometimes if you just sit still and let music heal you, you'll be—I don't know—you'll be okay." She looked around at all of us. "Help me, you guys," she said.

Myra said, "It's true. It's always true." Christine nodded. Steve Landauer was staring at Karen. I knew I could say something but my throat closed up, my larynx just eclipsed. TV makes a very big difference in what you can do. Ezra whispered to me, "The *Requiem*." I sat staring straight ahead. Mozart was working on his *Requiem* when he died, and it's very great music. It's a set of prayers for the dead, all in music.

Larry Ladley nodded his head at Karen. "And sitting next to Karen is sixteen-year-old Steve Landauer. Tell me, Steve, how do you see yourself ten years from now?"

Steve Landauer stared at Larry Ladley. Larry Ladley's eyelid twitched again. Then Steve Landauer stared straight ahead at the camera and held perfectly still and said, "I see myself playing in Carnegie Hall. I can't tell you what concerto I'm playing. I can't see what it is." He looked back at Larry Ladley. I could see his shoulders get relaxed.

Larry Ladley smiled again. There was something mean in the way he smiled. "Tell me, Steve, how do you know that's where you'll be?" He winked at Steve Landauer.

Steve Landauer got rigid and looked straight ahead at the camera again. "Because. Because I can't see myself doing anything else."

I could feel everybody looking at Steve Landauer and then looking away from him.

"Well, that's determination for you. We can all say we knew him when, can't we?" Larry Ladley's eyes went very fast down to the sheet of paper in front of him and up again. "Next is Myra Nakamura. She plays the koto. Myra, what's a koto?"

She looked as if she was always having to explain it to people. "It's a Japanese instrument with thirteen strings, it's kind of like a lute. You hold the string down with one hand and pluck it with the other."

Larry Ladley asked, "And how many koto teachers are there in Roseburg?"

"One. My grandmother."

"So. The koto is a family affair."

"Well, sort of," she said.

Larry Ladley said, "Ezra Jones is fourteen. His favorite composers are—well, one of them—I've never heard of—I hope I get this right—Giovanni Battista Fontana. Who was he, Ezra?"

Ezra's eyes got very big and then settled down. He crossed his arms. "Fontana was a seventeenth-century composer. He wrote a violin sonata and some other works. It's not certain when he was born. He died in 1630."

"That's very interesting, Ezra. Now, I believe you live in Culver, Oregon. Refresh us: Just where is Culver, Oregon?"

"It's ten miles south of Madras, and it's one mile west of Highway 97 on Highway 361."

Larry Ladley said, "And how would I get to Culver to hear

you play your violin all by yourself on one highway a mile west of another highway?" He winked at Ezra.

Ezra looked back at him. "You'd take a Trailways bus. It'd let you off in Madras. Then we'd come and pick you up." His glasses were sliding down his nose. He pushed them back up with his left hand, and then crossed his arms again.

"And your other favorite composer is Ernest Bloch. Tell me, Ezra, is that the same one this competition is named for?"

"Yes."

"Tell us a little bit about Ernest Bloch, Ezra. Don't make it too complicated."

Ezra uncrossed his arms, looked down at his shoes, and then up again. "Bloch lived the last years of his life in Oregon, at Agate Beach. He was Swiss, a Swiss Jew. His music has kind of dark tones that come from somewhere, kind of mysterious. . . . And religious too. He wrote some concerto grossos, and . . ."

Steve Landauer said, "And some unaccompanied violin suites."

"Right," said Ezra. "And he was working on a viola suite when he died."

"Which was—?" said Larry Ladley.

"On July 15, 1959," said Ezra.

"Is that so? And right here in Oregon, and I didn't know anything about him. Just shows how we oftentimes don't pay attention to what's in our own backyard." He looked down at the pages. "And our youngest fiddler today is Allegra Shapiro, who's twelve. Allegra, I believe you have a pet with an interesting name. Tell everybody your cat's name."

"Heavenly Days," I said.

"Does Heavenly Days like to listen to you practice?"

"Sometimes," I said.

Larry Ladley looked around at all of us. "Kids, I'm going to admit something. The only thing I play is the radio. I never learned to read music. How would I learn to do it?" Nobody said anything. "I mean, all those little black dots, they're like a secret code—" He chuckled.

"Did you ever want to?" Christine asked. A camera moved very fast toward her.

"It's best if you do it when you're little," Karen said.

"I bet you're right," he said. "Well, tomorrow one of these fine fiddlers will be the winner of the Louis Bloch Competition, and I want to wish all of you good luck. Stay with us. We'll be right back."

We got up to leave. Larry Ladley stood up and said, "Thanks, guys. Good luck. See you in Carnegie Hall." He was talking to all of us in general.

The tall woman from the very beginning, the one with the questionnaires, walked along with us to the elevator and said thank-you several times and good-luck several times. The elevator door opened and we all got in. It closed. We started down, nobody talking.

"What an incredible jerk. Jerk. JERK," Christine said. She was in the back of the elevator. Everybody turned around.

"Oh, not completely," said Myra. "When he asked about learning to read music—he was like a helpless little kid."

"That doesn't excuse him for being a jerk," said Karen.

"It helps," Ezra said.

We laughed. The elevator stopped. The door didn't open.

Ezra pushed the "Open door" button. Nothing happened. He pushed it again. Nothing happened again.

"You think Larry Ladley's in charge of elevator maintenance too?" Karen said.

We waited for something to happen. Karen Karen banged with her fist on the elevator wall. Ezra said that wouldn't help. Then she pressed the alarm button. We stood around looking at each other. I got the idea that the elevator was really stuck.

"Do you get the feeling nothing works around here?" said Karen. "This is a very disorganized place."

Nobody said anything.

"The whole world might get blown up and we'd never know," Myra said.

Nobody said anything. We all got quiet, and we stayed that way for a long time. We took turns leaning against walls. Only two people could sit on the floor at once. It wasn't a very big elevator.

Ezra looked around and said, "My teacher says, 'Is not moost be rooshing rooshing rooshing zeez notes because is coming an earthquake. . . .' " He said it very fast, accenting the words with a kind of sideways movement of his jaw. We burst out laughing, all except Steve Landauer. He looked around at us very fast and then looked back down at his shoes. "She's Romanian," Ezra said.

I suddenly realized we could be playing I'm Neek. We could play it if I didn't mention the name of it. "My teacher wears sweatshirts with things on them," I said. I told them about "Dvořák alive! Terrorizes couple in Tampa!" and "The *What* Quintet?"

Christine said, "I have this little tiny student, he says,

'All you make me play is E-flats, I'm gonna fwow up E-flats.' "

"My violin teacher doesn't trust anybody," Myra said. "She thinks people steal things out of her house. One day she couldn't find this old wool skirt, and she said her maid stole it. And then once it was a kitchen pan."

We laughed and then got quiet again.

"Once she thought somebody'd stolen her toothbrush."

Ezra said, "Hercules got so mad at his music teacher he brained him with his lute." Everybody looked at Ezra. "Killed him," he said. We laughed and then we were all quiet.

Steve Landauer kept himself away from us by not looking at any of us, not laughing, not doing anything but looking at the ceiling and the floor. He kept his hands hanging down at his sides. Once in a while his hands fisted and then unfisted. I'm not sure he even knew they were doing it.

After a few minutes Karen said, "I don't see a single scared face in this whole elevator. Isn't anybody afraid we're gonna go crashing to the bottom?"

"That'd take care of practicing for today," Ezra said. "But we can't, really. There's a safety brake at the top."

"What do you mean?" asked Myra.

"Well, an elevator works by a system of counterweights. They're supposed to regulate the operation, but in case there's a malfunction or an accident, the heavy-duty brake grabs ahold at the top and holds everything still. It's mounted on the shaft of the main lifting motor."

"What if there's a power failure?" Myra asked.

"The elevator has its own generator," Ezra said. "It's driven by an AC motor; the lifting motor is on direct current; so is the generator."

"I bet you get A's in science," Christine said.

"Or ride in lots of elevators," said Myra.

"Nope. Never rode on one before," Ezra said. He looked up at the ceiling. Everybody looked at him. He shrugged his shoulders.

We were quiet again. "I wonder if they know it's not running," Myra said. "Do you think anybody even knows we're here?"

Christine said, "Who could care about six people stuck in an elevator with all the big important things going on in the world?"

Ezra said, "Somebody whined at Beethoven that one of his quartets was too hard to play. And Beethoven said, 'Do you think I care about your lousy fiddle when the spirit moves me?' "

"The spirit around here has moved them to get on with their business. They'll figure out something's wrong when they want to go home," Karen said.

"I wonder if Daddy's getting upset," Myra said.

"And my mother," I said.

"My car's probably towed away by now," said Karen.

Everybody got quiet again. I looked around and tried to picture all of them playing the violin. Christine and Steve Landauer were easy; I'd seen them. But the others. I looked at the violin bruise on the left side of their necks and tried to build a mental picture from there. Myra had a kind of way of standing that made a little bit of space around her. As if she was wearing some kind of perfume that sent waves out to separate her from unperfumed people, but I don't think she was wearing any. Ezra had huge, dangling, bony hands, and his brain was filled with all those different things, as if there were so many rooms up there—a room for elevator workings, a room for things Beethoven said to people, a room for composers most people have never heard of, a room for what Hercules did to his music teacher. Karen Karen was maybe the most mysterious; the way she was on TV, asking Larry Ladley why he'd laughed at her. I looked at her hands, which she was holding folded in front of the flowered dress; I couldn't picture her playing the violin any more than I could picture her windsurfing or driving a car or dancing.

"You know, what's going to happen is, they're going to find us in about five thousand years," Karen said.

Ezra nodded. "We'll look like the Easter Island statues."

Myra said, "They'll wonder what these six sacred figures represented."

"—in a curious box that seemed to go up and down," said Christine.

Myra said, "I haven't even made a will. I wonder who'll get my gerbils."

Everybody laughed and shifted position except Steve Landauer. The elevator was getting really warm.

Karen pushed herself slightly toward him and said, "How come you don't talk to any of us?"

He closed his face and said, "I do." Then he looked past her at the elevator wall.

"No, you don't. We're all in this together—we're all supposed to compete against each other tomorrow, and we're all wondering what's going on, and we're all being very good sports about whatever it is—and you're hunkering over there like a cucumber—"

She stopped. She looked surprised. So did he. I think I held my breath. I think some other people did, too. She and he stared at each other.

"A cucumber?" he said. It was a question.

Myra laughed first. Then Ezra. Then Christine and I. I think we shook the elevator. I'd never be able to describe to Jessica and Sarah the look on Steve Landauer's face. If he really had been a cucumber, his skin would have wrinkled up for just a second and then smoothed out again. He looked as if he was hunting inside his brain for something he couldn't remember. He looked as if the word "cucumber" was going around and around in his head. The whole elevator was filled with laughter, and he was looking up at a corner where the ceiling and wall came together.

"Lighten up, Landauer," Ezra said. The laughing changed, got softer.

Steve Landauer looked cornered. He stared at Ezra. He shifted his weight from one foot to the other. Then he looked at the ceiling again.

Christine said, very gently, "Steve, when did you know you were going to be a concert violinist?" Then she said, fast, "You don't have to answer. . . ."

Everybody was looking at him. His eyes were moving sideways back and forth. I held my breath again. "I don't know," he said. He looked down at the floor. Everything was quiet. That was evidently his answer. People started shuffling around a little bit; nobody said anything. Then he opened his mouth again. "It didn't come on me like a flash—from the eye of God or anything. I just—" He moved his weight from one foot to the other again and looked at his feet. I could hear everybody breathing. Steve Landauer took a breath like a gulp, and said, "It's better than being a cucumber."

Everybody was still looking at him. Suddenly there was a sound of hammering somewhere in the elevator shaft. Everybody looked up. There was a very tiny bit of laughter.

Karen said, "Steve Cucumber, important figure in late-twentieth-century music—Sonata for Tossed Salad in G—"

"Suite for Elevator and Hammer in A Minor, his longest work—" said Ezra. The hammering went on. Everybody wasn't staring at Steve Landauer anymore.

"You haven't heard my greatest piece, 'Serenade to a Talk Show Jerk,' " said Steve Landauer.

We looked at him. It was an astonishing surprise. We laughed. He pretended for a couple of seconds that he hadn't said it; he tried to look down at the floor as if we weren't even around. There was more hammering. The elevator was full of laughter. Steve Landauer started laughing as if he didn't want to but was doing it anyway.

I looked around. Six people with their private worries, all in competition against each other, people who might be hating each other, all laughing our heads off. Then everybody got quiet.

Myra started clapping her hands. I didn't understand. Then Christine joined her. Then Ezra. Then Karen and I. Steve Landauer looked flustered, as if he didn't get it. But he did get it, he'd have to be a moron not to get it. We weren't clapping because somebody decided to hammer on things in the elevator shaft.

By the time we got out of the elevator, the lobby was full of parents and flashing lights and TV cameras, and the woman in the lace collar tried to make an apology speech while we pushed out past her, and she sort of got shoved out of the way.

I'd decided I could get through the rest of my life very happily without ever being on TV again.

13

I was awake at 4:42 A.M., watching the clock. I did some exercises where you listen to the arches of your feet relax, and then you do the same with all the rest of you in small bits, all the way up to your hair. A Yoga lady on TV does them, and she has this very spiritual smile and an extremely superior attitude. Like we're mere earthlings and she's got an advanced spirit and we're all several incarnations behind. I lay in bed and practiced what she says in her perfumy voice, "Focus attention on the very center of your head. Feel yourself breathing in through your ears, out through your ears, in through your ears, out through your ears." The birds were getting up in the trees outside. She also says to "breathe out through your feet," but Sarah says we have to draw the line somewhere.

I told Heavenly Days that her name had been said on TV yesterday. She went on licking her thigh.

Pretty soon it would be over. By the time it got dark again I'd be eating dinner, and somebody would have won the Bloch Competition.

What if Myra won first, Ezra won second, and Karen and Christine and Steve Landauer and I were left standing there holding our bows?

Except that if Myra really did have such terrible stage fright, something would probably happen. Her bow might bounce, she might forget something. So she'd be left holding her bow, too.

But Christine was concertmaster of a whole orchestra; she had acres of poise, and she taught violin to little kids. "I'm gonna fwow up E-flats." I remembered being really little and having Mr. Kaplan play harmony with me when I played scales. Those were our little duets. When I was five years old playing my little screechy scales, Christine was twelve, probably playing Beethoven sonatas. She would logically win.

But then there was Ezra. Never rode in an elevator. Fourteen years old. His favorite composer, or one of them, somebody who died in 1630. Knew about Hercules and the lute. And Larry Ladley was so mean to him. Those things don't automatically make a good violinist, of course.

Myra Nakamura. Her hands were graceful. Not that graceful-looking hands would automatically make anybody a better violinist. But she'd had so much public exposure too. So much mileage. Starting with her stage fright, and going around playing for all those clubs and churches. And she had that kind of exotic air space around her. Playing the koto would develop a whole different part of her brain. Wouldn't it? Maybe she had an advantage over everybody. Except Steve Landauer.

While Steve Landauer was flying all around the country, playing everywhere he went, Myra had been going around Roseburg, Oregon, working on her stage fright.

And Karen Karen. The beauty queen in my dream, the chunky girl in Trout Creek Ridge, and on television practically telling Larry Ladley he was a jerk, and so feisty in the elevator, getting Steve Landauer to stop being a cucumber. She must have been desolate when she couldn't even practice because of her fingers. I think she loved Mozart more than any of the rest of us did. That would mean she'd play the concerto with more something than the rest of us would. What would it be? When you really truly love something— you do it differently. More of your blood beats into it.

But Steve Landauer. Just the thought of him made me turn over in bed with a lurch, it was a reflex. I dumped Heavenly on the floor in my haste.

I had a hunch he was the only one of all of us who really was determined to be a concert violinist. That was going to be his life. And he was good enough to be the "very exciting young player" in a piano quintet. At least for one concert. He probably was a prodigy.

I lay on my stomach and thought about Deirdre. I tried to imagine her being young and in school and being a prodigy. She probably was weird too. Geniuses are. There's a lot more going on inside them. More wires to get crossed. Maybe more blood going to their brains, or going there faster or something. And then I imagined her holding her baby in her arms and then I saw her screaming in our music room and I saw my mother rocking her.

Steve Landauer had four mothers.

I turned my head to the right, and I felt Heavenly settle beside my stomach, and the next thing I knew the alarm clock went off and it was morning.

Bro David was the first person I saw that day. He was

standing in my bedroom doorway in pajama bottoms and a Trail Blazers T-shirt. "You know you were on the late news?" he said.

"Get out of here," I said.

"Everybody tumbling out of the elevator. Your boyfriend Landauer and everybody. They made it look like a party."

I sat up in bed. "David, is that true?"

He nodded his head. "A different channel had it on. I forget which one."

I pushed the back of my head into the pillow and closed my eyes. I could hear him walking across the room. He sat on my bed. "You know what you have to do today," he said.

I didn't open my eyes.

"You have to go for it. You've worked real hard. You deserve to have fun with old Wolfgang."

I kept my eyes closed and nodded my head.

"And it's not the end of the world."

I looked at the dress I'd decided to wear hanging on the outside of my closet. It was just a blue dress, medium blue with medium sleeves. I would put it on and go and play the competition and come home again. I looked back at Bro David. "Thanks," I said. He walked out of my room.

Play for Elter Bubbe Leah. I'd promised her.

Play in my most personal way. Honor the nineteen-year-old boy who gave us this concerto. Let my own angel out. Give 100 percent, not 110 percent. Don't go all the way over the top. Remember everything I've ever learned and simultaneously forget it. The divine inspiration of the NBA.

At breakfast there was a big bouquet in my water glass with a note pinned to a zinnia leaf:

*These were handpicked from several people's gardens
who don't know they're wishing you good luck in the
Great Allegra Shapiro Violin Performance.*

*Our great passionate love,
Jessica and Sarah*

*P.S. We'd rather do Mr. Trouble's laundry than turn
pages for that Landauer.
P.P.S. Ezra is adorable!*

I suddenly remembered the piece I'd played in the audition for the Prep Orchestra when I was a little kid. It was the second movement of a Schubert sonatina, and it was in D major. I looked into my glass of orange juice and could almost see the notes. There was a B-flat at the top of the right-hand page. I wore yellow socks that day, and Mary Janes.

Way back in June, I hadn't wanted to know what any of the other players looked like. Now I knew them all. I could picture them in their pajamas, I could imagine them drinking orange juice.

"Morning, everybody." My dad came walking through the kitchen with grease all over his hands.

Bro David was right behind him, carrying some kind of oily car part. "Buy Oat Floats, kiddies," he said. He says that nobody ever says "Morning, everybody" except TV dads, so when Daddy says it Bro David does a commercial. They disappeared into the dining room.

"Why do you think they're going to fix the car in the dining room?" my mother asked.

I didn't say anything. I picked a flower out of the glass and moved it to the other side of the bouquet.

If Elter Bubbe Leah hadn't made her only daughter get on a boat and go away forever so she'd never see her again, Daddy wouldn't be walking through his house saying good morning to everybody today. Bubbe Raisa wouldn't have met Zayde Shapiro in the standing-room line at the Metropolitan Opera and they wouldn't have gotten married and had Daddy, and he wouldn't have met Mommy, and Bro David and I wouldn't exist.

Daddy came back through the kitchen carrying the oily thing David had been carrying, on his way outside. He came over to where I was sitting, and he held the oily car part way out away from me, and he bent over and kissed me on my neck, on the chin-rest bruise. "Everybody, good morning," he said to my neck. I put my arms around his neck. Naturally, he didn't know anything about the private arrangement I had with his grandmother's purse.

Everybody left. My mother went off to water flowers, and I sat at the kitchen table.

The phone rang. "Allegra, sweet one, this is your big day," said Deirdre, all excited. I'd forgotten that even her speaking voice is so beautiful. It flows out. "Remember, what's down inside you, all covered up—the things of your soul. The important secret things. Are you listening to me?"

"Yes," I said. "I am."

"The story of you, all buried, let the music caress it out into the open. Promise?"

I didn't say anything. How could I promise a thing like that?

"You'll know when it happens," she said. "You can't make it happen. And remember the Celtics. I wish you love today."

"Thanks, Deirdre. You, too. You want to talk to my mother?"

"No, sillybones. I called to talk to you. Say hi to every-body."

I ate some breakfast. I stared at the hummingbirds outside the window. I went to the music room.

My mother walked in, sat down, waited for me to finish the Kreutzer Étude no. 39, and said, "Remember all day long today: You need to enjoy this. Enjoy, dear." And when my parents dropped me off at the building, my dad said, "You're now in a position to take delight in doing this thing, Allegra. The concerto you can play upside down and backward—now go ahead and take delight in it."

"Wish me love," I said while I was getting out of the car.

"Love," said my mother and my father, almost at the same time.

I walked in the door thinking about David warning me not to let it make me a crazoid. I could feel a buzz in the Green Room. And yet nobody was talking. Maybe it was the six violin cases in the room; maybe it was just all those same people who'd been stuck in the elevator together stuck here together again the very next day. Whatever it was, somebody could have plucked the air, the way you'd pluck a string, and it would have twanged.

There was a big bulletin board on the wall with blank white envelopes thumbtacked on it. We were each supposed to take an envelope. It had a number in it, and that was the order of playing. "These are jumbled. There's no order to the way they've been placed on the board," said a lady who was evidently in charge of us. She had a neck chain attached to her glasses, and she had a violin bruise on her neck. Maybe it was a viola bruise. "And where's Allegra Shapiro?"

"Me," I said. I whirled around from unzipping my case.

That wasn't the answer to her question. But it was what came out.

She looked at me, almost as if she'd expected somebody else, and said, "There's a message for you on the board. Oh—and—everybody? Listen: There's a smaller number on the corner of your card. That's your practice-room number. You'll wait there till you're wanted."

I took a blank envelope, and on the opposite side of the bulletin board was a smaller one with my name on it in Mr. Kaplan's writing. I think I could get very old and be in a rest home and I'd still know his handwriting. My number was four. In the other envelope was Mr. Kaplan's note:

May you have great, great fun with this beautiful song today.

"One. How could they do that to me?" Myra Nakamura stood at the side of the bulletin board, holding up her number.

"They had to do it to somebody," Karen Karen said. "I really, truly, cross my heart, didn't want Number Six." She held up her card with the six on it.

Christine opened her envelope, took out her number, and held it up for everybody to see. "How did they know two is my unlucky number?"

Ezra said to her, "You really think there's any such thing?"

She laughed. "I do badly at the second lesson of a new piece, I have terrible second dates with guys, I'm the second oldest in my family. . . . Let's see what you got."

He held up his Five.

Steve Landauer had taken an envelope off the board and walked away from everybody.

"Where are you in this thing, Allegra?" Ezra asked me.

I showed him my Four.

"Let's see—" Christine was looking around and checking us off with her eyes. "That means—Number Three is over there." She nodded her head toward where Steve Landauer was standing with his back to us, flexing the fingers of his left hand. He looked as if he was probably staring at a wall. The rest of us looked around at each other. Christine said, "I didn't know they'd use a screen. I mean, I hoped, but I didn't know for sure."

Everybody looked at her. "Really? Are they really? How'd you find out?" Karen Karen asked.

Christine said, "The woman with the envelopes told me. They're using a screen. Somebody insisted at the last minute. One of the judges. I don't know. It's very unusual."

It was a strangely happy moment right then. Five people, and another one over in a corner, all knowing more or less how long we'd have to wait to play, and knowing we could be really anonymous behind a screen—we wouldn't have to look at the faces of the jury. And nobody would have an extra advantage for looking perfectly poised.

We looked around at each other and made relieved faces. Even Steve Landauer almost glanced out of his corner. I had probably more than an hour to wait in room 104.

Room 104 had a grand piano, and a piano bench, and a straight chair, and a window looking out on the street. I put my violin case on the floor and looked out the window. People were down there going along in their lives. I could come in last in the Bloch Competition today and it wouldn't

·225·

make any difference to them. Ernest Bloch was already dead, and the winner of a competition named after him couldn't make any difference to him. Nuclear war could break out and we'd all be dead in a few days, and then nothing would make any difference anyway.

I pulled the piano bench over near the window and sat on the end of it, and I leaned my chin on the windowsill. People are always saying, "Don't sweat the small stuff," and then somebody always says, "It's all small stuff." I watched a little tiny kid being pushed along in a stroller on the sidewalk across the street. I could win a dozen competitions, and I wouldn't bring Deirdre's baby back.

I could play an entire concert in Carnegie Hall and have Itzhak Perlman wish he could play like me, and I wouldn't take away Mr. Trouble's brain damage or find him his Waltzing Tree.

I could play the violin better than Anne-Sophie Mutter or anybody else in the world, and I wouldn't make the people who were dead at Treblinka live to ripe old ages.

The little kid in the stroller started crying and reaching out around the stroller for something to make him happier. I had three little groups of notes going around in my mind, and they wouldn't stop. I even heard them when the baby in the stroller cried. I'd probably played those little groups of notes five thousand times.

I got up off the piano bench and squatted down and opened my violin case. "Everything doesn't have to be a matter of life or death." "Everything does have to be." "Why are you yelling at me?" "Because I love you." I breathed in and out the way the Yoga lady says to, and unzipped the pocket of my case where I'd put Elter Bubbe Leah's purse. I laid it on the piano. I tuned my violin.

I played the cadenzas, all three of them. Then I did some stretching exercises. I rolled my neck around, I did some of Sarah's ballet leg lifts, I swung my arms. I played D-major and A-major chromatic scales for a while. I closed my eyes and tried to remember exactly what the embroidered design on Elter Bubbe Leah's purse looked like. I tried to imagine somebody's fingers embroidering it in Poland almost a hundred years ago. That was still younger than my violin. I opened my eyes and found out I'd gotten everything right except one little leaf at the lower-right-hand corner of the design. I stared at the purse for a while. Nothing was in my mind; I was just staring.

Somebody knocked, and the lady from the Green Room said, through the door, "Allegra, about twenty minutes, half an hour till you're on. Number Two broke a D string. May I get you anything?"

I opened the door and looked at her. I couldn't remember the words at first. Then they came to me. "No, thank you," I said. I stared at her. "Broke a D string?"

"Oh—she replaced it and finished the concerto. Don't look so worried. It doesn't disqualify her. Of course not. Of course not, dear. We'll let you know when it's time," she said. "You may leave your case and things here while you play." She smiled a little bit and went walking down the hallway. I watched her feet go up and down on the floor, and then I closed the door.

As I looked at the keyboard of the piano, my mind tried

to empty itself; it tried to pour all my thoughts down a chute of some kind. I could feel them sliding away. Like a big balloon deflating, like a tank of something emptying. I felt my eyes bug out with the shock of it, and I saw my arms reach out to catch what was emptying out of me. I stood there looking at the space between my arms, and tried to find Mozart. I closed my eyes and looked for the first movement first; there it was, with its cadenza. Second movement. Third. They were there, with their notes in order, with Mr. Kaplan's blue markings on the pages.

Very strange, my mind doing that. I picked up my violin and played the third-movement cadenza. It was there, solid, it hadn't gone off anywhere. I wrapped Elter Bubbe Leah's purse in its tissue paper and put it back in my violin case. I went down the hallway to the bathroom. I looked at myself in the mirror. I was just a person in a blue dress standing in dim light in a public bathroom next to a towel machine. I turned around and went back to room 104 and sat down with my violin and bow in my hand.

The envelope woman came and got me, and we walked down the hall and then down the stairs and then through a heavy door. Suddenly the lights were very bright and the floor was very polished and there was a line of screens on my right. Several screens were lined up so the jury couldn't see any part of me, even my feet. The woman pointed to where I was supposed to stand. I went to the spot and stood. It was the place Steve Landauer, Number Three, had just walked away from. I suddenly remembered Alice in Wonderland getting smaller and smaller. I propped myself firmly on my feet, looked down at them; they were the same size they'd been five minutes before, and I knew I wasn't shrinking.

I decided to look at the vertical line down one of the screens.

A man's voice came from the other side of the screens: "Number Four, you may begin when you're ready."

I thumbed my strings and heard the D string a shade flat. While I was tuning it I closed my eyes and saw Elter Bubbe Leah's photograph with the purse and the goose and the broom, and into my vision came a teenage hand with a quill pen in it, just at the edge of the photograph. Music being written. I listened in my mind for the rhythm and I took a medium-size breath and started.

The start was a good one; notes came up out of the violin on time, in time, things weren't blurred, it was fun. Through the notes, I saw Elter Bubbe Leah shooing her geese up a slope with her broom in Poland; the notes went scooting along. It was strange: I was able to hear every note clearly, every group of sixteenth-notes, every little sforzando, and at the same time I was seeing a movie of pastures and the little house in Suprasl.

The second movement. How many times Heavenly and I'd gone to sleep listening to it, with our arms around each other. I reached inside my body for the key change and the rhythm change and I felt for the gentleness of it. I saw Leah, a little girl in a long white nightgown, climbing into her bed by candlelight, and I took a medium-size breath and played. The notes sounded like little flickerings of flame from the candle, little bright lights floating in a dark room. I played it for her to drop off to sleep in her feather bed with her braids spread out on the pillow.

The third movement, the Rondeau. If you turn on the radio just in time to hear this movement, you think it's such a happy thing, those alternating sections, dances. And yet, when you pay close attention, there's a kind of fragile sound—as if something's going to break somewhere but you don't know where. And little silences come up between the sections. I looked into what was going on in my mind and I saw the early morning waking Leah up with the sun coming in, a blessing. I took a medium-size breath and began. She woke up in the sunshine and she was a real girl in a real house, and I could see the grass and flowers growing as she walked outside, and I could feel the solid ground under her feet, and during the cadenza she was scampering along, very happy. And I got so carried away with the little girl in the story in my mind that I played an E-sharp a little bit askew, my finger came down on it too sideways. But I was happy. I was happy with the sounds of Mozart coming up out of the wood, and as I moved toward the ending it felt right. The last three notes came out just the way I liked them, balanced, even, each one of them getting softer until the last one just skips away into the air.

I took my violin down off my shoulder. I was in Portland, Oregon, and I'd just finished doing what I'd promised and feared to do. I was twelve years old, standing with my two feet on the floor and my arms hanging down. I might never even tell anybody about Leah and her goose and her feather bed in my mind. A whole story of her had happened inside the music. I looked down at the scroll of my violin. It's like a seashell, as if there's such a story inside that you could never find out all of it.

A man's voice came from the other side of the screen. "Thank you, Number Four."

14

The jury wanted to meet with us in the Green Room. The woman who'd been in charge of us told us to tell the jury our names but not our numbers, even though the winner had already been decided. "That's our policy. We want this to be the fairest competition in America," she said.

After we introduced ourselves, we sat all in a line. I sat between Myra and Christine, facing the jury, which was two men and two women.

One of the judges stood up. He was one of those round men you see in orchestras. A round head, and a round stomach and big hands. He was wearing a tweed kind of jacket, and he had frizzy white hair and grizzly white eyebrows. He sort of patted his stomach and said to everybody, "First, we want to thank you all. You'll each receive a tape of today's performances. All six of the finalists have—at the very least—met our expectations, proving once again"— he laughed—"that not all of the fine student musicians are in New York. Each player has, in turn, brought members of the jury to the edges of their chairs. We would like to share with all the contestants our commentary and the results of this year's competition." He lifted the clipboard in front of him and then put it down again to explain some more.

"We've worked very hard to make the Bloch the fairest possible young musicians' competition. The screen, while it deprives us of the pleasure of watching you, does away with visual distractions. Likewise, we have no invited audience. It is our feeling that audience applause—much as all of you deserve it—has a slightly distorting effect. It can tip the balance, sometimes." He looked hard at all of us. "And so, even if we recognize some faces"— he looked at Christine— "we truly don't know whose number is what." He smiled.

"Ernest Bloch would surely have been pleased to be here today. Those of us who remember him, with his beret and his pipe, almost feel that he is."

Then he lifted his clipboard again and began to read.

"Number One: A genuinely fluid performance, strikingly attentive to the musical fabric, sharply coherent phrasing, the melodies seem to bleed into the air.

"Number Two: Splendid command of the subtleties of the piece; even with the unfortunate interruption to replace a string—even despite that—the concerto flows out in a stream connecting the instrument and the listener in a series of crystalline moments.

"Number Three: Extraordinary combination of power and tenderness, extremely uncommon in young musicians; a sound that is radiant with paradox, gleaming in its coercion of notes into statements of art.

"Number Four: A staggeringly soulful rendering, almost ethereal shaping of the themes, portraying the simultaneous whimsy and tragedy of the Mozartean vision.

"Number Five: A pure, artless, supremely intelligent rendering, in which the buoyant surface of the music is at all times supported by an animated inner pulse.

"Number Six: The mature depth of this interpretation, the vigor of its treatment of the musical ideas, and the astonishing sense of kinship between composer and player—these constitute an almost magical effect.

"In short, ladies and gentlemen, there wasn't a clinker in the bunch." He smiled at us. I think he beamed.

We were evidently supposed to laugh. Most of us did. The other people in the jury looked around at us and smiled and shifted in their seats.

"And now, our decision. Young people, this job is never easy. . . ." He nodded at us as if he were saying yes. "This is always mysterious and exciting for the judges. Well. Here is the news. The second-prize winner, who will be the alternate in case the first-prize winner is unable to play in January—" He looked up and down the line of us. "Isn't this an awful moment, everybody?" He chuckled. Nobody said anything.

"Number Three."

Everybody went "Euuhh?" Just a little sound, not loud.

"Number Three, stand up and show us who you are," said the round man, cheerfully, looking down the line of us. He really didn't know.

Steve Landauer stood up. He wasn't smiling. Or he was almost not smiling. He looked as if he thought there was a mistake.

A woman read from a list, "Number Three is Steven I. Landauer. Steven is sixteen years old." Everybody clapped. Still he didn't smile. Christine whispered, "He's mad." I looked at his mouth. She was probably right.

"Congratulations to you," the round man said. "Now, Mr. Landauer, we want you to stay good and healthy until January, in case . . ." He laughed. Steve Landauer didn't. He sat down while people were still clapping.

The round man said, "And the moment everybody's been waiting for, our first-prize winner, who is scheduled to play the concerto with the Symphony in January. We might say this is the performer who hit the ball all the way out of the park." He looked down at the clipboard and then pushed it against his chest again. "Number Six."

I felt Christine and Myra say "Oh . . ." together. I think I said it with them. Karen Karen. I instantly felt a little tiny hurt inside, and I knew there was a part of me that had wanted to win. My hands started clapping, along with everyone else's, and I remembered that she was exactly the age Mozart was when he wrote the concerto. And she loved his music so much, and she probably deserved the prize most of all. She stood up, grinning and gasping.

"My gosh," she said. "Gosh. Gosh. Oh, gosh." Her whole dumpiness suddenly looked gorgeous. I can't explain it. The flowers all over her dress were almost vibrating.

The woman said, "First-prize winner is Karen Coleman. Karen is nineteen years old."

All the judges were standing up and everyone was crowding around Karen Karen. "Thank you, everyone, for a splendid afternoon," one of the women judges said. We stood up. I wondered how Myra and Ezra and Christine felt. I wondered if they'd counted on winning, if they'd spent the whole summer wanting to win.

Christine and Steve Landauer and I had just a little bit of time to get ready to play the concert in the park.

Christine gave me a hug. "Well, Allegra, we made it through this afternoon, didn't we? Can I call you Staggeringly Soulful from now on?"

Her hug felt good. I laughed. "You played crystallized moments," I said. "I don't even know what those are."

She whispered, "I don't either. Crystalline."

"Oh. Crystalline. Well, you played them."

People were moving and shuffling around; there was a sound of a lot of people talking and some laughing. Somebody hugged Karen Karen and her glasses fell off sideways. There were shoulders and violin cases and people hugging each other and shaking hands and a combination of smells almost like a locker room. Somebody called Christine "Christine Moments," and one of the women had Ezra backed into a corner and was telling him about her grandfather who made violins. Myra came over to me and said, "Are you in?"

"In what?"

"In the fan club to come hear Karen play in January. We'll all sit together and cheer." Looking at her, I thought about each of us going to our next lesson, picking out a new concerto to learn.

"Sure. Yes. Sure. Of course," I said.

We laughed. "See you then," she said.

Elter Bubbe Leah might have been a very old lady, very peaceful, sitting in a rocking chair somewhere.

My mother was waiting for me outside the building, sitting in the car reading a book. It was still hot. I got in the car. We looked at each other. I leaned against the seat and closed my eyes, and she started the engine. "The Trout Creek Ridge girl won first," I said. "Broken fingers and all." I wanted to spend the whole evening at home, cuddled up with Heavenly Days, instead of playing a concert in the park.

"And how do you feel about that?" she asked. She put her hand on my knee. I opened my eyes and looked at it. It was a bug-saving hand, a symphony-playing hand, a gear-shifting hand. Middle-aged, I suppose. She used to change my diapers with it. It went waggling up along beside her head when she was happy to see people. It was the hand she'd held tight to Deirdre with. It was a Kansas hand that had gone all the way to New York to get to Oregon to have me.

"I feel okay about it," I said, looking at her hand. "Pretty much." She squeezed my knee and took hold of the steering wheel. We didn't say anything for a while.

"The alternate was all scowly and pouty. Guess who it is," I said.

"I don't know. Christine?"

"Mommy, *think*. Think who wouldn't even be happy with second prize."

She drove along thinking. "I haven't a clue."

"My new stand partner."

She opened her mouth wide and drove along with it hanging there. "Oh," she said. She closed her mouth. "Well. How many judges?"

"Four."

"Well. Four judges can't be wrong. Good for him."

Daddy was making spaghetti and Bro David was garlicking the bread when we walked into the kitchen. Bro David had a pastry brush lifted above the loaf of bread, and my father was shoving pasta into the big pot of boiling water. They stopped and held still, nothing moved but the steam coming from the pot. Bro David is taller than Daddy, and neither of them ever wears an apron, and for some reason they looked like Boy Scouts standing there.

I told them the results. They looked at me.

"I'm fine," I said. "I played it well. You'll hear me on the tape, they're sending everybody a tape." They were looking at me to see how I really felt. It hit me that the three people standing there in the kitchen might never want to hear that Mozart concerto again in their lives. I laughed. "I'm *fine*," I said. Their faces relaxed, and they went on getting dinner ready.

I wasn't exactly fine. I was tired, and I was disappointed, and I was happy for Karen, and I knew that I knew my Elter Bubbe Leah better than anybody would ever believe, and what I said was almost true: I *would be* fine. I just wasn't exactly all fine yet.

I ran upstairs to put on my Youth Orchestra dress and had a one-minute hug with Heavenly. My mother tied a big apron on me so I wouldn't spill spaghetti sauce on my dress and we had dinner in a hurry. Everybody was in a good mood, or seemed to be. Something was over. School would start tomorrow. Bro David and I would be running around early in the morning arguing over the bathroom. I looked at him across the dining-room table, and I thought about what an amazing coincidence it was that Kansas and Poland had come together to get us hybrids, shoveling spaghetti into our mouths.

For a moment during dinner, I stopped and closed my eyes and listened. Garlic bread being crunched, little clinks of forks on plates, the sound of somebody wiping a hand on a napkin. Slurps of marinara sauce going into mouths. I opened my eyes. Daddy was holding the basket of garlic bread toward me and he was staring at me. Little Leah with her braids spread out on the pillow in her bed in Suprasl appeared for an instant, and Daddy and I looked at each other, not interrupted by anything, and I said inside my head that this was my father, and then I took the basket from him and we continued our dinner.

ᏗᎣ

Sarah and Jessica had saved a place for my parents on a big blanket with exactly three rows of blankets in front of them. Even though my mother and father were full of spaghetti, I could see them munching on Sarah's Healthy Nut Things.

Word had gotten around about the Bloch finals, and people backstage were calling Christine "Christine Moments," and I saw three people, two violinists and a clarinet player, try to congratulate Steve Landauer on winning second place. Every single time, he pretended he was looking for something in his violin case or his pocket. He barely said thank-you.

Mr. Kaplan came around the end of the stage, with his sort of stooped-over walk, and we spotted each other and he put his left hand up like a sign. He came close and put both his hands on my shoulders. "Did you enjoy this afternoon?" he asked.

"Yep. I did."

"The judges were quite taken with you."

I didn't say anything.

"I spoke with one of them." He put on a quoting voice, very bass and harrumphing: " 'That Allegra Shapiro. She's Fleur's child?' I said 'Yes, and Alan's as well.' 'Quite remarkable, Kaplan. But quite young.' " He leaned toward my left ear, and went on in a softer harrumphing voice: " 'A most inspirational performance, Kaplan. Most inspirational.' " His right hand applied a bit of extra pressure to my left shoulder, and he said, in his own voice, "Almost as exciting as the softball play-offs, eh?" He stepped back to see my reaction.

A big, face-breaking smile came up out of me. I would never in the world tell him about the pictures of Elter Bubbe Leah's childhood that I saw through the notes while I was playing the concerto. I might tell Bubbe Raisa.

"I'm very, very proud," he said. "I'm going to sit with your parents now. Have a good show."

Somebody came by and bumped my elbow on the way to the stage. I said, "Yes. Sure. Thanks, Mr. Kaplan."

He lifted his hand in his flat-handed wave and walked away. I walked up the steps onto the stage.

Steve Landauer's chair was missing its little rubber thing on the bottom of one leg and didn't sit squarely on the platform. He tore off a corner of the music folder and folded it up and stuck it under the uneven leg. The chair still didn't balance. He got very frustrated with it and sat and muttered while we tuned up.

After some speeches about how wonderful it was that the Youth Orchestra could fill in while the Symphony musicians were locked out in the labor conflict, we started playing.

As usual, Mr. Trouble was dancing. The concert went along. People clapped hard, the breeze lifted the pages just enough off the stand so that I was using four clothespins. I put the Sibelius *Valse Triste* up and Steve Landauer shook out his left hand, hanging it down beside his chair. He was still annoyed that the chair sat crooked on the stage, and he jiggled it forward and back a bit to get a firmer grip.

I slid my mute up and put it on the bridge. The instructions say "con sordino" and that means put your mute on. Steve Landauer didn't put his on. I guess he'd forgotten. I pointed with the end of my bow to the words. He put his mute on instantly, without looking at it. He kept his eyes concentrating straight on the conductor. Steve Landauer has very good peripheral vision.

The conductor stood very straight and still so that to the audience it looked as if he was just waiting, and he held up two fingers and turned them back and forth, and made happy and sad faces, to remind us of the double meaning, and we began.

I saw Mr. Trouble out of the corner of my right eye, and he was wondering how to dance with those first low plucked notes in the basses. He was waiting. I thought about how he was so good at waiting. In a way, he'd been spending his whole life waiting.

When we start playing the melody, using our bows, the suspense begins. Then there's a rallentando, a slowing down, and then at letter C there's an a tempo and the very strange silences begin. I don't know any other piece, of all the pieces I've ever heard, that has a silence like that. It's between the second and third beat of the waltz rhythm, and it makes you hold everything up in the air for a moment. Absolutely nothing happens. Like a huge question mark but nobody tells you what the question is. You have to figure it out by yourself.

That moment lets you think so much, your mind can go so fast in that little instant of no sound. You can imagine every question you've ever thought about: Why did Deirdre's baby die? Why did Elter Bubbe Leah get annihilated at Treblinka? Why did Jessica's father die in the volcano? How did Mr. Trouble get the way he is? Will anybody ever be in love with me? You can let it get your mind very overwhelmed.

What I began to notice was that Mr. Trouble got absorbed,

too. He started dancing, then I saw him stop and stare at the conductor. His head was going up and down, in rhythm with the conductor's arms. Then he started dancing again.

But he kept stopping. Dancing then stopping, dancing then stopping. He stopped and looked up at us playing, then danced again, his same dance. Then he stopped and looked down at the ground, and then danced again. He kept doing that.

We finished playing the piece and people clapped and we stood up. I very fast put the next music on top. Out of the side of my eye I saw Steve Landauer's leg jerk a little bit, then he almost backed into me. I looked down. Mr. Trouble was standing right below us. He had his veiny hands up on the edge of the boards of the stage. "Miss Allegra," he said.

I bent down in front of Steve Landauer's legs to hear him.

"That there Waltz Tree," said Mr. Trouble in his croaky voice. Even in his old watery eyes I could see he had such happiness. They were shiny in the stage lights. "That there Waltz Tree."

"*That's* Waltz Tree?" I didn't take it all in at first.

"Yes sir, Miss Allegra, that there song," he said. He nodded his head up and down and kept doing it. "That song. Waltz in Three. That's the one."

Valse Triste. Waltz Tree. Of course. I didn't know what to say. I just hung there, bent over with my violin hanging down. Suddenly there were tears stinging my eye sockets. I tried to smile at him, and then I realized everybody had stopped clapping and the orchestra had sat down again and we were supposed to play the next piece. I scooted backward across Steve Landauer into my chair.

We finished the concert and stood up for the applause.

Steve Landauer said, without turning directly to me, "That guy grabbed my pants. He actually grabbed them. Is he missing some marbles?"

I breathed in and out slowly before I answered him. "Not really," I said.

෴

My parents and Bro David and Jessica and Sarah were all standing beside my violin case on the platform backstage. When I walked around the corner they all started singing, to the tune of "For He's a Jolly Good Fellow":

> "A Most Inspirational Play-er
> A Most Inspirational Play-er
> A Most Inspirational Play-errrrr
> Which nobody can deny . . . ."

Except that Bro David just held up his fingers making ditto marks instead of repeating the words three times.

While Jessica and Sarah were hugging me, I said, "I'll tell you the incredible Trouble story tomorrow. It'll be something to do during lunch."

"Is it the kind of thing eighth-graders talk about?" Sarah asked.

"Trust me," I said.

෴

My mother wanted to come into my room and brush my hair before I went to bed. Even with school starting the next day. "Just a few minutes," she said. I was in my pajamas. We sat down on my bed, with my back to her. She began brushing.

It felt good, the sound and the feel of the long strokes down from my scalp all the way to the ends. "I've always loved the smell of my children's hair," she said.

"I probably smell like a crowded park full of greasy chicken," I said.

"You smell wonderful," she said.

"Deirdre called me this morning," I said. I told her about it, but not completely everything. Not exactly. I said she'd wished me love.

"Allegra," my mother said, "Deirdre is one of the finest, most profoundly loyal and loving people you'll ever want to meet."

We sat on my bed feeling sorry for Deirdre for some minutes, listening to the sound of the brush going through my hair. Then she said, "You know what would make almost all the difference with Deirdre?"

"What would?"

"Now, I don't mean anybody ever saves you—don't get me wrong. I don't mean somebody swoops down and lets you out of your own unhappy life. Not at all, not ever." She breathed in and out slowly. "That doesn't happen. But. Sometimes somebody can be a connection." I was carrying the secret of the velvet purse connection with Poland and Suprasl and New York and the shiny, dusted radio for the opera, and Mr. Trouble and his found song and his happy old eyes shiny in the stage lights, and my mother and Deirdre hugging each other on the floor, and my head was full of tumbling pictures of people doing things all invisibly connected with other people.

"Are you talking about Deirdre or what?" I said.

"I'm talking about Deirdre, yes. What would really help

her would be one good man. A man of principles and fairness and— Not the kind that suddenly takes a hike when the going gets sticky. A persister. That's what I mean."

The most persistent person I could think of was Mr. Trouble. He must have been looking for *Valse Triste* for more years than I'd been alive. In fact, he was exactly what Jessica said, about China, about the bamboo. Bending without breaking.

"Somebody who'd appreciate her. Help her hold her pain. Allegra, her pain's too much to hold all by herself." I could hear tears coming into my mother's throat. "Do you know, every time she sings she's asking—maybe asking the universe—oh, I can't say it exactly— Every single time she sings, she's giving her pain a voice, and she's asking what it means."

"Do you think pain *means* anything?" I said.

The brush strokes slowed down but they stayed steady. "Yes. Yes, I do."

"What happened to the husband she had?"

My mother sighed a middle-aged sigh. "Oh, he was—I suppose you could say the grief was too much for him. It made him into a not-nice person. He ended up walking away."

I remembered Deirdre in her elegant blue dress, screaming.

"Well, what do you think pain's supposed to mean?" I asked.

"Oh, I don't know," she said. She brushed rhythmically, not missing a beat. "I do know it connects the whole human species." More brushing. "I just don't know why."

We were silent again for a few strokes. "Allegra, what in the world was your buddy Mr. Trouble up to when he leaned on the stage? What was he saying to you?"

For a moment, I had a feeling of the world so full of millions of people, all of them with their own secrets, and they were all so important. Everybody. "Remember he lost his Waltz Tree?" I said.

"Right. His lost song."

"Well, think. Isn't it obvious?"

"What? Isn't what obvious?"

And suddenly it was funny. "Mommy, think. What were we playing?" And I got started laughing. My mother stopped brushing. Everybody and their secrets. Nobody could translate anybody else's secrets, they'd all sound meaningless if they tried. I was laughing harder and harder. It was a song about Death, about dreaming you weren't going to die, it was so tragic, and I was thinking of all the millions of secrets and everybody going along not knowing anybody else's.

I turned around on my bed to look at her. "Mommy, what was on the program?"

She scrunched up her face, thinking. I bet people do that on the tundra, and in Africa, and in Siberia, as much as we do it in an electrified place like Portland. Face-scrunching. A human sport. I watched her. The scrunches were moving around her face. Then her mouth opened wide. She said it really slowly, even with a little bit of the silence between the beats. "*Valse Triste*. Waltz Tree. Oh, Allegra." Tears came into her voice. "Oh . . ."

My mother was crying and I was laughing. I thought it was very strange for a moment, and then I realized it couldn't be the other way around.

"Allegra," she said, "I admire you."

"You do?"

"I do. You're a person of empathy and drive and—" she thought for a second, "and courage."

"What's empathy?"

"Oh," she turned my head away from her and started brushing again. "It's not sympathy, that's different, but they're close. Empathy is when you can feel for somebody—not because you think you should, not because it'll make you a better person—but when you can feel somebody's feelings because you haven't closed yourself off from them. From those feelings in yourself. E-m-p-a-t-h-y."

"Mom, can I go visit Bubbe Raisa for Rosh Hashana?" I said.

She sniffled. "What an inspired idea! Sure, why not?"

"And Deirdre too, at the same time?"

"Yes." This was the woman who wouldn't let me ride my bike in the neighborhood park, and she was going to let me fly to New York. We got up off my bed, and she put my hairbrush on a chair. We kissed good night. She called me her Most Inspirational Daughter and left my room.

I wrote "empathy" on the clipboard. And I looked at my list.

tenacity	*hinterland*
annihilate	*pernicious*
ambivalence	*flippant*
sabotage	*ominous*
simultaneity	*arrogant*
trauma	*empathy*

I imagined that the first assignment I'd get in English class the next day would be to write an essay or make a collage demonstrating "mastery" of all the words on the list. They're always talking about mastery at my school. I put the clipboard on the floor.

Way last June, on the day Mr. Kaplan had told me about the Bloch finals, when he'd looked at me in a way I couldn't describe, it was empathy. That's what it was. And then later, he'd said people talk too much about mastering a song, but what's more important is to merge with it—I sat on my bed and told myself I finally understood what he meant.

I turned down the covers.

You can be half Jewish. Maybe whole Jews or whole Gentiles wouldn't understand. But you can be. I am.

Under my pillow was a cartoon from Bro David. It was a tree, and on every single branch was hanging a violin. The caption said, "Martin Luther gets a better idea." And in neat small letters, "Congratulations to the Most Inspirational Player in the Ernest Bloch Competition," and there was a figure of me playing the violin with my softball uniform on. This time he'd made me my normal size.

I turned off the light and turned on the radio.

I tried to visualize the Juilliard String Quartet in the picture in Mr. Kaplan's studio. I thought of their second violinist, the one who'd tipped me over the edge to be willing to play the Bloch finals. I couldn't remember his name.

It was because of the Oregon Symphony lockout that Mr. Trouble had found his Waltz Tree. If Jessica hadn't danced with him upriver in the hinterland, we wouldn't have known his name. If Sarah hadn't gotten the courage to ask him questions, I wouldn't ever have heard about his lost song.

But it had started with Deirdre: "Why on earth doesn't somebody dance with that man?"

If my bow had landed with the hair toward me, I'd have

ended up learning a completely different Mozart concerto, way last year. I wouldn't have ever met Myra and Karen Karen and Ezra, and Steve Landauer would have been just a stand partner who treated me like his servant.

Somebody else would have been a finalist in the competition, maybe might have won it. Somebody was right now probably angry and upset, not being in the finals. I wondered who it was. Boy or girl. Old or young.

I lay down and pulled Heavenly under the covers. School would begin the next morning and I'd be exhausted. Somebody had requested "So What" by Miles Davis on the radio, the same record I have.

Karen Karen and Deirdre and Mr. Trouble were all related, too. There was something between them, a thread. And Myra Nakamura and Mr. Kaplan and Jessica and Sarah and Ezra. There wasn't a single person I could think of who wasn't connected to a whole bunch of other people I could think of. I thought of the blind woman in the airport bathroom trying to turn the water on and not knowing the secret code. If she knew it, she could be more connected with everybody else. But she was connected anyway.

I looked at the green light on the radio.

"So What" ended and the announcer started to talk. "The next tune is a request all the way from Culver, Oregon, for Allegra from Ezra, George Gershwin's 'Embraceable You.' " My head went alert on the pillow and Heavenly jumped. The song started to play. I sat up, like sounding some kind of alarm, and Heavenly dove off my bed. The song went on playing, just a regular request by a regular person for another regular person. The music just played, right on the radio in the middle of the night, from a studio somewhere, and I was sitting up straight in my bed, and I discovered that my whole body, all my cells and everything, jumped open and stayed that way long enough for me to know it was happening, and then everything closed, my lungs and everything went back to the way they were, and I got out of bed and danced in my bedroom to "Embraceable You," and I smiled in the dark, and I was very proud. I put my hand on my heart and it was jumpity-jumping along, just a regular heart all excited.

"Embraceable You" is a very beautiful song.

It ended. And I suddenly knew why Mr. Trouble had reminded me of something vaguely, the very first time I saw him: the Green Violinist in the painting. Mr. Trouble didn't have a violin, he had a song inside, needing to come out, and his face was twisted, and he was raggedy and his shoes didn't match, and he was all alone in the open air, dancing and dancing and dancing.

Ezra. Requested a song for me. Such a beautiful song. In the middle of the night. It was romantic, a romantic thing to do, and I wasn't even embarrassed. At all. I stood in my dark bedroom and looked at the little green light on the radio and I smiled. I curtsied in the middle of my room and got back into bed.

Of course I would want to tell him first of all my real name, Allegra Leah Shapiro.